I0581940

MURDER
ON THE
MEDINA

A FEN MAGUIRE MYSTERY

MURDER

ON THE

MEDINA

A FEN MAGUIRE MYSTERY

BRUCE
HAMMACK

Chapter One

Two cypress knees sticking up from the far bank of the Medina River had stopped the body from floating farther downstream. Former sheriff Fen Maguire looked at the lifeless form and let out a low moan. *If this causes me to miss Thanksgiving, Thelma and Bailey will roast me instead of a turkey.* Fen stopped the path of such a thought. As a seasoned lawman, he knew disappointment had no place when it came to duty. Somewhere was a family who would be feeling much more than disappointment on this holiday.

He slipped his cell phone out of his jacket pocket and located a name in his contacts. It didn't take long before the man's voice asked, "Fen? Is that really you?"

"It's me, Rusty. I hate to ruin your day, but I'm looking at a body in the river."

"You're joking." Sheriff Rusty Irons waited for a count of three and said, "No, you're not. You don't joke about bodies in rivers. Male or female?"

"Can't tell. The body is face down and he, or she, is against the far bank."

"What's your location?"

"Behind the River Oak Inn. I've booked a room here."

"I'm on my way with help. Is anyone else nearby?"

"No one but me."

Fen heard the sheriff's movements as his breathing increased and the jingle of keys sounded. "Expect to hear a lot of noise coming your way."

After the call ended Fen looked at his watch. It took twelve seconds for the first siren to break the quiet of Bandera, Texas, the self-proclaimed cowboy capital of the world, a town of about a thousand souls. The screams of more emergency vehicles soon joined the first.

Sheriff Robert "Rusty" Irons parked his half-ton, four-wheel-drive pickup truck in the hotel's rear parking lot, walked past a small asphalt parking lot for motorcycles only, and crossed a wooden footbridge. He quick-stepped across a grassy, flat area about the size of a football field, coming to a halt close to where Fen stood on the east side of the tree-lined bank of the Medina River.

"That was a fast response time," said Fen.

"I was a few blocks away at the Cowgirl Coffee Company getting my morning cup of motivation."

The sheriff reminded Fen of the stump from a sawed-off oak tree. He wasn't tall, but he was dense and never seemed satisfied that he had to wear boots to reach five-seven. It hadn't surprised Fen to learn that Rusty had a drawer full of belt buckles proving his aptitude for steer wrestling.

Fen pointed to a spot on the far bank. Words weren't necessary. The sheriff took a long look as Fen watched for a reaction. As expected, Rusty scowled.

Two additional officers arrived in quick succession—one male and the other female. Fen noted the female looked in much better physical condition than the male officer. A silver

Stetson covered her hair, except for the tight, raven bun at the base of her neck. He guessed her age to be thirty, give or take a couple of years. The sheriff's department uniform and winter jacket hid most of her curves. Out of habit, Fen glanced at her left hand and found it void of a wedding band.

Rusty's first instructions went to the male officer. "Scooter, put up yellow tape a hundred yards upstream and twenty-five yards downstream."

The man nodded like he understood, then asked, "Why not a hundred yards downstream?"

Rusty closed his eyes and opened them again. His voice barely masked his impatience. "Which way is the river flowing?"

"Uh... from right to left."

"Correct. The likelihood of discovering a primary crime scene is much better upstream."

"How far up the bank did you want me to go?"

"About a hundred yards. Stretch the tape between trees and bushes and stay outside the area. Also, tape off the foot-bridge and don't let sightseers past you. I'll send someone to tell you what to do next."

The female deputy didn't need to be told what to do. She already had yellow tape tied off downstream and was working her way toward them.

Another deputy sheriff arrived, this one with chevrons on his collar. Rusty turned to the female officer instead. "KK, call your team and tell them where to put in and where you want the ambulance."

"I'll put in at the park and have the ambulance go there."

The sheriff addressed his sergeant. "Put the next deputy to arrive at the footbridge and have Scooter report to me. I don't want anyone but first responders on this floodplain."

Having been in law enforcement for twenty years, Fen

knew things would slow down from this point on, even though emergency vehicles would continue to arrive. The sheriff looked at Fen and answered an unasked question.

"KK is Kathy Krump, but nobody calls her Kathy. She's not been a deputy long in this county but has certification as an EMT, plus she's our Swift-water Rescue Leader. She's who we call when the Medina gets angry like it is today."

"You're lucky to have her," said Fen.

The morning dragged on until the sound of an outboard motor caught Fen's ear. The Zodiac rounded a bend in the river with KK operating the boat. She looked different wearing a helmet and a life jacket.

The engine throttled down and brought the inflatable watercraft to within inches of the body on the far bank. With practiced skill, she held the boat still while instructing two beefy firefighters to take pictures of the body still in the water.

One firefighter made an obligatory check for the victim's pulse and shouted, "He's deceased." After snapping photos, he put the camera back into a waterproof pouch and slipped it into a compartment on his vest.

The river hadn't yet crested its banks, so the trip across took mere seconds. KK nestled the boat against the bank in front of Fen and Sheriff Irons, while instructing firefighters to secure lines fore and aft.

Fen and Rusty moved toward the bank, making sure not to slip into the river, which was still rising. Fen sought higher ground where thick roots shot outward from a massive cypress tree. He wanted to get a look at the victim who now lay face up in the bottom of the rubber boat. Thick whiskers on the victim's chin answered a previous question about gender. He was a lanky man with long black hair that covered much of his face.

The justice of the peace had arrived and moved to inspect the body. Fen surrendered his spot.

"Somebody hold me by the back of my belt. Two or three of you form a chain if you have to. If I go into the Medina this morning, I expect you to come in after me."

Several first responders complied, and the wiry older man hovered over the boat as he made a cursory exam. He stood upright and said, "I don't know him."

"Does anyone recognize him?" asked Rusty.

Fen watched the first responders. KK looked away for a moment. No one else reacted after seeing the man's face.

The JP took over again. "Take him to the park. I'll go through his pockets there and make a preliminary ruling on the cause of death."

"Hold on a minute," said Fen. "Can you look at the back of his neck before you leave? One of you in the boat, lift the hair out of the way."

KK had gloves on and performed the task.

"There," said Fen as he leaned forward while holding onto a tree branch.

KK bent over and examined the spot Fen had noticed.

The justice of the peace spoke as he squinted. "Well, I'll be. How did you see that?"

"I was looking for it."

"What is it?" asked a voice behind Fen.

KK gave Fen a piercing look. "It appears to be the entry wound of a gunshot."

The JP looked over his shoulder. "This changes things. I'll take a better look when you get him out of the boat, but right now, this looks like a homicide." He shifted his gaze and said, "KK, look in his pockets for identification."

All eyes were on KK. She located a wallet in the victim's back pocket, opened it, and pulled out a driver's license. "The man's name is Clay Trueblood."

KK produced an evidence bag and slipped the wallet in it.

Sheriff Irons asked, "Does that name mean anything to anyone?"

The sergeant said, "It rings a bell, but not a loud one. It might have been a traffic stop from a long time ago."

No one else had anything to add. KK looked up toward Fen and in a loud whisper asked, "Who are you, and how did you know to pull his hair away from the back of his head?"

Rusty answered. "This is Sheriff Fen Maguire."

"Former sheriff," said Fen.

The sound of the boat's engine coming to life put a temporary end to further conversations, and people moved away from the riverbank.

Rusty and Fen walked toward Fen's easel and sketchpad that he'd covered with a thick piece of plastic. The current sheriff of Bandera County hooked his thumbs in the front pockets of his jeans. "I'm hearing you're not as former of a lawman as you want people to believe. Would it be asking too much of you to take a ride with me down to the park where the ambulance is waiting? My sergeant can handle things here."

Fen knew he needed to set some boundaries to avoid any misunderstanding. "You need to know I'm leaving town in the morning. All I can give you is the rest of the day."

"Fair enough," said Rusty.

Fen reached for a camp stool he'd been sitting on while sketching. "I'll need to take my work up to my room."

"No problem. I'll talk to my deputies and get men searching on both sides of the river. Let's see if we can't find the original crime scene."

Chapter Two

Rusty walked through the open door of Fen's motel room. He looked at sketches taped to the walls. "You're a genuine artist, not an amateur."

"Don't sound so surprised. I've been painting and sketching all my life. I'm here to find interesting locations, take photos and do rough sketches. This winter I'll paint an oil on canvas and try to make something come to life."

Once outside, Rusty asked, "Was that your wife's picture on the nightstand?"

"My late wife, Sally."

"She was beautiful."

"Yes, she was, inside and out."

Rusty's chin dipped. "Sorry. It must be tough being single again."

Fen pressed the key fob to open his truck. He located his slicker suit, which he kept rolled into a tight ball and tucked behind the rear seat. He finally responded to the words of concern. "The first years were the worst. Time, getting older, and painting help me cope with losing her."

Fen kept talking but took the conversation in a completely different direction as they made the short drive down Main Street. "Did you know this isn't the first person I've found face down in a river?"

"I've heard some rumors," said Rusty.

"My ranch is on the Brazos, northeast of Austin. A body in the Brazos was the first case I helped solve after the voters of Newman County failed to reelect me."

"It must have been tough to lose your wife and your job as sheriff."

Fen gave a weak nod. "It was stay with Sally as she slowly died or run a reelection campaign. I chose the first option and don't regret a minute of staying by her side."

They turned right off Main Street and observed a waiting ambulance with lights flashing. Otherwise, the city park was void of activity.

The sheriff parked close to the ambulance and looked upward. "More rain is coming soon. We'd better put on our rain gear while we have a chance."

Outside, the sound of an outboard motor caught Fen's attention. "That must be KK. I'm surprised it's taking her so long to get here."

"The river makes a big loop to the west between here and your motel. Runoff from the heavy rains has swollen the river and made it possible for KK to travel so far upstream in the Kodiak. She's the only person I trust enough to navigate the Medina." He pointed. "Did you notice the short dam when we drove up?"

"I saw it and heard it. There's a lot of water going downstream in a hurry."

The sky suddenly cried large, cold drops. Fen hastened to slip into his slicker suit and affix a plastic cover over his felt

Stetson. The downpour drowned out most of the sound from the still-distant outboard motor.

Rusty and Fen moved to the edge of the river, which was now running faster and edging onto the floodplain. Rusty said, "I was afraid this would happen. The tall hills to the north and west are steep enough to force rainclouds upward and they dump a lot of water on rocky ground. So far, it hasn't been enough to cause much damage, but that could change soon."

Fen looked at the river. "Does the Medina flood often?"

"Rarely, but the floods have come close to wiping out the town a time or two. Hurricanes and tropical storms are our biggest enemies. In 1978, a tropical storm dumped several feet of rain in two days. Hurricane Harvey hit in 2017 and took twenty-seven lives in Bandera, Kerr, and Kendall Counties. Army helicopters picked people out of the tops of trees and dropped them off on high ground behind the county court-house here in Bandera."

Fen put in a word of encouragement. "I watched the weather this morning. They say the rain should move out before dark."

Rusty kept his gaze locked on the river. "My biggest concern is people driving through low-water crossings on the backroads. They forget the power of running water. It doesn't flood often enough to justify building massive bridges on county roads. Property damage won't be a problem with this storm, but cars and trucks being swept off creek crossings may be."

Fen looked upstream. "Here comes the Zodiac."

"And not a minute too soon," said Rusty. "The rain is really coming down."

Fen watched the approaching boat for a few seconds, but something else caught his attention. He squinted and made sure the brim of his Stetson blocked the driving rain as he pointed. "Look!"

Rusty's gaze followed to where Fen pointed. "Is that a log?"

"If it's a log," said Fen, "it's wearing a red jacket."

Rusty responded with an expletive. He moved to the edge of the bank, formed his hands into a waving X, and pointed across the river.

KK continued toward the bank, but one firefighter must have seen what Fen and Rusty saw. He turned and hollered something to the female deputy. Her gaze shifted, and the craft made a quick change of course and increased speed.

Rusty kept his gaze on the object that floated ever closer to the waterfall going over the short dam. It was a race to see if the red object would tumble out of sight before the Zodiac could reach it. KK piloted the craft to within a few feet of the low-water dam. She spun the boat in a tight one-hundred-eighty-degree turn and held the boat still in the swift current. The two firefighters who'd retrieved the first body hung off the side of the inflatable boat and grabbed any part of the object they could. Slowly, the boat moved forward against the current and headed to where Fen, Rusty, and two ambulance attendants watched and waited.

A last burst of power from the outboard motor beached the craft enough for the cadre of first responders to drag the object ashore. Flowing blond hair told Fen this was no log, but victim number two of the day.

Rusty spoke into his phone. "Leon, I have another customer for you. KK and the firemen just fished a second body out of the river. It's a female this time, with what looks like a similar wound to the back of her head. She's lying face down on the bank. We won't move her until you get here, but you'd better hurry. The river's rising."

After several first responders removed the first victim from the Zodiac, KK looked at Fen. "I need to get this boat out of the water. Can you go to my truck and back the trailer down the ramp?"

Fen spoke as the rain continued to fall. "Glad to. Give me the keys."

KK pitched them to him. She clicked the idling engine into reverse and gunned it until the bow slid off the slick grass. Fen moved with head down through the rain and soon had the boat's trailer backed down a concrete ramp, making sure it didn't go too far into the river. KK slid the boat onto the trailer with precision and motioned for Fen to pull forward. Once the trailer was well out of the water, Fen put the truck in park and went to lend a hand to secure the craft to the trailer.

The two made quick work of the task, and Fen climbed into the passenger's seat while KK climbed into the driver's seat.

Fen's words stopped her before she could put the truck in gear. "Let's sit here and have a little talk."

KK's wet eyebrows knitted together. "What is it?"

Fen didn't hesitate. "How long before you tell Sheriff Irons you know the first victim?"

A look of panic flashed across KK's face, but only for a couple of seconds. She hung her head for a moment, then righted herself as her chin quivered. "How did you know?"

"The same way I knew to look for a gunshot wound to the back of the head. Ten years as a state trooper and another ten as a sheriff taught me to watch for reactions. You looked away when you saw the Texas star tattoo on Clay's chest. If I was guessing, you have the same tattoo."

Her hand went to her chest. "A long time ago he was my fiancé."

Fen froze her with a stare. "Never lie about your past if you value your career. Tell Rusty about your past relationship with the victim."

"Do I have a choice?"

"Rusty will eventually find out on his own. I won't say a word, but I know I won't have to. You'll do the right thing."

She looked at the gathering along the riverbank. "I have a favor to ask. Let me tell him later. The river will continue to rise today, and my job is to save lives. This double murder has to wait."

Fen quirked a smile and said, "You're right, but your time will be up as soon as the water goes down."

Fen's phone buzzed and broke the tension his terse words caused. The photo on the phone's screen showed the smiling face of a petite, blond young woman. "Bailey, are you on the road yet?"

"I'm walking to my truck. My last class was a complete waste of time. Have you left Bandera?"

"Something came up. I won't leave until tomorrow morning."

"How many bodies this time?" asked Bailey, the off-again, on-again college student.

"Two so far, but the day is still young." Fen cut his gaze toward KK as he said, "All the rain we've had this week has swollen the Medina River and she gave up her secrets today."

Bailey let out a cackle. "What rain? It's dry as a desert here today."

"I'm closer to Mexico than I am to you. This is the second day of heavy rains, and the Medina is about to flood."

"No matter how many bodies, rain or shine, you better be here for Thanksgiving."

"I'll try to remember that. Tell Thelma I should be home tomorrow by mid-afternoon."

Bailey didn't hesitate. "You'd better be. I'm not covering for you this time. The only thing I'm telling Thelma is exactly what you said about not coming home before tomorrow and finding two bodies."

"That will be enough for me to earn a fried bologna sandwich instead of one of Thelma's chicken-fried steaks." He paused long enough to take a breath to say, "I need to go. Things are busy in cowboy country."

"Yee-ha!" said Bailey before the call clicked off.

KK asked, "Your daughter?"

Fen shook his head. "A stray I picked up, but she's the closest thing to a daughter I'll ever have."

"She must be special."

"Very special," said Fen.

KK's radio came alive with the sheriff using her call sign. She keyed the microphone and responded.

The sheriff's voice came out loud and clear. "Can Sheriff Maguire hear me?"

"Yes."

"Ask if he's willing to go with you upstream and look for the original crime scene. If this rain keeps up, we'll lose all evidence. I'm having to pull everyone else to block roads with low water crossings."

Fen nodded, and KK relayed the message. She looked at him after Rusty issued a quick thank you. "Looks like we're going boating. Park the truck and trailer on higher ground than last time. I'll have a life vest waiting for you to put on."

Chapter Three

The yellow rain gear was a souvenir from the sheriff's department of Newman County where Fen had served. KK spoke to him through the latest wave of driving rain. "Is it legal for you to be wearing that with SHERIFF in bold letters on the back?"

"I never gave it much thought. The only time I wear it is when it's pouring rain. I keep my peace officer certification up to date, so I guess it's legal enough."

He used a stick to snag a piece of cloth floating down the river. After examining it, he dropped it into the boat and gave a quick explanation. "A baby's one-piece outfit. Not what we're looking for. It wouldn't fit your former fiancé or the woman."

KK took her turn. "It always amazes me how much trash comes downstream during and after a hard rain. Don't people ever throw things in trash cans or dumpsters?"

Fen kept looking from one bank to the other. KK finally said, "Your neck will be sore from all that turning back and forth. What are you looking for?"

"Whatever doesn't look like it belongs."

"Like what?"

"If you were to kill someone and wanted to dump the body in the river, where would you do it?"

"Probably on a bridge."

"Why?"

"I wouldn't have to carry the body very far, or not at all."

Fen kept scanning the banks as his hat shielded his eyes from the rain. He glanced over his shoulder and said, "That's an excellent answer, but bridges are highly visible. What's another way?"

KK took more time answering, obviously rolling ideas around in her mind. "Park under the bridge late at night, kill them and dump the body there."

Fen nodded his approval. "That's exactly what happened to the man who ended up on the banks of my ranch, but I don't believe that's what happened here."

"Why not?"

"The water's too high and has been for at least a day. Unless there's a tall bridge ahead of us, there'd be no place to park except on the bridge or on either side."

KK shrugged. "I give up. How else could it be done?"

Fen asked, "Have you ever tried to carry someone down a muddy riverbank?"

She maneuvered the boat around a decent size tree branch before saying, "I can't say that I've ever tried it. It sounds like a good way to have your feet trade places with your head."

"Exactly," said Fen. "I'm looking for a place with steep banks where someone either dragged a body down the bank or tried to carry it and plowed a path in the mud."

He picked up on the story he started about a prior murder he'd solved. "My ranch is on the west bank of the Brazos River. This murder reminds me in some ways of that one. The victim got hung up in the branches of a tree that fell in the river. The first responders had a hard time getting him up the riverbank. By the time they had him on solid ground, it looked like a herd of pigs trekked up from the river."

KK dodged some more flotsam and asked, "You said you own a ranch?"

He kept looking from bank to bank. "Part ranch, part farm, part pecan orchard, and my homestead. The river bottom is too wide and rich not to have it under cultivation. There's two thousand acres for farming, a thousand acres for cattle, and another thousand acres in old growth woods, pecan orchards, and my home."

"Must be nice," said KK with envy seasoning her words. "All it's missing is a hundred oil wells."

"There's nowhere near that many," said Fen with a straight face.

KK's mouth gaped open before she closed it partway and said, "I looked you up on my phone while you were parking my truck and trailer. Your paintings sell for a ton of money."

"Only half a ton," said Fen. "But it wasn't always that way."

"Still," said KK. "You don't have to be sitting in an inflatable boat, in the rain, headed up a river in Nowhere, Texas."

"Don't worry," said Fen. "It's all yours after I get back to the hotel. I'm leaving tomorrow."

"That may be, but why are you here now helping me?"

Fen turned to face her. "I made a promise to my late wife that I'd stay busy. That's why I farm, ranch, paint, and sometimes help people like Sheriff Irons."

KK proved she wasn't one to back down when looking for answers. "I still don't understand. You aren't obligated in any way to help us. You could have given your statement and gone about your business."

Fen lifted his shoulders and let them fall. "It's simple. I'm really good at only two things—painting landscapes and catching criminals, especially killers. Sally made me promise that I'd keep doing both after she died."

He looked at the banks again and asked, "Now, do you understand?"

"I understand enough to know I need to listen to what you say and learn from your experience."

"That's good," said Fen as he pointed toward the bank. "Either a pig came down that bank in the past day or somebody pulled a body down it and walked out caked in mud."

KK's gaze shifted and focused on the matted grass and gouges in the mud. "Holy smoke," she said as she throttled back and pointed the boat to the bank where Fen tied the bowline to the branch of a tree.

"Good job," said Fen. "You picked a spot where we won't track up what may be the primary crime scene. Do you know where we are?"

"Not far downstream from a concrete bridge and close to a picnic area on this side of the river."

"How close?" asked Fen.

"Close enough to carry a body."

"Let's look."

They both slipped a little getting out of the boat but didn't go down. They had to pull themselves up the bank with the aid of bushes and saplings. It wasn't too steep, but the rain and mud made it a tricky ten yards.

Once on higher ground, Fen said, "You lead. I'll walk in your tracks."

They hadn't walked over twenty paces when Fen shouted, "Stop!" He pointed. "Behind that cedar tree, on the ground, I see cloth."

"I'll check it out," said KK.

"I'll stay here unless you need me."

As he watched the young deputy walk forward, Fen realized he'd already violated the first rule of investigating a murder —secure the crime scene. He had no police tape to mark off the area and was improvising procedures to gather evidence.

KK made a looping path along the downstream side of the bright green tree that looked more like a bush. A gasp came forth once she reached the other side. She followed it with an expletive before shouting, "It's a windbreaker."

"Anything else?"

Her response came back hard. "A stupid, empty bottle of cheap whiskey."

Fen didn't mind her snapping at him. In fact, it was a good sign. Keeping emotions bottled up was a recipe for nightmares. "Take pictures of everything where it is."

When she pocketed the camera, Fen asked, "Anything in the pockets of the windbreaker?"

"No, but I recognize the logo on the front. It's from a dude ranch west of town. I brought small evidence bags and one plastic grocery bag."

"Bag it up," said Fen. "We don't have much time to gather evidence. When you're finished, come out the same way you went in."

A few minutes later she walked toward him with head down, making sure she made no new footprints. As she reached him, Fen asked, "Do you want to call Rusty or would you rather it be me?"

"I'll do it," said KK. "You've already called in one homicide today."

She used her cell phone instead of the radio clipped to her life vest. She put it on speaker, and Rusty answered with a question. "Did you find something?"

"Sheriff Maguire found what he believes is one of the original crime scenes. It's not far upstream, down the bank from the Silver Spur. He spotted a windbreaker that I've bagged."

"Is water over the bridge?"

"It was over it when I came downstream with the first body. I had to raise the motor to float over it."

"Do you have your camera with you?"

"Yes. I took pictures before I bagged it."

"Good job."

KK asked, "Do you want us to continue upstream?"

"Ask Fen what to do next if you're unsure, but you have to preserve as much evidence as possible before it's too late."

The trip down the steep bank involved sliding more than walking. So did entering the boat, which required a face-first leap of faith. Once seated, Fen pointed. "I'll look. You pilot the boat and look when you can. Holler if you see anything of interest and I'll do the same. Our object is to fill evidence bags. We only have one shot at this before the rain compromises everything."

The race against time and nature was on. The faint sound of a siren sounded from the direction of the park. KK said, "The JP must have finished. Let's hope that's the last time he's needed today."

As they passed Fen's motel the rain was coming down in sheets, sometimes sideways. The thought crossed his mind that he could be warm and dry in his room, painting a scene of a rocky canyon north of Bandera. Instead, he was wiping the cold rain from his face. He refocused on the riverbanks. In the distance, a road dipped toward the river and disappeared into muddy water on both banks.

KK shouted above the drum of the rain against the boat. "We can't go any farther upstream. The bridge is barely under water and has concrete rails."

Fen hollered. "Pull over and let's get out again."

"There's a spot on the east bank."

KK once again brought the boat to rest in a spot that

allowed them to get out without being swept away. Fen secured the bow-line while she did the same to the stern. With the engine off, they could converse without the whine of the motor. KK took three steps away from the water and said, "There's a parking lot at the top of the riverbank. This is where young people come to drink and find out about the birds and bees."

They climbed the bank and found themselves standing in an asphalt parking lot with picnic tables scattered around the edges. A path led away from picnic tables into a heavily wooded area. Fen looked at small piles of soggy toilet paper off the sides of the path. Empty beer cans accounted for other evidence to be collected if he spotted any indication that this was a crime scene. Up to this point, he'd led the way, but he came to a sudden stop. "You lead and I'll follow. As the Brits would say, 'This is your patch.'"

Forty-five minutes later, they returned to the parking lot. KK let out a huff of frustration. "Nothing but beer cans, cigarette butts, a roach clip, and toilet paper."

Fen said, "It was a long shot."

A determined look came into KK's gaze. "Didn't you say it would be easier to dispose of a body by killing them on the bridge?"

Fen nodded and said, "The bridge is almost under water. Any evidence is long gone."

"I know, but let's look along the road until we run into the river."

A nod served as a partial response. "Might as well. We can't get any colder than we already are."

They each took a side of the road. Slow steps took them down a gentle hill to a steeper decline in the road. A glint caught Fen's eye. He came to an abrupt halt and squatted.

"KK," said Fen in a firm voice. "I hope you have another bag for evidence."

She appeared by his side. "What is it?"

"It's a .22 revolver."

She let out a gasp, followed by, "Holy burritos, I can't believe it."

Fen stood. "What do you think happened?"

KK looked at the edge of the water before her gaze reached the center of the bridge where she locked onto a spot. "The killer and the victim parked in the lot. They walked to the middle of the bridge and the killer shot the victim with that pistol you found then tossed it in the bushes."

"That's the simple version of the story. Now all we have to do is find out who and why."

Fen then pulled out his phone and made a call. "Rusty, I'm wet, cold, and we've located what appears to be the first crime scene. Is there any way you could send someone to pick me up and take me to my motel?"

"Put KK on the phone. I'll come myself and buy you a steak dinner tonight."

Chapter Four

The trip by road back into town took only a few minutes, as opposed to the longer route by boat on the serpentine river.

"Just pull over; I'll walk to my room," said Fen as they approached the motel he was staying in.

"Thanks again for all your help," said Rusty. The radio came to life again, which prevented Fen from responding to the salutation. He stepped out and firmly closed the door. Staccato lights and the piercing wail of a siren marked the end of Fen's day in law enforcement. Rusty was already rushing to his next emergency.

The walk through the rain to his room seemed almost surreal, as did the relative quietness. It was like he'd ridden on a sling-you-around carnival ride with flashing lights and boisterous noises only to be put into a soundless, dark room. It was too quiet, too fast, so he turned on the television and looked for weather updates. Muddy boots came off, as did the yellow rain gear.

He shivered. The yellow outerwear had only partially protected him from the rain. His shirt around the cuffs and collar was soaked. Leaving the wet clothes in a pile to be dealt with later, Fen stepped into the shower and sighed as hot water peppered down on him. He soaked in the warmth of the water until steam filled the bathroom and the untanned parts of his skin turned pink.

Fen had finished drying off and was parting his hair when his phone issued a mechanical announcement of an incoming call. He looked at the caller ID and engaged the device. "Hello, Thelma. How's everything on the home front?"

"Don't you worry about things along the Brazos. It's the Medina River I want to know about. The weather channel is saying you'd better get to high ground."

"I'm safe."

"I doubt that's true. You probably heard heavy rain was coming, and stayed an extra day to go swimming. Why didn't you come home last night like you were supposed to? Now you're in the middle of a flood and Thanksgiving is only a few days away." Her voice came up an octave. "And what's this I'm hearing about a murder?"

Fen couldn't help but smile. Thelma, his overprotective housekeeper, had made a promise to his late wife Sally that she'd look after him. To say that Thelma took that assignment to heart was one of the biggest understatements in the history of mankind.

He gave straight answers to her questions. "I didn't come home yesterday because I had one more sketch to draw of the river. Bailey already told you that."

"It should have come from you."

Fen allowed the complaint to bounce off him. "The weather didn't cooperate with me this week. It's been overcast, rainy, and dreary, which is fine for close-up and mid-range paintings, but not for panoramic views of the steep hills and canyons around here. Besides, I told you I'd probably spend an extra day or two."

He took a breath. "As for the murder, the first body was in the river near the hotel I'm staying in. I was minding my business, making sketches when I noticed it."

"What did you say?" demanded Thelma. "The first body? How many are there?"

"Just two."

In his imagination, Fen could see Thelma's hands squeezing his neck. She let her words fly. "Not only do you have your feet dangling in a raging river, you're hunting for a mass murderer." She sucked in a breath. "And don't waste your breath telling me you haven't been in the middle of things. Every time you go out of this county, there's a dead body that finds you. I'm thinking they wait to get killed until you get past our county line."

The conversation needed to end. "I'll be home tomorrow."

"Ha!" said Thelma. "I'll believe that when I see it."

Fen stared at his phone that had suddenly gone silent. It wasn't the first time Thelma had ended a call without warning and it probably wouldn't be the last. She could act downright prickly when he didn't meet her expectations. What he never doubted was her loyalty to him and his late wife.

Fen was buckling his belt when the rumbling of his stomach made him realize how hungry he was. The day's adrenaline rush had waned, and his blood sugar must be pointing toward empty. He was looking at reviews of local restaurants when his phone buzzed in his hand.

This time the call was from Bailey, the budding artist and college student who had a combination apartment and art studio over his garage.

He answered her call with a quip. "How much steam is coming out of Thelma's ears?"

"Not that much. Sam told her to knock it off. You should be safe coming home tomorrow. It's amazing how she listens to him."

Fen added, "Most of the time he does it with a look instead of words. Is she having hot flashes again?"

Bailey chuckled. "I hadn't thought of that. Perhaps she ran out of the anti-grumpy pills the doctor prescribed."

"Find out," said Fen. "We may not make it through Thanksgiving without them."

A couple of seconds passed before Bailey said, "Lou called. She said she tried to call you twice within the last thirty minutes."

"Ah," said Fen. "She's trying to sniff out a story to publish. I was in the shower."

"Do you think there's a chance we'll be involved in the investigation?"

Fen expected the question from his protégé, who like Lou, an investigative journalist, had become a regular member of his investigative team. "I guess anything is possible, but the sheriff is competent. Do you know what that means?"

"Yeah. We won't get involved until he hits a wall and asks for help."

"It's more complicated than that, but you're right. The sheriff will have the first shot at solving the murders. Other members of law enforcement may take a crack at it next. Unless I'm asked, I keep my big camel's nose out from under the tent. Either way, I'll be home tomorrow and we'll have a nice Thanksgiving."

Fen's phone chimed. He pulled it away from his ear and looked at the screen. "Lou's calling. I'd better talk to her."

"Try to be here before lunch if you don't want to endure the wrath of Thelma for missing another meal."

He punched the screen and said, "Hello, Lou. I was just talking to Bailey. Before that, I was in the shower when you called."

"Cut the small talk," said Lou. "There's a double homicide and a flood. That adds up to juicy stories. Give me the lowdown."

"I'll give them to you, but the flood won't amount to much because the weather is clearing late today. As for the murders, you can't publish anything juicy yet."

Lou had a certain way of huffing through both her mouth and her nose that made her sound like a mule snorting. This time was an exceptionally loud snort. "Why did I ever agree to your terms? Don't you know I'm a starving reporter?"

"No, you're not. You did better than most women by clipping your three ex-husbands for divorce settlements. Plus, you sell more magazine articles and feature stories than anyone I know. That doesn't include the cushy job you have with the local newspaper."

"Cushy? Are you kidding? It's beans and rice, supplemented by rice and beans at my hovel of a home. Now cut the comedy and give me the scoop."

"Remember the terms of our agreement? Do you promise not to reveal your source or print anything until I say so?"

Another huff. "Yes, master. Whatever you say."

Fen gave her a step-by-step accounting of the day from the time he set up his easel until the sheriff dropped him off at his motel.

"Is that all?" asked Lou.

"That's all so far."

She was habitually unsatisfied with incomplete stories. "You should have insisted on staying with Sheriff Irons."

"I was wet, tired, and hungry. Now I'm only tired and hungry."

"Where are you going to eat?"

"I haven't decided yet."

"Make it a bar and strike up conversations with people. I'll need some filler material. Get quotes from locals."

"Lou," said Fen with force. "Do you want a dinky story today or something that might be profitable for your books?"

"Can you guarantee a full short story?"

"No."

"You haven't given me anything to write since spring. Only the Lord knows why, but I've hitched my wagon to your star. I'm confident publishing stories and books of you solving murders will fund my retirement, but at the rate you're going, I won't be able to afford a tin cup for people to put loose change in."

Fen countered with, "Perhaps you should find husband number four. This time, choose a very rich man and stay married to him."

"That's plan D. D for desperation. You're still plan A."

Fen ended the conversation with, "Have your feet under my dining room table on Thanksgiving or be prepared to explain to Thelma why you couldn't make it."

"Fen Maguire, you don't play fair." The phone once again clicked off without a salutation.

With nothing left to do for the rest of the evening, Fen winnowed out the one good idea he'd heard from his conversation with Lou. He checked the local establishments for what looked like a place where locals might gather, drink, and talk. He could nurse a beer for an hour or so and perhaps pick up on the local gossip. News of the murders was bound to have tongues wagging.

He purposed to take a sketch pad and pencils with him

tonight. Nothing broke the ice like drawing a quick sketch or a caricature of someone and giving it to them. But first, he needed something to tide him over and a nap sounded better than leaving his room. He spied a pizza box on the dresser and the microwave sitting on top of a small refrigerator. Two slices of a supreme thin crust seemed to call his name. Perfect.

Chapter Five

The online photos of the TRAIL BOSS STEAK AND GRILL restaurant intrigued Fen enough to lure him to a building on 11th Street. The white wooden structure sat one block off Main Street at the intersection of Highways 16 and 117. Neon signs in the windows told him all he needed to know about the restaurant. One read *Steaks* and the other, *Whiskey*. Unlike the bar down the street, this establishment didn't have wooden rails out front to tether horses to, but his one-ton dually pickup truck looked right at home parked on a street lined with other pickups.

Inside, Fen took stock of his surroundings. Worn wooden floors told the tale that the building hadn't always been a restaurant, but the decor didn't give away its past. Rusty tin covered some of the walls, while another was home to a mural depicting a cowboy herding cattle in the Hill Country. A bar with stools for about a dozen patrons caught Fen's eye. Beer taps rose like stalagmites and rows of bottles sparkled under lights that reflected off a mirrored wall.

A server asked, "Booth, table, or the bar?"

"A booth against the wall, if you have one."

"What's the matter? You afraid someone might sneak up on you?"

"It's an old habit," said Fen.

The woman gave him a narrow-eyed look. "Are you a lawman?"

"I used to be." He wanted to change the subject so he said. "Now I'm an artist."

The woman looked to be in her mid-twenties. She'd squeezed a plump, shapely figure into jeans that hugged every curve. She had a pleasant, friendly smile, and wore a simple, gold wedding band on the ring finger of her left hand.

The woman directed him to a booth. "An artist? We get quite a few through here. Tourists are suckers for western art."

Fen reached into the pocket of his shirt and pulled out a business card. "I'm more of a landscape artist. Sometimes I'll put in cattle and horses, but my paintings are more about the land. I go all over Texas looking for unique settings."

The woman read the card and said, "Fen Maguire. That name rings a bell. So does your face. Are you famous?"

"Not much."

He could tell by the way she studied the card that she didn't buy his answer. She shrugged. "How 'bout a cold beer, or would you prefer something to take the chill out of your bones?"

Fen settled into the booth and said, "I didn't have much lunch, so I'd better save the beer for dessert. How about a mug of hot coffee and a glass of water? I'd also like a T-bone cooked medium rare, with a baked potato, and something green."

"Salad or green beans?"

Fen didn't hesitate. "Salad."

"Good choice. The green beans taste like they dip them in wallpaper paste."

Fen smiled at her. "What's your name?"

"Gladys Mae." She wrinkled her nose in distaste. "I know —it's old-fashioned. I was the last of eight children. Mama and Daddy ran out of names, so they named me after a great aunt."

Fen looked at her and said, "My full name is James Fenimore Maguire."

"Your mother must have loved *The Last of the Mohicans*." Gladys Mae stuck her order pad into the pocket of her apron and said, "I'll be right back with your coffee."

Fen scanned the almost empty room, taking his time to fix in his mind the faces of the patrons. It didn't take long to complete the mental discipline of remembering faces. He wondered if the sparse crowd was due to it still being early in the evening. Things might pick up a little later if the torrential rains and the proximity to Thanksgiving hadn't taken its toll on all the town's restaurants. Still, he had a chatty server to talk to. Perhaps he could mine some information from her that might help lay the groundwork if—

Gladys Mae interrupted his mental wool gathering by sliding a mug of coffee onto the table in front of him. "You don't impress me as a cream or sugar man. I'll get some if you want it."

"No thanks, and you're right. Black and hot is how I take my coffee."

She wiggled her eyebrows. "Like when you were a highway patrolman?"

A smile parted his lips. "Someone's been on their phone doing some snooping."

"I didn't get very far and I'm dying to know more. You're more than a little famous."

Fen looked up at her as he took out his phone. "Do you mind if I take a picture of you?"

She pushed wavy hair away from her face. "Why in the world would you want to do that?"

"I want to draw a sketch of you."

A cackle came forth. "There are longhorn steers they parade down the street with better looks than me."

"Nonsense," said Fen. "That ring on your finger tells me someone thinks you're fine and dandy."

"Scooter and I could both use a gym and a makeover."

Fen tilted his head and asked, "Did you say your husband's nickname is Scooter? Would that be Deputy Scooter?"

"That's him. He's hard to miss. Did you meet him?"

"He was one of the first to arrive on the scene earlier today."

Gladys Mae's eyes widened as she slapped her forehead. "You're Sheriff Maguire."

"Former sheriff," said Fen. "Close your mouth and I'll take your picture. After my meal, I'll do a pencil drawing of you."

Gladys Mae did as instructed but struck an awkward pose. Fen pointed his phone away from her and said, "Turn your head to the left like you're watching Scooter come through the door unexpectedly."

Her face lit up with a smile, and Fen knew it would make a delightful keepsake. She turned back to him. "Scooter will be here in a little while. He'd love to sit with you, if you don't mind."

"Not at all. I'd enjoy talking to him."

"I'm going into the kitchen and read the rest of your bio. I still can't place where I've seen you before."

As Gladys Mae scurried back to the kitchen, she told another server to take the table where an elderly couple had settled in for an early supper. Fen took out a sketch pad and thought to himself that he might have hit the jackpot concerning information about the murders.

He lost track of time as he swiped with a pencil while shifting his gaze from the photo on his phone to the sketch pad. Gladys Mae returned with a medium-rare steak that barely fit on the plate with a loaded baked potato that looked as if it had to fight for its share of porcelain real estate. The salad arrived in a bowl and had to sit beside the plate, like a pinch-hitter waiting for his turn to bat.

He put the sketch on the seat beside him but left the phone on the table. Gladys Mae said, "I'm almost through reading about you, Sheriff. We'll talk after you've finished."

Fen already had a firm grip on a knife and fork. "I've nowhere to go and nothing to do tonight. But don't neglect your customers on account of me."

She looked around. "Ain't hardly anyone here. The rain has them all homebound." She paused. "I remembered where I knew you from. You solved that murder in Kerrville about a year and a half ago. Didn't you get shot in the leg?"

"Not then, but a bullet to my knee ended my career as a state trooper. A woman tried to shoot her husband and hit me instead. I hobbled around for ten more years as a sheriff. In Kerrville, I twisted wrong and finished the job the woman who couldn't aim straight started. One knee replacement surgery later and here I am, almost good as new."

"I'll leave you alone, so you can enjoy your meal. I told the cook to take that scrawny T-bone off the grill and give you the best cut of meat in the cooler."

Fen looked at it. "And the biggest. Thank you, but I can only eat half." An idea came to him. "Why don't I cut half of this off the bone and give it to Scooter? He'll be starving when he gets off."

He knew an objection was coming, but it didn't sound very convincing. "Oh, I couldn't do that."

"Sure you can. It's my gift to Scooter in appreciation of his hard work today."

She snickered. "He puts in long hours, but hard work and Scooter Gillespie rarely go in the same sentence. Don't get me wrong, he's a good man and a better husband, but if the government had a branch of service called the Chair Force, he'd be a general."

"Bring me a to-go box and I'll give that man of yours a treat," said Fen.

She winked. "Thank you, Sheriff."

Fen added half the baked potato into the container but kept the salad. He figured Scooter was a meat and potatoes kind of guy, anyway. After pushing the plate containing only a bone away, he got to work on the portrait. Normally, he would have done a caricature, but he wanted to do something more for Gladys Mae and Scooter.

The pencil strokes came fast as he already had the outline of her face, the profile of her partially turned countenance, and the shape of her hair. She was one of those women who the longer you looked at her, the prettier she became. He imagined her as a fun-loving teen with dreams of traveling and swimming in the azure waters of the Caribbean. That excitement still registered in her eyes.

Instead of the Caribbean, Fen drew a background scene of Gladys Mae looking out to sea on South Padre Island, the closest thing Texas has to a sun-kissed island paradise, and reachable in less than a day's drive.

It took him about an hour to complete the drawing, but it was an excellent likeness and told a story. He hoped she and Scooter would like it.

Scooter made a less than grand entrance when he came in. He almost made it to Fen's table before sneezing. "Danged rain and cold," he said as he dug a red bandana out of his back pocket and blew his nose.

Gladys Mae came from the other side of the room. "Honey, you're soaked to the skin."

"Yeah," he said with a drawl thick as refrigerated honey. "The seam of my slicker britches split while dragging a woman out of her car. The car was half in and half out of the water. There was no time to go home and change. At least the rain's finally stopped."

Fen looked at the round, honest face. "Are people taking the flooding seriously?"

"The road traffic is next to nothing, and the highway department and county road crews finally got barricades up at the river and creek crossings that usually flood. They're predicting the river to crest by daylight."

Gladys Mae asked, "You don't have to go back to work, do you?"

"I have to go back after I eat. Somebody's got to do it when the Medina gets angry."

"What about putting on a dry uniform?"

"No time," said Scooter.

"That ain't right," said Gladys Mae. "You're already half sick."

He waved off her complaint. "Tell her, Sheriff. Days like this go with the job."

"He's right," said Fen. "Life and property come before personal comfort."

Scooter smiled. "That doesn't mean I can't stay in the truck and run the heater when I'm parked at a barricade with my emergency lights on. All I have to do the rest of the night is stay awake and respond to any calls from dispatch."

"You'd better take a full thermos of coffee," said Fen.

Gladys Mae turned and said, "Your supper should be ready by now. I'll bring it and coffee."

"Milk, please," said Scooter. "I'll be drinking coffee all night."

Fen asked, "When did you get to work this morning?"

"My shift started at 6:00 a.m."

"When do you get off?"

"The same time, if I'm lucky."

Gladys Mae returned with the meal and milk. She placed it in front of her husband and said, "Do you want some rolls?"

"This will do me just fine. I wasn't expecting anything this good."

His wife looked at Fen with appreciation shining in her eyes. "The sheriff here was generous enough to share his big steak with you."

"Wow. Thanks, Sheriff. That was mighty kind of you."

Fen said, "Have a seat, Gladys Mae. I have something for you." He picked up his sketch pad, signed the drawing, and handed it to her.

Her chin quivered. She pulled a napkin from the dispenser on the table and dabbed her eyes.

"Let me see," said Scooter.

Gladys Mae handed him the drawing. He looked at her, then at Fen. "Did you do this?"

"Of course he did," said Gladys Mae. "He's a famous artist."

"I don't doubt it. You must have told him we went to Padre Island on our honeymoon."

She shook her head and cried some more.

"Honey," said Scooter, excitement lacing his voice. "Let's go back this summer."

Green eyes sparkled. "Do you mean it? Can we?"

"I don't see why not. If we go on our anniversary, it'll be plenty warm."

"Warm? It will be downright hot."

"Even better," said Scooter as he wiggled his eyebrows up and down in a suggestive manner. "We'll stay in our room like we did last time."

Instead of scolding him, she winked. "You still know how to sweet talk a country girl."

Before things became any more uncomfortable, Scooter said, "By the way, expect a steady stream of first responders to come in tonight. They'll be tired, wet, and hungry. I'm the first to be relieved."

Gladys Mae rose and said, "I'll put this drawing somewhere safe and tell the cook the night might not be as slow as we thought."

As she walked away, Fen took in the information and asked, "Do you think Sheriff Irons might come in?"

"He should be here in a little while," said Scooter.

Chapter Six

A steady stream of first responders came and went for the next hour and a half. Thanks to either Scooter or Gladys Mae, word was out that the visiting sheriff was giving away free drawings of anyone who had braved the weather to keep people from harm or had worked the two murders. Between the radio chatter, the humorous caricature sketches, and Fen being a former sheriff, he gleaned real-time information on the flood, and some additional information related to the female victim.

Sheriff Irons arrived and two deputies who'd not been in a hurry to finish their apple cobbler and second cups of coffee made haste for the door. The sheriff spoke to the men's backs, "Thirty minutes means thirty, not forty-five. Spread the word that I'll be here until closing."

Rusty slid into the booth opposite Fen, took off his hat, and rubbed his eyes. "It's days like this that make me question my choice of a career."

Fen countered with, "Think of all the stories you'll have when you retire."

"That's if I live through today. The county commissioners are all for my people working extra hours while the water's rising, but it won't be long before the river goes down and they'll want to know why I approved so much overtime. That's not counting why I didn't prevent a double homicide. They'll be riding me like I was a horse at one of the dude ranches. They'll probably want everything solved before Thanksgiving."

Fen took the opening to verify something he'd heard from an ambulance attendant. "I understand the female victim is a local woman named Misti Palmer."

Rusty rolled his eyes. "I should have known that wouldn't stay confidential for long. Was it one of my deputies?"

Fen shook his head. "An EMT. He sat in the next booth and his voice carried. In a town this size, it was bound to come out, no matter what you said or did."

"I know you're right, but it still isn't fair to the next of kin."

"And who might that be?"

He leaned forward and let out a harsh whisper. "Elton Palmer, one of the most ornery, cantankerous county commissioners you'd ever want to meet."

Fen raised his eyebrows. "That sounds like ten pounds of trouble in a sack meant to hold five."

"I went to his ranch to tell him myself, but his foreman told me he left after receiving a phone call. I have a bad feeling he's giving serious thought to who he can blame for Misti's death."

Fen tilted his head. "Was she his only child?"

"There's an older brother named Cliff. Elton lost his wife when Misti was seven years old. A horse threw her and Deloris landed wrong. Misti was with her. I think seeing her mama die sort of flipped a switch in that little girl's brain. Over time, she became more and more rebellious. Elton's spent a lot of time and money keeping her and Cliff in trucks and out of jail."

Fen leaned forward. "What's your theory involving the two deaths?"

"I don't have one."

Fen tilted his head, which Rusty followed with a non sequitur. "You look well rested. Did you get a nap today?"

Fen responded with a sheepish grin.

"My phone hasn't stopped ringing, and I can't tell you how many radio transmissions I received today. Ask me about theories in a day or two. Right now, I'm having a hard time keeping my head above water."

"Fair enough," said Fen.

Rusty let out a sigh. "Sorry. I'm usually better at dealing with pressure. I can tell you this much. An anonymous witness called today and claimed she saw a cowboy named Brent Stone and Misti Palmer together at the picnic area a week ago."

"Do you believe that's possible?"

"He's the type she went for. According to the police chief in Kerrville, Brent was one arrest away from a long bus ride to prison. Now he's our problem."

Gladys Mae delivered a cup of coffee and a glass of water to Rusty without him asking for it. She placed a hand on his shoulder. "*Someone*," she shifted her gaze to Fen then back to the sheriff, "opened their wallet to pay for supper for all the first responders tonight."

Rusty looked at Fen. "That's mighty generous of you."

Gladys Mae beamed. "It's the most big-hearted thing I've seen in all my years of waitressing."

Fen glared at the young woman. "It was supposed to be anonymous. A hot meal is payback for all the times individuals and businesses helped me with a meal and hot coffee."

What Fen didn't say was he had an ulterior motive for telling Scooter to pass the word that supper would be free for any first responder who helped during the flood or worked the double murders. He had an inkling that he and his small, unusual team of sleuths would return to help Rusty solve the murders. A free meal and some caricatures might go a long way in getting people to talk.

A big *if* accompanied the impromptu decision to treat so many to a free meal. He needed someone to ask for his help, and he'd already done more *inquiring* than he should.

Out of the blue, Rusty said, "Uh-oh. Here comes trouble looking for a place to happen. I was hoping it wouldn't happen tonight."

Fen followed the sheriff's gaze as it rested on two men wearing mud-caked boots, spurs, rain gear, and soggy cowboy hats. They walked a straight line to the bar, ordered shots of whiskey, and unbuttoned their long black coats. "Those two look like they were in the weather most of the day."

"Probably moving cattle to high ground," said Rusty through clenched teeth. "The one in front is Brent Stone."

"Is he on probation or parole?" asked Fen.

"Not at the moment, but it's only because we couldn't catch him when he was on probation. He's slippery as a greased eel." Rusty took a sip of coffee. "Worst of all, he and Misti Palmer used to be the talk of the town. Everyone thought they'd run off and get married, but her daddy had other ideas."

"Do you know why they broke up?"

"Sure," said Rusty. "Everyone knows. Elton Palmer put his foot down, and it landed on Misti and Brent. No one knows for sure what he said or did, but it was enough for Misti to go back to college in Tennessee for a year and for Brent to spend three months in jail. There was also talk about Elton threatening to write Misti out of his will."

"Do you think he'd do that?"

Rusty lifted his coffee cup and spoke before he took

another sip. "I wouldn't put it past Elton, but that's a moot point now that she's dead."

Fen shot a glance at Brent. "He's got that rebel look about him. I wonder how he'd react if I did a sketch of him?"

Rusty raised his shoulders and let them fall. "It probably depends on what kind of mood he's in." He looked around the room. "There's plenty of help here. If he gets rowdy, my deputies will put a quick end to it."

Fen gave his head a nod. "This might be interesting. Keep an eye on me and send in the cavalry if he hates artists."

Fifteen steps was all it took for Fen to span the distance from the booth he was sitting in to the bar. He eased onto a stool, leaving one open between him and Brent. Instead of starting a conversation, Fen opened his sketch pad to a blank page and began sketching the two cowboys.

Occasional glances in the mirror behind the bar allowed Fen to sketch the men. He was about six minutes into what he thought would be a ten-minute sketch when Brent turned to him. "Hey, old man. What are you doin'?"

Fen kept sketching. "I'm a professional artist. I came to town looking for interesting things to draw. The rain washed me out, so I'm finding interesting people to sketch. I've already sketched a waitress, several cops and a couple of volunteer fire-fighters. You two look like real cowboys, so I thought I'd draw a sketch of you."

Brent turned on his stool toward Fen. "Who gave you permission to draw me and my buddy?"

Fen shrugged and kept drawing. "The owner knows what I'm doing. Besides, I'm not drawing anything above your chin. With your heads down, your hat brims cover most of your faces."

"Give me that drawing," said Brent with menace in his words.

Fen kept drawing. "I don't think so, cowboy. How 'bout I buy you another round?"

Brent slid off his stool. "How 'bout I take that drawing and cram it down your throat?"

"No thanks. The day's been unpleasant enough without me having to teach you some manners. I found a murdered man in the river and a dead woman earlier today. Drawing people who are still alive will keep me from dwelling on how they looked when I go to bed tonight."

Brent squared off with fists clenched. "You're either crazy or a liar."

Sheriff Irons came from Brent's blind side and said, "He's neither. This is Sheriff Fen Maguire. He found Clay Trueblood's body in the river this morning."

"That's a shame," said Brent, his fists relaxing some. "I don't know anyone named Trueblood."

Fen slid off his stool and stood beside the sheriff. "Have you been in the saddle all day?"

"Yeah. What of it?"

"Look around," said Rusty. "The place is crawling with lawmen. Two people died today. I already told you about one. The other is Misti Palmer."

Brent took a step back and whispered, "No. That can't be."

Fen caught a movement out of the corner of his eye. A gruff voice shouted, "Why can't it be? You killed both of them."

Fen saw the reflection of a grizzled man in the bar's mirror. He held a pistol in his hand and was in the process of raising it when Fen took two steps to his right. This put him between Brent and the man he thought to be Elton Palmer, with his back to the deceased woman's father.

"I don't know who you are," said Elton. "But if you don't move, I'm going to put a bullet through you and into that piece of trash you're protecting."

Fen watched in the mirror as Rusty drew his pistol and spoke in an urgent but restrained tone. "Elton, you're an inch away from killing an innocent man, and even if Stone is guilty, you've no right to kill him."

"Tell the first one to move. I've got no beef with him."

Fen raised his hands and turned to face Elton. "I know what it's like to lose someone who's the most important person in your life. I've felt the same rage you're experiencing, but blindly striking out at someone who may be innocent will only make matters worse. Put the pistol away and let Rusty do his job. He and I will take Mr. Stone and his buddy to jail and start getting answers."

"Are you really a lawman?" asked Elton.

"Retired, but still a certified peace officer," said Fen.

Rusty added, "Sheriff Maguire can be your friend or your worst enemy." He took a step toward Elton and stopped. "Now, put your pistol on the table to your right and back away from it."

"Do I have your word that you'll take Stone to jail?"

Rusty didn't hesitate. "Sheriff Maguire said we would. His word is good as gold."

Fen added. "We'll detain him for being drunk in public and threatening physical harm. You missed his threat to cram a drawing down my throat."

"What about my daughter?" shouted the grieving father.

Rusty took over. "We'll find out if he has an alibi, and I'll keep him locked in a cell until I can check it out."

Brent regained some of his bravado and asked, "What about this crazy old man? He threatened me with a pistol."

Elton raised his pistol and was taking aim again. Fen knew he had to act, so he spun around and sunk his fist into Brent's belly. The cowboy folded in half like a sheet of paper as air shot from his lungs.

The results were exactly what Fen hoped for. The distraught father no longer had a shot at Brent, and the fierceness of the blow shocked Elton into inaction. Meanwhile, Rusty took another step toward the man and shouted, "The pistol goes on the table, Elton. There are three deputies behind you with pistols pointed at your back. Two of them are good shots. That means you and I both stand a good chance of getting shot if you don't do as I say."

Rusty gulped a breath. "Sheriff Maguire and I are taking Brent and his buddy to jail and you're going home. You can come by my office in three days to get your pistol." He paused. "For the last time, put it on the table."

Elton pointed his pistol at the floor and walked to the table. He placed the revolver near the middle and stepped back.

Brent was still reeling from the punch in the gut but managed to eek out, "Arrest him."

Fen responded by grabbing the shoulders of Brent's mud-stained, black coat and jerking it halfway off, pinning Brent's arms to his side. Fen then shoved the coughing cowboy into the bar and pushed his neck until Brent's face lay against the polished wood. "I could use some handcuffs," shouted Fen.

Two deputies responded and took over, while a third deputy unloaded Elton's pistol, gathered the shells, and stuck the pistol in the pocket of his jacket. This left Rusty free to speak to the county commissioner. "Go home, Elton. There's been enough heartache for one day."

The grieving father released a mournful sigh and nodded. "I'll go, but I expect a report tomorrow on what you found out."

"I'll promise you this," said Rusty. "I'll call the district attorney tonight and give him a full report of our interview with Brent. I'll also tell him about you coming into a place that sells alcohol and threatening Brent with a loaded pistol. He may want to press charges against you. If he does, deputies will be out tomorrow and you'll go to jail."

"That ain't right. He oughta' be arrested for threatening me now!" shouted Brent from the bar.

One deputy ended the conversation with, "Brent, it's still rainy and slick outside. It would be a shame if you slipped and fell on the way to my truck. I suggest you save anything else you want to say until Sheriff Irons and Sheriff Maguire talk to you."

Chapter Seven

It wasn't long before Fen and Sheriff Irons sat on one side of a table with Brent Stone's running buddy, a young man named Roger Blankenship, sitting opposite them. The interview room seemed cold, which came as no surprise. Comfort in small town jails wasn't high on anyone's list of priorities.

Unlike Brent Stone, Roger wasn't earning frequent flier points for visiting the county lock-up. He verified this by saying, "This is my first time to come here. I sure hope it's my last."

Rusty stared at the young man and said, "Roger, if you don't enjoy sitting here, I suggest you find someone besides Brent to hang around with." He pulled a card from the pocket of his shirt. "I'm going to read you your rights and record this interview."

After completing the formalities and saying that former Sheriff Fen Maguire would join him, Rusty gave Fen a nod.

Fen asked, "How long have you and Brent been friends?"

Roger sat straight in his chair and said, "I wouldn't call him a close friend. He and I work at the same dude ranch. He's been there off and on for a couple of years. I started about a month ago. I ran out of money for college and came home to work until I could go back to school. Since August, I've been slinging pizzas at a place in town. Working at the Lucky 7 pays better, plus the food and a bunk keep my expenses down."

"Were you with him yesterday?"

"All day," said Roger. "The owners had a farrier out to put new shoes on about half the horses. I can trim a hoof if it's only one or two horses but staying bent over all day kills my back. I'd rather clean the stalls, so that's what I did. Brent made sure the farrier didn't have to wait for the next horse."

Fen detected no evasion. In fact, Roger was volunteering more information than requested. This was a good sign, so he continued with another open-ended question. "What did you two do after work yesterday?"

Roger hesitated before saying, "We drank a few beers."

Fen pushed his luck with an accusation. "And smoked a joint or two. Did you do anything harder than weed?"

Roger examined his dirty fingernails. "No. Just a couple of joints and we split a six-pack." He raised his gaze to look at Fen. "How'd you know we smoked dope?"

"I didn't until you told me, but you did well by not trying to lie about it. Keep telling the truth and nothing too bad will happen to you tonight."

Rusty took over. "Where did you have this after-work party yesterday?"

"At the roadside picnic area on the east side of the river, on the way to Medina. The cops wait until after ten to stop and hassle anyone. We finished smoking and drinking about eight o'clock. That's when I came to town and ate a burger."

Rusty asked, "What about Brent? Did he leave then, too?"

Roger shook his head. "He wanted to stay and smoke another joint."

Fen asked, "Why didn't you stay and join him?"

"I was buzzed and hungry. That pot he scored was powerful, and I can't afford to wrap my truck around a tree. We drove our own trucks." He looked Rusty in the eye. "You may not believe this, but I seldom drink or smoke dope. Like I said, I'm saving to go back to college."

Rusty asked, "Did Brent say anything about meeting someone at the picnic area?"

A shake of his head was all Roger gave for an answer.

"Did he mention anything about Misti Palmer?"

"Not yesterday or today, but he had plenty to say about her last week."

Fen took his turn. "When last week?"

"Sunday, after the last guest checked out."

"Keep talking. You're doing good."

Roger puffed out his cheeks. "I'm not very proud of it, but Brent and I went to the same picnic area after we got off work. Brent knew of a couple of girls from San Antonio who met us there. Those girls came ready to party and Brent came prepared."

Fen asked, "Cocaine?"

Roger nodded. "Cocaine, beer, and pot. The pot was low-quality, lots of seeds and stems. I stuck with beer, but the girls went for the nose candy."

It was Rusty's turn again. "Let's get back to what Brent said about Misti Palmer. What exactly did he say about her?"

"He talked about Misti before the girls arrived, after he took a big snort of coke. That stuff loosened his tongue like nothing I've ever seen before. One minute he'd be talking about the good times they had, and the next, he was cussing her and her daddy." He paused for a few seconds. "I sort of tuned him out, so I don't remember exactly what he said, but it alternated between love and hate."

Fen thought there might be more. "Think hard, Roger. Did Brent say he wanted to harm Misti or her father?"

"He's a guy who pops off without thinking. It doesn't matter if he's stoned or sober."

"What about Misti's boyfriend? Did Brent mention him?"

"I didn't know she had a new boyfriend. He didn't mention that. Are you sure?"

Rusty gave Roger a hard stare. "Let's get something straight. We ask the questions. You answer them to the best of your ability."

Fen played good cop. "Let's start over with the last question. Did Brent mention anything about Misti having a new boyfriend?"

"No, but he's been real moody the last few days. I asked him what was wrong, and he cut me off. Yesterday was the first day he asked me to do anything with him all week."

Fen moved on. "Tell us about today."

"It was a miserable day of moving cattle in the rain. Brent wanted ninety proof anti-freeze, and I wanted a hot meal." He looked at Sheriff Irons. "I don't know if you noticed it or not, but I didn't drink any whiskey at the bar. I gave my shot to Brent."

Rusty said, "We noticed." Without skipping a beat, he asked, "Have you ever heard of a man named Clay Trueblood?"

Roger responded with a simple, "No, sir."

Rusty turned to Fen. "Any more questions for Roger?"

"One or two more." He shifted his gaze to Roger. "Where were you last night after you ate your hamburger?"

"At the dude ranch. There's a bunk house the hired hands can live in. We work from before dawn until after we wash, dry, and put away the supper dishes. In between, we take the guests on trail rides and do everything else related to ranch work. The steady rain meant no trail rides, so we spent much of the day taking turns talking to customers about the ranch and doing chores."

Fen nodded that he understood. "What about Brent? He doesn't impress me as a dishwasher or one who likes to talk to customers."

A faint smile pulled on the corners of Roger's mouth. "You nailed him on helping with the dirty dishes, but he'll talk the ears off customers. In fact, he's darn good at making up tall tales and he can play the guitar and sing. When it's not raining, he's the one who builds the campfire for the after-supper sing-along of old cowboy tunes. They let him do it for health reasons. His idea of washing dishes is to rinse them with warm water. He does a terrible job on purpose, but he makes a perfect campfire every time. Besides, he's been there longer than most. There aren't many guests from January until the end of April, but they keep Brent and one other cowboy on year-round."

"When did Brent get back to the ranch last night?"

Roger gave a contemplative look at a spot high on the wall above and behind Fen's shoulder. "I can't say for sure."

"Why not?" asked Rusty. "It's a simple question."

Roger answered with a defensive tone in his voice. "I'm not trying to dodge the question, Sheriff, but when I work, I work hard, and when I sleep, I'm out like someone drugged me. Last night I showered, made it to my bunk, put on a sleep mask, plugged in earbuds, and listened to waves coming ashore. I'd tell you when Brent came into the bunkhouse if I could, but I can't."

Fen said, "Thanks for cooperating. That's all the questions I have."

Roger seemed to gather his courage and asked, "Am I being arrested?"

Instead of giving a direct answer, Rusty said, "You'll go with a deputy, write a formal statement of what happened tonight, and sign it. I'll talk to you again after I speak with Brent. Be thinking of anything you failed to tell us."

Rusty rose and motioned for Roger to do the same. They left the room, and Rusty returned with Brent a few minutes later. After taking a seat, Brent asked, "Can you loosen these cuffs?"

"It depends," said Rusty. "Do you plan on cooperating with our investigation?"

"That depends on you, Sheriff. Am I under arrest?"

"Not yet. You're being detained, so I need to read you your rights."

Brent scoffed, "I've had those read to me enough times I can quote them."

"Then one more time won't come as a surprise to you."

Following the reading and Brent affirming he understood, he asked, "Does my detention have anything to do with Misti and that guy being killed?"

Rusty looked to Fen so he could field the question. Fen looked straight into Brent's eyes. "Do you know either of the victims?"

"Of course I know Misti. I already told you I don't know any Trueblood." Brent shook his head and rocked in his chair. "I still can't believe it." He kept repeating the phrase and pulled at his handcuffs to no avail before shouting, "Get these off me."

"Not until you calm down," said Rusty.

Fen looked at the sheriff. It was time for them to change roles and Fen to play the bad cop. "You'll get nothing of value from him tonight. I suggest you put him in a cell and try again in the morning."

"Wait," said Brent. "I need to know what happened to Misti." He squirmed in his seat. "At least put the cuffs in front of me. I have to know what happened."

Fen and Rusty traded glances. "It's your party," said Fen.

Rusty moved to stand behind Brent. "Lean forward until your face and chest are on the table. If you do anything stupid, you'll earn a long stay in a cell, and I'll make sure you don't hear anything about Misti. Do we have a deal?"

"Yeah. Anything you say, Sheriff."

Fen walked around the table and grabbed a handful of the back of Brent's shirt collar to make sure the cowboy's head and chest were pressed hard against the table. Once one side of the handcuffs was loose, he pulled back on the collar and brought Brent upright in his chair. "Hands in front of you and lace your fingers together like you're praying."

Brent complied, and Rusty clicked the cuffs together. Rusty said, "I'm not double locking these. If you struggle, you'll only make them tighter. It's been a long day and we're in no mood to play games."

"I understand. What happened to Misti?"

Fen took his turn as both he and Sheriff Irons returned to their seats. "What do you think happened to her?"

"How should I know?" said Brent with a strained voice. "All I know is she dumped me."

"When was the last time you saw her?" asked Fen.

"It's been at least a month."

"That's a lie," said Fen. "Try again."

It was a guess, but an accurate one. Fen knew in a town the size of Bandera, the chance of them not seeing each other was remote, if not impossible.

"All right," said Brent. "I saw her at a dance hall three weeks ago. We danced and drank a few beers. She went her way, and I went mine."

Fen shook his head. "You're digging a deeper hole for yourself. You moped around the ranch this week. That tells me you either saw her or talked to her since then."

Brent's eyes darted from side to side. "I didn't. I swear it."

Fen shifted his gaze to Rusty. "He's telling the truth, but I didn't ask the right question. Do you have his cell phone?"

"That and a knife, along with his wallet, keys, and belt."

"Check the phone for texts."

Brent scowled at Fen. "You win, but I didn't lie. We started texting each other three weeks ago. You won't find anything older than that." He leaned forward. "Now tell me what happened to her."

"Someone shot her in the back of the head," said Rusty. "Who do you think that was?"

Fierce anger shone in Brent's eyes, and he spat out a name. "Clay Trueblood. Find him, and you'll have your killer."

Fen's narrowed his eyes. "You said you don't know a Trueblood."

Brent's eyes widened, his mouth opened as if to say something, then closed.

Rusty spoke in a soft voice. "Whether you knew him or not, we don't have to look for Mr. Trueblood. Sheriff Maguire found his body in the river earlier today. What I need you to tell us is where you were last night."

The man's dark eyes darted from side to side. Fen wondered how long it would take Brent to figure out he was suspect #1 if he didn't have an airtight alibi.

The seconds of silence dragged on before Brent said, "I'm not saying anything else without an attorney."

Fen pushed back from the table. "That's probably a good idea. It will give Sheriff Irons plenty of time to discover where you were and what you were doing. It would be easier if you told him, but that's between you and your attorney."

Rusty stood, walked to the door, and instructed a deputy to put Brent in a cell. Things weren't looking good for the rebellious cowboy, but Fen wasn't sure of Brent's guilt. If he had a fireproof alibi, Fen and his team might be back before Christmas. If not, the cowboy would live in a prison cell until he was a very old man.

Chapter Eight

Fen woke with the first rays of sunlight peeking through a gap in the curtains of his motel room. He reached for the framed photo of Sally and wished her a good morning. After brushing his teeth, he returned to bed, stacked a pillow on top of the one under his head, then balanced the photo of his love on his stomach and conducted a ritual he started the day after she died.

"Good morning again, sweetheart," he began. "As you know, I'm in Bandera. I came to sketch landscapes, but it seems another murder case has found me." He paused then continued, "That's not exactly true. The sheriff hasn't asked for help yet, but I think he will. There's a cowboy named Brent Stone who needs a good alibi, or they'll arrest and charge him." Fen took a breath. "I'm not convinced he did it, but it's early in the investigation and the high water is delaying everything."

He pinched his eyebrows together. "Can you hold on a minute? You know me and how I love to talk to you while sipping my morning coffee. I'll be right back."

The coffee maker proved to be a single-cup machine with a flimsy plastic tray and an elongated, tiny bag of coffee that slid into it. He poured a paper cup full of water into the back of the machine and waited until the hissing and sputtering stopped.

Armed with stimulation, he returned to Sally's photo. He sipped the black brew and waited for inspiration before resuming the one-sided conversation. "Bandera is a fascinating place. You'd like it. I'm sorry we never came here. In some ways it's modern and in others, it's like going back in time about a hundred and fifty years. Back then, the cattle roamed free and real cowboys rode through the canyons and rounded them up for trail drives. The county has several dude ranches that cater to people wanting to have a taste of the old west."

He looked away as a thought struck him. "Some things haven't changed, though. There are still lawmen and those that break the law." He let out a low chuckle. "I hope there aren't lawmen who break the law."

He took another sip. "I'm rambling this morning. You know how I get when there's a murder. My mind works overtime. Do you think I should call Lou and Bailey this morning and have them do a background check on Brent Stone and a couple of other people who interest me?"

He waited for an answer that didn't come. Instead, he stared deeply into the face of the blond-haired, blue-eyed beauty. How he wished she had chanced getting a second heart transplant, but her sense of fairness told her it wasn't right that she should get two replacement hearts while there were so many waiting to get their first.

He finished his coffee in silence and placed the cup on a nightstand. A thought exploded in his mind and he jerked his gaze back to the photo. "What do you mean I should call Audrey on the way home? That's not the deal we made. I called her on the way to Bandera. She'll think something's wrong if I call her this close to Thanksgiving."

Sally seemed to look back at him with something like loving mischief in her smile. He tilted his head and said, "The holidays are special, and I'd rather spend this one with you."

Time seemed to stand still as he stared at the photo. He finally said, "All right. I'll call her, but I'm still yours for the next several years, and that includes this Thanksgiving and Christmas."

The spell of two-way communication broke as Fen lay Sally's picture on the bed. He retreated to the bathroom, showered, shaved, and packed his belongings into a suitcase, along with Sally's picture and memories of happy days.

His stomach let out a rumble of protest as he finished putting his easel and other art supplies into the camper shell that covered the bed of his truck. He hadn't tried the restaurant across the street yet, but the name intrigued him.

THE HEN'S NEST was the kind of café that Fen loved to frequent when he was away from home. As he stepped through the front door, the words intimate, rustic, friendly, and tasty came to mind. He would soon discover that the owner was a woman who took great pride in serving fresh, locally sourced food, and had a wide streak of independence running through her. Quality came first, and she made sure the coffee cups didn't drop below half full. Servers hustled under her watchful eye.

"Here's a menu, sir," said a slender Hispanic teen with a Texas accent. "You look like a cowboy who could use a cup of coffee."

"Yes, ma'am," said Fen. "I have several hours of driving ahead of me."

"Where are you going?"

"Back to Newman County, on the Brazos River. If I don't

make it back before Thanksgiving, there's a good chance I'll be tarred and feathered."

She chuckled. "Your wife?"

Fen shook his head. "My housekeeper and a young lady a little older than you. Her name is Bailey and we sort of adopted each other a couple of years ago. She's home from college."

The girl gave him a sideways look. "You look familiar. What's your name?"

"Fen Maguire."

She snapped her fingers. "You're the artist and lawman."

He nodded. "I'm surprised you've heard of me."

She swept a hand around the room. "See those paintings? Last summer I almost starved to death trying to make a living as an artist until I realized bacon, eggs, biscuits, and gravy sell better." She narrowed her gaze. "I heard it was you who found the bodies of that no-account man from Kerrville and Misti Palmer yesterday. I also heard you knocked the stuffing out of Brent Stone last night and helped Sheriff Irons lock him up so he can't cause any more trouble."

Fen didn't argue but said, "Sheriff Irons is running things, and I'm leaving today. I just gave him a hand yesterday."

The door opened and KK walked in. She made a beeline to Fen's table and said, "Good morning, Sheriff. Mind if I join you?" She looked at the server and said, "Juanita, how are you?"

"Fair to middlin', KK. Turn your cup over and I'll fill it. You two holler when you're ready to order."

Fen turned his attention to KK. "You look tired."

"That's because the river didn't crest until a little while ago." She scanned the room. "It seems you're the talk of the town this morning. Everyone's saying you kept Elton Palmer from killing Brent Stone and then got Brent to confess to both murders."

Fen chuckled. "They'll be disappointed when the truth

comes out. Brent didn't confess to anything. If he has a decent alibi, he won't be in jail long."

KK dumped some sugar in her coffee and spoke as she stirred. "Elton Palmer may have something to say about Brent getting out of jail. He has a lot of influence in this county. The sheriff better find solid evidence, or Brent will spend thirty or forty Christmases in prison."

Fen asked, "Do you think he killed both victims?"

KK held up her hands like stop signs. "The sheriff didn't hire me to be a detective, and I like to keep things simple. If there comes a flood, I save lives and property. Otherwise, I do what I'm told and keep my head down." She gave him a sly smile. "Besides, I've only lived here for about six months. There's an unwritten rule that you have to be born in Bandera County or have lived here at least eighteen years to be counted as anything more than a move-in."

Fen knew of many small Texas towns that followed the same way of thinking. What KK really said was, most of the time, the judicial system followed state law. There was, however, a small cadre of people who could exert themselves into important matters, and Elton Palmer was one of the county's most influential people. While the law was unbreakable, certain people could bend it until it screamed.

Was this a simple warning to avoid the quicksand of county politics? Perhaps, but why did KK take it upon herself to tell him? After all, she'd stayed up all night and could have gone home for much needed sleep instead of tracking him to the restaurant. He wondered about her relationship with Elton Palmer. Could he have sent her to issue a subtle warning? Perhaps Elton wanted Fen to go home and not return unless it was to paint landscapes.

KK snapped her fingers and brought Fen out of his mental musings. She asked, "Where did you go?"

"Sorry. I was thinking about what you said. Believe me, I know all about small town politics. My former father-in-law developed a serious dislike for me, and it resulted in me losing my job as sheriff. I'm lucky I had art to fall back on."

A tilted head told Fen that KK didn't fully believe him. She confirmed it by saying, "I had plenty of down time last night waiting for some foolish person to be swept off a bridge or low water crossing. I spent a lot of it doing research on you. You have an interesting habit of showing up when police chiefs and sheriffs can't solve murders." She leaned forward. "All I'm saying is sometimes the powerful people in this county forget this is the 21st century, and they're not living in the 1850s when trials were sometimes deemed a waste of time."

Fen asked, "What are the chances Brent Stone won't live to go to trial if he's arrested and released on bond?"

KK took her time answering. "That may depend on the alibi. If it's beyond all doubt that he couldn't have killed Misti Palmer, I'd say his chances are about fifty-fifty. They go down fast if he can't account for where he was at the time she died."

Fen rubbed a hand across his freshly shaven cheek. "That certainly adds another dimension to the case. Sheriff Irons impresses me as an honest lawman who'll do all he can to keep Brent alive."

The woman sitting across from Fen gave her head a hint of a nod. "The sheriff will do all he can, but he can't be everywhere at once."

"Do you think Rusty will arrest Brent Stone before he's able to check on an alibi?"

KK shrugged. "All I know is the safest place for Brent is in jail."

Fen sensed his eyebrows coming together. "Why do you say that?"

"There are only forty deputies to cover the entire county.

To supplement, the city of Bandera has a town marshal and five additional deputy marshals. They're responsible for taking prisoners from jail to court appearances. They're state certified law enforcement officers, but they don't answer to Sheriff Irons." She gave him a knowing glance but didn't elaborate on what she thought of the division of law enforcement duties.

Fen said, "I see what you mean. In most counties, the sheriff's department provides deputies as courthouse security and prisoner transfers along with their normal law enforcement duties outside of the city limits."

"Right," said KK. "With only a thousand people living in the town of Bandera, there's no city police department. Sheriff Irons, his deputies, and State Troopers handle law enforcement, unless it's in the county courthouse or emergencies."

Fen filed the information away and concluded this rural Texas county really did resemble a frontier town from years gone by. He understood how people could settle disputes in ways that bore little resemblance to modern norms.

Juanita made her way back to the table with hot coffee and an order pad. "Are you two ready to order?"

KK pushed away from the table and stood. "Not me. All I want anywhere near my mouth is a toothbrush and pillow."

"I'm ready," said Fen, as he received a nod of goodbye from KK. He shifted his gaze to Juanita and said, "I'll take the J.T."

"Good choice if you're going to drive for four hours. That comes with three eggs, four strips of crisp bacon, two waffles, and hash browns."

"Perfect," said Fen.

Juanita asked, "Do you think you'll be back soon?"

"It's possible," said Fen. "I've always wanted to paint a snow scene of this part of the Hill Country."

Juanita laughed. "Snow? There's not much chance of that,

but it would make a unique painting. Longhorn cattle in a snowy canyon would be something you don't see every day."

"I'll talk to the weatherman and order us both a foot of snow. You need to add a snow scene to the wall."

Chapter Nine

Fen did significant damage to the plate of food Juanita delivered to him but couldn't finish all the hash brown potatoes or the second half of the waffle. He left a large tip on the way out, filled his truck with diesel, and began his trip home. It took him about an hour before he didn't feel miserable from his gluttonous meal.

A quick look at his phone showed an incoming call from Bailey. He engaged the call and the young woman's voice came through the truck's speakers. "I can hear the hum of your truck's engine. I hope you're on your way home."

"I am, and the only reason you said that is because Thelma's worried."

"I was having my doubts, too. Do you realize that tomorrow is Thanksgiving?"

The question didn't deserve an answer, so he remained silent until Bailey asked, "How's the investigation progressing?"

"One suspect is being detained. The most popular theory is the killer is now behind bars."

Bailey must have detected a hint of uncertainty in his voice. "You don't sound convinced. What is your gut telling you?"

"That I ate too much breakfast. It's a good thing Thelma gives us half-rations the day before Thanksgiving. Has she started cooking yet?"

Bailey treated him to a laugh that reminded him of the ringing of the smallest bells in a handbell choir. "I was told to eat cold cereal and then banished from the kitchen. I'm in my room, working on the portrait that's due before Christmas. The husband wants me to fudge a little on the size of his wife's nose. We had a bit of disagreement about how much."

Fen nodded even though she couldn't see him. "That's a risk you take because your preferred medium is hyper-realism. Most people want portraits that soften people's imperfections and depict a dominant positive trait or characteristic."

"That's what I tried to do, but this woman has a beak like a pelican."

Fen thought for a few seconds and said, "Have you considered light and shadows to enhance the woman's physical attributes and minimize the nose?"

"Uh... no, but that could help."

"I'll look at it when I get home, which should be about noon."

"How's the traffic?"

"Not terrible, but heavier than usual. Add another thirty minutes to my ETA."

Bailey hesitated, then spoke in a soft voice. "There's something else we need to talk about, but it can wait until you're not distracted."

Fen was ninety percent joking when he asked, "Is there a warrant out for your arrest?"

Bailey shot back, "How did you guess?"

Fen burst out laughing. "There's no warrant. Thelma would have called me if there was."

"Good point. You also know I wouldn't get caught even if I did something bad enough to go to jail." She gulped a breath. "Don't break your brain trying to discover what it is we need to talk about. It's nothing bad."

"Now I'm really worried," said Fen. "You sound serious and mature."

"That's because I am."

The call ended, leaving Fen to glance at the phone giving silent witness that Bailey had indeed ended the call. Something important was afoot. He reconsidered and said, "Correction. Something important to Bailey has happened or soon will."

After about twenty minutes of frustration, Fen abandoned his guessing about what Bailey might have done or wanted to do. She was a free-spirited twenty-year-old who was long in natural talent but sometimes lacked patience.

Instead, he shifted his thoughts to the early morning time he spent with Sally, his late wife. Normally, those times brought a strange mixture of fond memories, unexplainable peace, and stabs of loneliness to him, with emphasis on the last one. Not today. She wanted him to call Audrey, the only other woman who'd stirred his heart since he was a teenager.

Sally had made it abundantly clear in pre-death conversations that she didn't want Fen to spend the final third of his life as a lonely, miserable widower. As a result, he and Audrey were less than a year into a five-year plan of gradual courtship. The emphasis was still on the word *gradual*. Serious courting would take place eventually, followed by a brief engagement and nuptials. His and hers rocking chairs on the back patio were his idea for a wedding present.

In the meantime, he'd paint, help solve murders, and allow time to heal his grief.

Audrey also had unfinished business. She had a son to put through law school, help him establish a practice, find a wife, and begin his own family.

Fen sensed it would take a similar amount of time for Bailey to find her purpose in life and for Thelma to accept the idea that he would share his life with another woman.

He picked up his phone and told it to call Audrey. She answered on the second ring. "Good morning, cowboy. I wasn't expecting to hear from you so soon. How was Bandera?"

"Interesting. Two murders."

"I heard. It was nice of them to wait until you were there painting landscapes. Is it true you discovered both bodies?"

"It was blind luck, especially on the second one." He checked his speed then continued, "For a city attorney in a small town hours from Bandera, you're well-informed."

"I believe in looking after my investments."

"What kind of investment am I?' asked Fen.

"Time. Five years of waiting until I can hug you whenever I want to. Did you talk to Sally this morning?"

Fen lifted his foot from the accelerator that he'd mashed down when Audrey mentioned her desire to hold him then shifted back to Sally in the same breath.

Fen brought his emotions under control and said, "It's a rare day that I don't spend time with Sally. She wanted me to call you."

"That's amazing," said Audrey. "I was about to call you and make sure you were on your way home."

"Are you kidding? Thelma and Bailey would take turns hitting me over the head with frying pans if I missed Thanksgiving or Christmas." He then said, "Does John have to work tomorrow?"

"He volunteered to work a double shift tomorrow and on

Christmas day to give other officers time to be with their families, but the big news is he starts law school in January."

"I thought he wasn't starting until next fall?"

"That was the original plan, but they had an opening and he's looking forward to getting on with the next phase of his life. I'm excited for him."

Fen added, "Tell him I think he's making a wise decision."

"That will mean a lot coming from you. John and his mother both think you're pretty special."

"The same back at you."

"Fen," said Audrey, as a serious tone entered her voice. "I need you to give me a straight answer to something."

Fen gripped the steering wheel with both hands. "Ask away."

"I'm hearing there may be a rush to judgment concerning Brent Stone's guilt. What do you think?"

"I expected to hear this from Chuck and Candy, not from you."

"Never mind that," said Audrey. "What do you think?"

Fen gave the question serious consideration before saying, "I think Sheriff Irons needs to find out if Brent Stone has an alibi." He paused. "I also have a feeling that an alibi from an unreliable source might not be enough to save Stone from a life sentence or vigilante justice."

Audrey then said, "Expect to hear from Candy and Chuck soon."

Fen wagged his head as he checked the rearview mirror. "They're coming for Thanksgiving dinner tomorrow."

"I know," said Audrey. "I spoke with them early this morning."

The conversation hadn't gone the way Fen thought it would, but it didn't disappoint him. He ended the talk by saying, "There's a lot more to you than a pretty face and curves in all the right places. Have a happy Thanksgiving."

"You're easy on the eyes, yourself. Enjoy the holiday and your time back in Bandera."

Fen could usually compartmentalize his mind to think of one item at a time. Not so for the rest of the trip home. Like four varieties of popping corn in the same hot oil, thoughts of Bailey, Audrey, Sally, and the murder took turns exploding. The result was a hodge-podge of thoughts and feelings. Some were pleasant, some confusing, and all a little perplexing, especially when they *popped* close together.

The result was a strong desire to get home and settle his overstimulated brain by retreating into his studio, putting on Beethoven's Pastoral Symphony, mixing colors, and painting until he could hear nature sounds come from the images on the canvas.

He stilled the clattering engine with a turn of a key and walked toward a side door. Thelma met him with hands tented on her hips as he cleared the hall leading from the garage. "It's about time you remembered where you live. I hope you're not hungry because the kitchen is closed and off limits. You wouldn't have time to eat, anyway. You have cowboy work to do. Sam's near oil pump #3. He's trying to pull a calf from the momma cow I told you to sell last year."

"Which one? Every year, you make a list of a dozen or more after Sam and I agree on which ones we need to sell."

"The black baldy I call Skinny-Minnie. Anyone can see her hips are too narrow."

Fen shook his head. "She's produced healthy calves for the last four years. I'm surprised she's having trouble."

"It's because of that new bull. Bigger isn't always better. You should have stuck with Old Reliable."

If there was one thing Fen could always count on with

Thelma, it was her ability to share her opinions on almost any subject. Being right wasn't nearly as important to her as was stating what she thought.

That was one side of Fen's sometimes cantankerous cook and housekeeper. On the other side was a fiercely loyal woman whom Sally'd met when Thelma was an inmate and cook in the county jail during Fen's tenure as sheriff. It's said that love covers a multitude of sins and that was certainly true as Sally loved Thelma into becoming a much improved version of herself. Fen sometimes wondered how many other rough edges his wife would have taken off Thelma had Sally lived.

Instead of unloading his truck or checking in with Bailey, he went to the driveway and fired up his four-wheeler. He took the dirt road that ran along the top of the river bottom. Below him he saw the Brazos River Valley, complete with flat fields and sprigs of winter oats poking up toward the sunlight. As usual, Sam, his ranch foreman, had plowed and planted straight rows of a crop that would be harvested in the spring.

He passed this rich farmland on his left and turned to the west on another dirt road. The off-road machine rattled over pipes that were pieces of discarded oil well drill stems welded to form a cattle guard. His climbed and descended gently rolling hills until he saw Sam's and Bailey's trucks parked near a pump jack extracting oil from a field dotted with cattle.

A black cow with a white face paid no attention to him as she licked her newborn calf. Fen climbed down from his four-wheeler and spent a few minutes in wonder as the calf struggled to rise. The cycle of life in animals still amazed him.

Bailey approached. "I never tire of watching new life come into the world. It's good to have you home."

Sam joined them before Fen could respond to Bailey's words. As usual, Sam didn't speak first, so Fen said, "It looks like I got here in time to do nothing. Thelma said you were pulling a calf."

Sam shook his head. "My wife knows how to cook. I know animals and the land."

Bailey added, "Don't feel bad, Fen. She talked me into believing there was an emergency, too." Bailey's gaze went back to the calf. "It was worth the trip to watch it being born."

"You're right," said Fen. "A gentle rain and a newborn calf are always welcome on a ranch."

Bailey wiggled her eyebrows. "So is a double murder to solve. When are we leaving for Bandera?"

Chapter Ten

If Fen were a betting man, he'd have placed a wager that Bailey would corner him as soon as she could after returning home from watching the calf come into the world. She didn't, which told him something important was bothering her that would require a closed-door meeting. Her opportunity came after he cleaned out his truck. They built their own lunch meat sandwiches and retired to his studio. Instead of discussing what was really on her mind, she brought her unfinished portrait from her combination art studio and apartment over the garage.

Fen took a long look at the portrait and photos of the woman that the husband had provided. Bailey was right. Even after reducing the size of the woman's nose, the sheer volume of it seemed to jump out at him.

Fen put an optimistic spin on his critique. "You've already done a great job of softening the overall look. Have you thought about my suggestion of using a shadow?"

Bailey nodded. "I tried using a tree, partially opened

curtains, and a patio umbrella. She's such a pretty lady, except for that enormous honker."

Fen rubbed his chin. "Does she have a child?"

"No kids, but she's bonkers over her Ragamuffin cat. It has long, gray fur and the prettiest eyes you've ever seen. The woman's eyes are the same cornflower blue."

Fen said, "There's your answer. Show the woman holding the cat up to her face with her nose buried in the cat's fur. Emphasize both sets of eyes, the woman's hair, and the cat's fur. Make it a close-up of the two faces."

Bailey's eyes lit up. "I'll have to start over, but now that I know what to paint, it should be my best portrait. It will be hyper-realism at its finest." She smiled and sat once again.

Fen asked, "What about that other thing you wanted to talk about?"

"Do you mind if we wait until tomorrow morning to talk about that? I need to get started on sketches of the eyes to get the dimensions perfect."

It wasn't what Bailey said that bothered Fen, but what she left unsaid. Most people would write off Bailey's reluctance to face a big decision head-on as normal behavior for a college student. They'd be right if it was most any other woman her age. Bailey was truly a one-of-a-kind, with confidence oozing from every fiber of her body. A deceased father and a drug-addled mother meant she'd gone most of her life making her own unguided decisions. The fact that she was now actively seeking advice and then delaying the conversation caused warning sirens to go off in Fen's brain.

"One more thing to think about tonight," whispered Fen. "I wonder if she'll still want to go to Bandera and help with the investigation or if she'll have time?"

He took out his sketchbook and looked through the landscape images he'd brought home, hoping to choose one or two that would stand out. It was a fruitless task. His mind shifted between concerns, like he was driving an old car with a three-speed standard transmission. First gear was the double murder and whether he'd be called upon to travel back to Bandera. Second gear was Bailey and the decision she needed to make. He shifted into third gear as his thoughts turned to Audrey and the future life they might live together.

He shook his head to chase all three thoughts away. Then, a realization hit him. The metaphorical car he was driving had a fourth gear—his painting. If he focused his thoughts on staying in high gear, the evening would pass productively. Otherwise, he'd waste time guessing what the future might hold.

It took time and effort, but he got his pretend car into fourth gear and kept it there until fatigue overtook him. After a quick talk with Sally, he turned off the bedside lamp and nestled under crisp sheets and a down comforter. He then gave thanks for the day and what the next one would bring. After all, when he rose, it would be Thanksgiving Day.

***

THELMA TREATED Thanksgiving and Christmas Days as the reddest of the red-letter days on the calendar. Her kitchen and the breakfast nook were strictly off limits until that night. Breakfast consisted of three choices of cold cereal, one banana each, coffee, and small plastic glasses of orange juice. Paper bowls and plastic utensils, along with the food and drink, sat on a sideboard in the formal dining room. Everyone knew this was a get-and-go service and Thelma didn't care where you went to eat breakfast. No one dared to sit at the table, which was already set for the feast that began when the grandfather clock in the hallway struck two o'clock.

Fen and Bailey ate in Fen's studio while Sam was a no-show for breakfast. Fen assumed he preferred to cook his own somewhere in the woods. Bailey asked, "What do you think Sam's eating this morning?"

"Either squirrel or rabbit," said Fen. "He also likes those packaged white donuts covered in confectioner's sugar."

"I may join him next year."

"You don't have to wait that long. Christmas is right around the corner, and we'll get a repeat of this morning's meal."

"Uh-huh," said Bailey in response, as she'd already shoveled in a bite of Froot Loops. What she meant by "Uh-huh" was anyone's guess.

It didn't take long for both of them to get their fill of cereal and shift to coffee. Fen issued a word of caution. "If you want to top off your coffee, you have four more minutes. Thelma is on a strict schedule, and she clears the sideboard at 7:00 a.m. sharp."

"I outwitted her this year. I brought my single-serve coffee maker home with me. It takes those little pods of coffee. It's only two days a year, but I didn't want us to have coffee withdrawals today."

"That's good thinking. I'll take you up on that later this morning."

They finished the poor excuse for breakfast, and Fen sipped his coffee as Bailey made a weak joke of doing their dishes. He sensed she was building courage to discuss something important to her, so he kept the conversation light. "How did your sketches of the eyes go?"

"Better than I hoped, but only after I realized how close-up the two faces needed to be and that I needed nothing in the background. I'm still debating on whether to make the background completely black or to make it lighter and out of focus."

"That's a tough call," said Fen. "Is the woman mostly serious or sort of happy-go-lucky?"

"Bubbly and always smiling."

"I'd say lean toward bright but stay in her color palate and make the background sort of glossy."

Bailey nodded her appreciation and then looked down at her hands. "There's something else I need advice about." She looked up and fixed her gaze on him. "I received two unique opportunities for summer work." She took a ragged breath then let it out. "Actually, there are three or four things I could do this summer, and I can't decide what's best."

Fen waited for details that didn't come. "Take your time and start at the beginning. We have all morning to talk about it."

She started slowly, as if the words were having a hard time forming in her mouth. "I overheard some art students talking about one of the cruise lines looking for artists to teach basic and intermediate classes on their longer cruises this coming summer. It's a pilot program to see how much demand there is. It's a premium line that caters to affluent people."

Fen leaned back. "I wasn't expecting anything like that. What have you done about it?"

"I applied in October and heard from them last week. The job is mine if I pass their background check." Her head dipped again. "I hope you don't mind, but I listed you as my mentor and guardian. Don't be surprised if they contact you. They want me to talk you into coming on a special cruise designed for serious artists and being one of the faculty."

"A specialty cruise?" asked Fen.

"Exactly. I didn't realize it, but there are so many specialty cruises."

Fen rubbed his chin. "Apparently, you haven't totally committed to this yet. What's the second opportunity?"

"One of my professors wants me to study in Rome this summer. It's an intense program of study and painting. It would be a big financial commitment, but I have the money to do it."

"That could be a life-changing experience," said Fen. "Why did you list it as a second choice?"

"I didn't," countered Bailey with fervor. "There's one and a half more and I want to do all of them."

"Sorry," said Fen. "I didn't mean to put words in your mouth. What's next?"

"I thought we could repeat the last two summers and work our booth at special events around the state. I realize I'm still building name recognition, and it takes a lot of work before people will recognize me as a competent portrait painter."

"You're farther along than you think," said Fen. "But you make a good point. We know what works for both of us, and there's a lot to be said for slow growth and keeping your name in front of people."

"Finally," said Bailey. "I've been thinking about how I can keep being useful to you when there's a murder to solve. If I sail off on a ship or spend my summer in Rome, I won't be around to help. That will drive me crazy, but there's no guarantee you'll have a case to work this coming summer."

Fen nodded in agreement. "There's also no guarantee we'll go back to Bandera to help with the latest murders."

A look of resolve came over Bailey's face. "We'll go. I feel it in my bones."

"Not until we're asked."

"Chuck and Candy will take care of that today."

Fen looked away. "I feel it in my old creaky bones that if they do, it won't be until after your final exams."

Bailey shook her head. "Your bones aren't old, and they don't creak. That artificial knee might, but not your bones."

"Let's compromise," said Fen. "Even if Chuck and Candy

tell me there's something for us to do in Bandera, you'll not come until after you finish the semester."

"I thought you'd say something like that. I made top grades so I could be free to help you or do whatever I wanted during my break. Another week of classes and I'll be exempt from finals."

Fen brought the conversation back around to Bailey's dilemma of too many choices. "Let's table the discussion on what you'll do this coming summer. That will give us time to think about it. Sally might give me a hint of what you should do."

A sly smile pulled at the corners of Bailey's mouth. "You might ask Audrey, too." She tilted her head. "When was the last time you spoke to her?"

Fen avoided a direct answer by saying, "We're on a two-calls-per-month schedule." He then went on offense. "Speaking of relationships, how's your love life?"

Bailey shot back, "Thanks for reminding me I'm well on my way to becoming an old maid."

"There's still hope," said Fen. "If a woman with a beak like a pelican can catch a man, surely a beautiful young lady like you can land one. Who knows? There may be a handsome cowboy in Bandera waiting to sweep you off your feet."

Bailey wrinkled her nose. "The idea of dating a feed-lot-Phil doesn't really appeal to me."

"What about a chuck-wagon Charley?"

"Nope. You're not even close." She pretended to touch the brim of an invisible cowboy hat. "*Adios*, partner. I'll leave the horses, cattle, and spurs for you and Audrey to play with. I have a date with canvas and paint. We'll talk more about summer jobs later."

Chapter Eleven

The time with Bailey ended on a positive note. Just talking about the choices seemed to lighten her load of worry. There was a time, and not that long ago, when she would have committed to take action based on feelings alone. He could almost see the bud of youth maturing into a flower of adulthood. What surprised him most was her acceptance of waiting until thought and time came together to guide her.

He intended to spend five hours painting but cleaned his brushes at noon when the first rumbles of hunger pangs came from beneath his belt buckle. The grand feast wasn't for another two hours, with the guests arriving thirty minutes before. He glanced out the window and realized the late fall day was far too pretty not to take advantage of. The half-mile walk from his home to his property's front gate would be a welcome stretch of the legs. While there, he could check the mailbox, just in case Bailey or Thelma hadn't done so yesterday.

In Central Texas, many years fall was an extension of summer and winter arrived much later than most people wanted it to. Short sleeve shirts weren't unusual around the holiday banquet tables and the sound of cool air coming from air conditioner vents provided background noise to conversations. A mostly-blue sky awaited Fen as he stepped onto the front porch. The light breeze that ensured he wouldn't break a sweat as he made his trip to the front gate smelled fresh while being neither hot nor cold.

The walking tour took him past an oil pump with a mechanical arm that neither slept nor slumbered as it drew oil from deep within the earth. A lone buzzard circled high overhead, caught a sideways breeze, and drifted out of sight without flapping.

The walk gave him a chance to start a mental list of pros and cons concerning Bailey's opportunity to spend her summer leading art classes on a cruise ship. He had to admit that the idea of being included on a specialty voyage with serious artists intrigued him.

His thoughts shifted to Audrey, and he wondered if she might somehow show up on the cruise ship. A shake of his head followed as he spoke to the gravel road. "A cruise might be in our future, but that can't happen for years. We made a deal and I'm sticking to it." He chuckled. "That doesn't mean I can't go with Sally this summer."

Fen glanced skyward. "Sally, what do you think? We talked about going on a cruise but never got around to it. This summer might be a good time."

No answer came, but he didn't expect one.

He arrived at a metal pole with a keypad attached. Four numbers in the proper sequence was all it took to trigger an electric motor to swing open a heavy metal gate. He walked across a cattle guard and kept going until he turned left at a mailbox mounted atop a thick wooden post. He pulled the metal tab on the mailbox and the front door lowered like a miniature drawbridge. Inside, he found a single, plain, letter-size envelope without a stamp or postmark. At first he thought the envelope was empty, but it felt too heavy.

He took his knife from the pocket of his jeans, flicked open the lone locking blade, and slid it under the flap. The sharpened steel produced a clean cut along the fold. It contained a letter that reminded him of a ransom note with individual letters cut from a slick-surfaced magazine and pasted to the single page of regular copy paper. It read **sTay ouT Of bandEra or ElsE.**

Fen refolded the page, put it back into the envelope, and slipped it into the pocket of his shirt. He patted a back pocket of his jeans and realized he'd left his mobile phone in his studio. "Probably just as well," he said to himself. "Chuck and Candy need to see this before I call Rusty Irons. I need to know what kind of threat I'm really dealing with."

Questions without answers churned in Fen's brain as he purposefully left the gate open and walked back to his home. Guests would soon arrive, and the cattle guard ensured livestock wouldn't seek greener grass on the other side of the fence.

Tires crunching gravel drew Fen's attention away from the unwelcome letter. A silver SUV rounded a corner and eased to a stop beside him. The passenger's side window made a whirling sound as it lowered into the door. "Did you lose your horse?" asked Chuck, his attorney and long-time friend.

"It's a holiday. My horse is watching a football game."

Candy, Chuck's wife, snickered before saying, "Hop in or walk; it's your choice."

Fen pointed to the letter in his shirt's pocket. "This was in my mailbox. It's a six word note warning me not to return to Bandera." He then climbed into the back seat and said, "We'll go to my home office and inspect it under a magnifying glass."

No one spoke on the short ride. Fen glanced at his watch as

he, Chuck, and Candy slipped into his home office unnoticed. This was crunch time for Thelma as she and Sam put the finishing touches on her culinary masterpiece. Her husband was the only living soul she allowed in her kitchen on this special day. Bailey hadn't come down from her studio, and Lou was seldom early to arrive for a social event. The only thing that would ensure her early arrival was a hot tip on a juicy news story, which he was short on today.

With gaze fixed on Candy, Fen said, "Sit at my desk. There's a box of gloves in the bottom left drawer and a magnifying glass in the top right." He took the note out of his pocket and laid it on the center of a brown leather blotter. "Turn on the desk lamp if you need more light."

Candy looked right at home, putting on blue gloves to handle the evidence. This further confirmed his suspicion that she was much more than a paralegal and secretary to Chuck. His guess was former CIA, or some other cloak-and-dagger government agency. He also believed the couple left national security politics behind and narrowed their focus to state issues. All Fen knew for sure was they'd contact him when a need arose for him to help solve murders that the local agencies couldn't, or wouldn't, handle.

His mind drifted to Audrey. He suspected her, along with Candy, Chuck, and others, of being involved in some sort of statewide organization dedicated to giving justice the occasional helping hand.

Candy gave a verbal analysis of the envelope before she withdrew the letter. "Standard stock like you'd find in any Walmart, Target, or office supply store. No writing, smudges, or postmark." She looked up at Fen. "When did you arrive home from Bandera?"

"Yesterday, not long after noon. Sometime between twelve thirty and one."

"Was there any other mail in the box?"

"Nope. Thelma or Bailey must have checked it yesterday. Sam never checks it."

"There's not much else I can tell you about the envelope other than it was most likely hand delivered by someone who kept it clean and dry. The person sealed it, but it's going to take a lab to discover if they used saliva, water, or something else."

Candy took the magnifying glass, pulled the light a little closer, and inspected the top edge of the envelope. "You keep the blade on your pocketknife sharp. There's hardly any raggedness where you sliced through the fibers."

She then slipped the letter from the envelope, held it up to the light and announced, "No watermark. Inexpensive copy paper, most likely purchased from the same source as the envelope."

Fen asked, "Is it likely someone bought it in bulk?"

Candy spread the letter flat on the blotter, and said, "Both products probably came from the same company and were mass-produced. How much someone bought is anyone's guess."

She focused on the individual letters adhered to the page. "This is interesting. The different fonts tell me the person took extra care. The curved edges of the cuts also show they used cuticle scissors to harvest the letters instead of regular scissors."

Chuck asked, "Anything else?"

"Yeah," said Candy. "It needs to go to a lab, be dusted for fingerprints, checked for saliva, and have an analysis done on the glue used to adhere the letters to the page."

Fen asked, "Can you build a profile of the person from what you have?"

Candy looked up at Fen and smiled. "Why don't you take a stab at it?"

"All right, I will," said Fen. "I believe the person who sent the letter is most likely a detail-oriented woman from Bandera

County who drove a very long way to put the letter in my mailbox. She's resourceful enough to know how to locate my home address."

Candy shot him a glance of approval. "Very good."

Chuck asked, "Why a woman?"

"Cuticle scissors," said Fen. "Do you use them?"

"Nope."

"Me either."

Chuck then asked, "Why detail-oriented?"

"She took the time to use multiple fonts."

Candy then asked, "What was her motive for sending the letter?"

Fen rubbed his cheek. "I can think of two possibilities. The obvious one is to scare me off. The second is to wave a red flag in front of a bull, and I'm the bull. She, or possibly he, has a streak of arrogance in them."

This brought a full smile to Candy. "My money is on option number two."

She paused then said, "Hold off on contacting Sheriff Irons about this. We'll take care of getting the letter to a lab and having it analyzed."

Fen pointed. "There's an evidence bag in the same drawer as the gloves. Do you want me to fill it out?"

"Please," said Candy.

"Do you think I'll be going back to Bandera soon?"

Chuck held up his hands. "That's anyone's guess right now."

Fen puffed out his cheeks. "I'd rather see Rusty solve it. It would be a nice feather in his cap. Besides, if I'm asked to help, Bailey will want to go, but she needs to finish the semester strong."

Candy came to his rescue. "Why don't you and Lou work on the case from here? Do some background work. Keep in touch with Rusty and share information on everything except the letter you received today. If he doesn't have the murders solved by the time Bailey is on Christmas break, I feel sure you three will go back to Bandera."

A knock on the door put an end to the impromptu meeting. Fen turned the handle and beheld Bailey and Lou with looks of expectation painted across their faces. Lou was the first to speak. "A wonderful Thanksgiving meal isn't the only thing I smell in this house. Please tell me you three have been cooking up an assignment that will help fund my retirement."

Bailey's words followed on the heels of Lou's. "When do we leave for Bandera?"

Fen looked at his watch. "We have ninety seconds to make it to the table before Thelma comes unglued. We'll discuss Bandera this evening. Until then, let's steer clear of the subject."

Lou shook her head. "That's the dumbest thing I ever heard. Thelma will see right through us."

Fen hung his head in thought, then looked at her. "You're right but let me broach the subject."

Bailey issued a warning. "There's less than a minute to get to the table."

Conversation ceased as all five quickly made their way to the feast that awaited them.

Chapter Twelve

Fen arrived at the table last and acknowledged Thelma's glare with a cheerful reply. He tapped the face of his watch and said, "Four seconds to spare."

She countered with, "You cut it close just to aggravate me."

He stilled any more complaints by raising his voice and saying, "Let's pray." A heartfelt and unusually long expression of thanksgiving followed. Thelma dabbed the corners of her eyes at the mention of Sally, the woman who helped save her from herself and convinced her of the reality of hope and a better future.

Conversation took a back seat to eating until everyone was at least halfway through their first helping of belt-stretching traditional dishes. Fen broke the ice by saying, "Everyone eat up. We might have hamburgers on Christmas Day this year."

Thelma's fork came down hard on her plate. "What do you mean? We'll have the same thing on Christmas Day."

"You and Sam might, but Bailey, Lou, and I may be in Bandera."

Thelma gave him a squinty-eye stare that said, *"Over my dead body."*

Fen cut a bite of turkey but didn't lift it to his mouth. "We might be back before Christmas. Then again, there's a chance we won't have to go. Isn't that right, Chuck?"

All eyes shifted to the attorney, who didn't return anyone's stare. "I'd say the chances are about fifty-fifty. Sheriff Irons is a good, competent lawman, but he's never worked a double murder."

Fen took over. "That's why Lou and I may need to do what we can to help him."

Lou jumped in. "When do we leave?"

"We don't. At least not for now. The primary suspect is already in jail, but I'm not convinced he's guilty." He lifted the bite of turkey. "He demanded to see a lawyer. If he has an alibi, and it's watertight, the sheriff is back to square one."

Bailey spoke up. "I didn't hear my name mentioned."

Fen popped the turkey into his mouth and started chewing. After taking a drink of sweetened iced tea, he said, "Your dance card is full until you finish the portrait and the semester."

"That stinks."

"No, it doesn't," said Thelma. "It's bad enough that Fen gets involved in murders all over the state. A proper young lady like you has no business putting yourself in danger. If Miss Sally hadn't told me she wanted Fen to keep working as a lawman, I wouldn't let him go."

This comment earned a hard stare from Sam.

Thelma backpedaled and mumbled, "At least I'd try to talk him out of it."

Fen put his fork down and said, "Here's how things stand for now. Lou and I will gather information as best we can and turn it over to Sheriff Irons. Bailey will finish the portrait she's working on and go back to college on Monday." He looked at her. "I'll keep you in the loop while you finish school, but you'll not do anything without checking with me first. Agreed?"

Bailey seemed to consider her options and nodded. "It seems I don't have a choice."

Fen cast his gaze to everyone around the table. "That's how things stand now, but if there's one thing I know about murder investigations, things can change quickly. I'll keep everyone informed if they do."

He smiled and put a lighter tone into his words. "We have something else that Bailey would like advice on. Some unique possibilities have opened up for her this coming summer. I'll let her tell you about them while I finish my first plate of this incredible meal."

Bailey's eyes opened wide. "I wasn't expecting to share this yet, but it seems I don't have any choice about a lot of things."

She placed her fork on her plate. "Thelma, don't take it wrong, but if I have seconds, I won't have room for the pies you baked."

"That's fine, hon. There's only so much that little bird belly of yours can hold. You cleaned your plate, and that's all I expect of you."

Bailey then launched into a long explanation of the ways she could spend her summer. Chuck thought working on a cruise ship as a teaching artist was a wonderful way to combine work, play, and a chance to see places she'd only read about. Candy seemed more in favor of her studying art in Rome. Thelma, as expected, thought staying under Fen's protective wings was her best choice. Lou cautioned her to avoid serious romances no matter which choice she made.

Eyes opened wide when Sam said, "Take long walks in the woods. Speak to the trees and sky. Hear the words of the river. Then listen to what your heart says and do what it tells you."

As for Fen, he sidestepped an answer by saying he was still

thinking about it. In reality, he'd thought about it quite a bit but hadn't reached a definitive answer. He did, however, accomplish his goal, which was to get the conversation off a murder investigation. After all, this was a day to give thanks, not discuss two homicides.

Following the meal, it was a custom in the Maguire house for everyone to exit the formal dining room and waddle to the great room where an oversize television came to life, with football games as the only selection offered. Low volume meant people could give comments on the good, bad, and ugly plays. Those not interested, could huddle together and carry on conversations unrelated to sports.

Lou chose a seat near Fen. "I know it's against the rules to talk about the investigation today, but when and where do you want to meet tomorrow?"

Fen kept his gaze fixed on the television screen. "Ask Candy if she and Chuck are planning to go to their office tomorrow morning. If they are, we can use their conference room or an empty office. Is nine o'clock too early for you?"

"You're joking. If there's any chance of a decent story coming out of this case, I'd be there at three a.m."

"You'd have a long wait."

Lou rose, resettled next to Candy, and launched into a soft-spoken conversation. Fen looked away from the television when a commercial came on. His gaze went to Lou, who gave him a thumbs-down sign. They wouldn't meet with Chuck and Candy until later. He responded with a nod.

Fen was almost asleep in his recliner when Thelma's rich, alto voice came to life with an announcement. "It's halftime. That means it's time for dessert, coffee, hot tea, and water. They're spread out on the dining room table. If you're too lazy to get up and serve yourself, don't look to me to bring you anything. For the rest of the day, you're on your own. I'm taking my selections of dessert to my little house out back. You won't see me until tomorrow and my kitchen better not look like a herd of wild pigs spent the night in it."

Fen shouted, "Let's give a round of applause to the best cook in the world."

Hollers and applause followed Thelma out of the room. She acted like she didn't want recognition, but everyone knew she lived for compliments.

Chuck and Candy were the first to leave, but only after the team he was rooting for fumbled away a victory with less than a minute to play. As expected, Chuck threw up his hands, released a few choice sentences about incompetence, then waited for Candy outside.

Candy shook her head as Fen rose to escort her to their car. "Chuck has the Midas Touch in reverse when picking winning football teams. I'm afraid to ask him how much he lost by betting on today's game."

"I had the same problem until Sally helped me find the cure," said Fen. "She called it couch therapy. It didn't matter if I won or lost, if she caught me gambling, it meant a week of me sleeping on the couch."

"That might have worked during the first ten years of our marriage. Now, I'm not so sure," said Candy. "He'd slink into the guest bedroom and sleep like a baby."

"Women underestimate their influence over their husbands," said Fen. "That goes double for you and Chuck. He's putty in your hands."

Candy hooked her arm in Fen's as they continued toward the car. "You certainly know how to make an old gal feel younger." She stopped at the front of the vehicle. "And speaking of women, have you spoken to Audrey lately?"

"We talked yesterday." Fen looked her in the eyes. "You can stop pretending you didn't already know that."

Candy's expression didn't change. She'd neither confirm nor deny his gentle accusation. Instead, she asked, "Do you two think you'll be able to stay apart the full five years?"

Fen looked to the west and the setting sun that seemed to set the clouds ablaze with red and amber streaks. He didn't want to lie to Candy, but he wasn't ready to renegotiate the terms of their agreement either. Instead, he found a way out of giving her a definitive answer. "Sally still speaks to me now and then. She'll let me know if we're to make changes."

Candy patted his arm. "Chuck and I will support you, no matter what." She gazed at him soberly. "Keep spending time with Sally every day and call Sheriff Irons tomorrow morning. I have an uneasy feeling about Brent Stone. I'm not sure if he's in more danger out on bond or in jail."

Fen's thoughts shifted immediately to the Bandera County Jail. "Do you think Rusty should try to get Brent transferred to a more secure facility?"

Candy raised her shoulders and let them fall. "There's a bond hearing set for Monday morning. It will be interesting to see if he stays in jail, is transferred, released on bond, or if the DA chooses not to indict."

Fen added, "Or if he makes it to Monday alive."

Candy opened the door and slipped into the car. She rolled down the window. "Come to the office at 8 a.m. on Monday and make sure Lou doesn't oversleep. We'll trade notes."

The window rolled up and Chuck gave a weak goodbye wave.

Back inside, Bailey waited for Fen's return. "I'll be in my studio the rest of the evening unless you have something for me to do concerning the case."

Fen shook his head. "The best use of your time is making that portrait something exceptional. If you don't forget about the case for the next couple of weeks, you'll take shortcuts and produce an inferior portrait. This is an opportunity to build your reputation. Don't blow it."

She let out a huff of exasperation. "Asking for help in deciding what I'm to do this summer was a waste of time. Everyone had a different opinion."

"That's because it's your decision. The way I look at it, you'll need to decide between good, better, and best. The problem is, you may never know if the one you chose was the best."

Bailey rolled her eyes. "I might as well flip a coin."

"You could do that, but I'd recommend gathering more facts about each choice. You're likely to find things that are a turnoff to you."

Bailey spoke in a semi-serious tone. "Any other pearls of wisdom?"

He gave her a straight answer. "You mentioned having a deadline before making a commitment. Do your fact-finding and set your own deadline before you're forced to. I'd say rank your choices at least three days ahead of time. If you have peace about your decision at the end of the three days, go for it. Do what Sam recommended and listen to your gut."

"You make it sound so easy."

"Making rash decisions is easy. Deciding between good, better, and best is always difficult."

"The only thing I'm sure of is I need to finish the portrait and make it super-special. I'll worry about next summer later. There's not room in my mind for the portrait, school, the murders, and what to do next summer."

"Good decision."

Bailey turned and headed for the door leading to her apartment/studio.

Fen reentered the living room where Lou sat alone. She

punched the remote and silence replaced the noise of a commercial. "What's the plan?" she asked.

Fen said, "I've made a list of persons of interest in Bandera and Bandera County. I want you to take half the list and do what you can with background checks on them. I'll do the other half this weekend. It's a holiday weekend, so we'll need to dig deeper next week."

"Give me the entire list," said Lou. "I have absolutely nothing to do this weekend. If you want to duplicate half the list, go ahead."

Fen nodded an affirmative response and added, "We're to be at Chuck's law office at 8 a.m. on Monday. I'll call Sheriff Irons tomorrow and have an update to share. I expect Candy and Chuck to have more information, too."

"Good," said Lou as she stood. "Any idea of when we might go to Bandera?"

"It's still an *if,* not a *when.*"

Chapter Thirteen

Fen pushed the covers back before dawn, dressed, and made his way to the kitchen where a surprise awaited him. Thelma hadn't made coffee. He couldn't remember a time since Sally hired Thelma that she didn't have coffee ready to serve at five forty-five every morning. Her absence was so unusual that he called Sam to make sure nothing was seriously wrong with his cook and housekeeper.

Sam answered and didn't waste time on chit-chat. "Thelma's asleep. I gave her medicine."

"Medicine? She hates doctors and never takes medicine. Neither do you."

"We don't take store-bought medicine. Old Choctaw recipes work better."

"How long will this medicine make her sleep?"

"Two nights and one day."

Fen considered the half-empty bottle of powerful painkillers in his bathroom cabinet. The label on the bottle read one tablet every eight hours, as needed. He asked, "Do I want to know what's in the potion you gave her?"

"It's best you don't, but everything came from what grows on this land."

"So do poisonous snakes and spiders."

Sam's lack of response made Fen wonder if he'd guessed two of the ingredients in Sam's witches' brew. His farm manager changed the subject. "I thought you and Bailey were hunting today."

"Too hot."

"Going shopping? Thelma said this is a big bargain day."

"Bailey and I will spend the day painting unless you need our help."

"I'll call if I do."

The call ended with no word of good-bye, which was typical for Sam. Black Friday meant nothing to him or Fen, other than it was the day after Thanksgiving and a good day to stay home to paint, or do chores around the ranch. Sometimes he and Bailey would go deer hunting if the weather cooperated. A high-pressure system meant warm temperatures over Central Texas this year. Sitting in a box-stand on stilts waiting for a deer to walk by while swatting late-season mosquitoes wasn't Fen's idea of a good time.

It wasn't long before he had coffee brewing, and Bailey made her appearance. Casual didn't come close to describing the rag-tag flannel pajama pants and paint-stained gray sweatshirt she wore. She shuffled into the kitchen with her small feet encased in furry house shoes that might have once resembled rabbits.

"Where's Thelma?" asked Bailey through a yawn.

"Taking a well-deserved day off."

"No way," said Bailey with absolute certainty. "Thelma doesn't take days off."

Fen countered with, "I called Sam to make sure she was all

right. He gave her one of his home remedies to help her get over all the work she did for Thanksgiving."

A look of panic came across Bailey's face. "I hope he's checking on her. There's no telling what he puts in those little green bottles. When I burned my hand so badly, the pain medicine the doctor gave me might as well have been out-of-date baby aspirin. Sam mixed up something that took me to La-la land. I don't think I could have made it through the skin grafts if it wasn't for that stuff. It tasted like a mixture of kerosene and rotten eggs, but all it took was one dose every twelve hours. Thelma made sure she measured it out and took the bottle away after each spoonful."

Fen tilted his head. "I suffered for years with a knee that popped out of place and hurt like someone was stabbing me with an ice pick. Thelma and Sam never offered to give me their pain medicine."

"That's because you insist on strictly obeying laws and rules. I have a broader interpretation. I look at felonies the way you do, but not the misdemeanors. The reward isn't worth the risk for taking a chance with felonies. Ordinances, minor traffic offenses, and silly rules are mostly optional. I count those like they're strong suggestions."

"That doesn't explain your history of stealing cars."

"Sure it does," said Bailey. "I never boosted a car, stole over two hundred dollars at a time, or sold marijuana after I turned seventeen. They sealed my juvenile records, so it was like those things never happened." She took a breath. "It's the same principle that's in the Bible where it says God 'takes our sins, casts them as far as the east is from the west and remembers them no more.' If He doesn't remember them, who am I to do otherwise?"

Fen couldn't help but chuckle. "I'll concede that you received a clean slate when you became an adult and you're not the person you once were. Going to jail for a misdemeanor isn't worth it."

Seemingly unconvinced, Bailey poured a cup of coffee. "It's impossible to follow every law, rule, ordinance, covenant restriction, and custom, so why not obey the big ones and use some common sense with the rest?"

The keen mind of the young woman was mentally working her way through some of life's toughest questions. While it was a good mental exercise, he had other things that needed his attention.

"Let's save this discussion for later and focus on more practical things."

"Like what?" asked Bailey.

"Like cooking and cleaning after meals. There's breakfast, lunch, and dinner. You choose first. Do you want to cook or wash, dry and put up dishes?"

Bailey's eyebrows came together as she considered the options. She sipped her coffee and placed her mug on the table. "There's an uneven number of meals and Thelma left the kitchen spotless yesterday. I suggest you and I are on our own for breakfast. Pecan pie on a paper plate is all I want. What about you?"

"I was thinking about left over fruit salad, sliced ham, and a piece of toast. That could go on a paper plate, too. For the other two meals, I say leftovers and heat them in the microwave or eat them cold. We could stack the dishes in the sink and not wash until after we finish supper tonight. I'll wash and you dry and put up."

"That sounds like a plan," said Bailey. "There's only one potential flaw. What if Thelma wakes up after lunch and finds dirty dishes?"

Fen raised his eyebrows. "Cleaning the kitchen after every

meal is Thelma's rule, not ours. I'm willing to deviate from the exact letter of the law if you are."

Bailey delivered a smile with a twinkle in her eyes. "I believe cleaning the kitchen after every meal is more of a suggestion than a rule. Besides, I still get a rush when I live on the wild side."

Bailey had her pecan pie and coffee while Fen ate a more complete breakfast. He cut off a bite of ham and asked, "How's the portrait coming along?"

"I made good progress last night. Do you want to look at the sketches before I start on the canvas?"

"You're advanced enough in your technique that you can tell when you're ready to switch from paper to canvas. There's only so much you can do with pencils and sketch pads. I'll wait until you're ready to mix colors for the background."

Bailey popped in a small bite of pie and spoke around it. "What are you doing this morning?"

"I'll call Sheriff Irons about nine o'clock. I'm hoping to find out if the suspect he has in jail will post bail on Monday."

"Bail for a double homicide?" asked Bailey.

Fen corrected her. "When I left, there was no evidence placing him at either crime scene. That means he's presumed innocent. The Thanksgiving holidays put a pause in the timeliness of the proceedings. The DA could drop charges completely."

"What are the chances of that happening?"

Fen shrugged as he smeared butter on his toast. "My gut is saying what happens Monday will surprise me."

Bailey huffed, "That tells me absolutely nothing."

"Sorry," said Fen. "I hope to know more after I speak with Rusty."

Bailey leaned forward. "Rusty Irons may be the silliest name I've ever heard for a sheriff."

"Politics is about name recognition. The name makes perfect sense for a small county with a western heritage like Bandera."

Bailey's scrunched nose and quick shake of her head told him his words fell short of convincing her. "I still think Rusty Irons is a goofy name for a sheriff."

He turned away from her. "Don't you have a painting to work on?"

She stepped toward the door. "That quick dismissal means you agree with me, but you're too stubborn to admit it."

Bailey stopped and spun around. "Did I tell you I know a guy from Bandera?"

This bit of information came as a surprise to Fen. "What guy?"

"You might remember Jeremy from the case we worked at Lake Palestine. He was one of the fraternity guys at the resort where we stayed."

"How could I forget? He was responsible for the fraternity choosing you as their honorary sweetheart after you drew caricatures of them. Are you still in touch with him?"

"Uh-huh. That's another thing we need to discuss. I'm considering changing colleges again. The idea of learning from several art teachers instead of one or two agrees with me." She waved off the statement. "It's only an idea, and it's fourth in my line of priorities. Finishing the portrait, completing the semester, and helping with the investigation come first."

Fen narrowed his eyes. "I suppose the college you're thinking of transferring to just happens to be the one Jeremy attends. Have you already called him?"

She played like the question was one she hadn't considered. "Why didn't I think of that?"

Fen clicked his tongue. "You either have or you're going to. Which is it?"

Bailey smiled. "Both. We've been calling and texting each other ever since that week we stayed at the resort. I'll call him later today."

"Why haven't you mentioned him before now?"

A look of mischief came into her eyes. "A woman has to have a few secrets. Besides, I just remembered early this morning that Jeremy grew up in Bandera."

It took Fen only a few seconds to process the new information. "See what he knows about Brent Stone, Misti Palmer, her father, and Clay Trueblood. Send a report to me and Lou."

A look of excitement came across her face and she opened her mouth to say something but Fen cut her off. "That's the one and only assignment you'll get until you're finished with the semester. Lou and I are meeting on Monday morning with Chuck and Candy. You'll be back at college by then, so get that report to us before you leave on Sunday."

As quickly as excitement filled her eyes, it was gone. "It's still a bummer that I have to stay at college instead of helping you with the case," said Bailey with a pout in her voice. She spun around and walked toward the door.

He'd expected her disappointment. Bailey's reaction had more to do with her overcrowded schedule, but he needed to stand firm. She was too close to finishing her semester with top grades. The portrait also commanded her attention, as did making life-altering decisions.

Fen instructed himself to focus on his own work in progress, as it was still too early to call Sheriff Irons. Years of practicing mental discipline paid off as he got in two hours of painting shafts of sunlight, which ignited a fall landscape of vibrant yellow and crimson leaves.

A quick glance at his watch told him he'd allowed more than enough time to pass before calling Sheriff Irons. He took his phone from his shirt pocket and told it who to call. Rusty answered in a calm tone. "Hello, Fen. Did you go hunting this morning?"

The laid-back greeting was what Fen had hoped to hear. It meant nothing bad had happened to Brent Stone. At least not yet. Fen wanted verification, so he asked, "Did your guest enjoy his Thanksgiving meal yesterday?"

"He ate like he hadn't a care in the world and slept the rest of the day and night. He's still not talking, and his lawyer won't see him until Monday morning."

"Have you identified any other suspects?"

"Not yet, and that seems to please Elton Palmer."

Fen asked, "Have you heard if he's pushing for bond?"

"He is, but the rumor is that it's a paltry amount. Nothing happened yesterday except too much food and football games."

"Was there significant damage from the flood?"

"Rising water swamped several vehicles. No injuries or loss of life other than a bull calf that was separated from its mother and couldn't get to high ground. A cowboy on a dude ranch almost saved him, but the calf panicked and ran into the river."

Fen heard Rusty try to stifle a yawn. It was all he could do not to yawn himself. He ended the conversation with, "It sounds like everything is quiet again in Bandera."

"Very quiet, but that may change at the bond hearing Monday."

Chapter Fourteen

Saturday morning arrived with Thelma back in the kitchen at her usual time and hot coffee ready to serve. Fen doubted his faithful cook would mention taking a day off to recover from overwork, and she didn't disappoint him. Since all the stars were back in their proper orbit, Fen poured his first mug of stimulant and retreated to his office to start his day by speaking to his late wife.

Thirty minutes later, he asked Sally to watch over Bailey and retraced his steps back into the kitchen where he found Thelma and Bailey staking out their positions on what Bailey should do about a summer job. He arrived in time to hear Thelma say, "A cruise for artists? Why don't they stay on dry land and paint? I can't think of a reason anyone in their right mind would get on a boat with thousands of people and paint."

Bailey came back with, "New places and new experiences stimulate creativity. Artists need that more than most people."

"That may be, but how do you expect people to paint with the boat rocking and rolling in the waves? I've watched enough documentaries to know the ocean bounces huge boats around like kites on a windy day."

"Not always, and even in choppy seas, large cruise ships have powerful stabilizers. It's not like I'd be on a boat with sails. Modern cruise ships are like floating cities."

"That's all the more reason not to get on one. Big cities are places people go to have bad things happen to them." She set a cast-iron skillet on the stove and adjusted the flame. "How many people will they cram on that ship you're talking about?"

"About four thousand for the one I'd be on."

Thelma shook her head. "That's like everyone in a county crammed onto a tiny boat. Think of all the dirty hands, runny noses, and people sneezing. It's a miracle half of them don't die on board and the other half pass away after they return."

Bailey challenged her by saying, "Studies show that illnesses on cruise ships mirror the number of illnesses in the general population on land."

"Not if you live on a ranch or a farm."

Bailey wasn't one to back down. "I don't think that's accurate, and I know for sure that farm and ranch accidents are much higher than other occupations."

"That may be right, but you and Fen don't count as ranch workers since you paint most of the time. You're safe as long as you stay on the ranch and don't go gettin' on airplanes and boats."

Fen broke into the conversation. "I haven't taken the time to give the choices adequate consideration. What I know at this point is Bailey will decide, and I'll support her."

Thelma grudgingly said, "I guess there are worse ways to spend your summer, but I still don't like the thought of you getting washed overboard."

A sly smile came from Bailey. "Would you rather I helped Fen solve murders all summer?"

A grunt of disgust came from Thelma. "Don't get me started on that. I'm wearing out my prayer rug hoping you don't take after Fen too much. Chasing after killers is more dangerous than going on a cruise or working on this ranch. You're the second-best artist I've ever seen, and it would be a shame if you did anything else."

"Thanks, Thelma," said Bailey.

With a temporary truce in place, Fen put a touch of optimism in his voice. "Yesterday was a great day for painting and today should be a repeat." His gaze fixed on Bailey. "I don't know about you, but I got on a roll and lost all track of time."

"Me, too," said Bailey.

"Did you remember to call Jeremy?"

Bailey gave her head a firm nod. "He's much younger than Brent Stone but knows him by his reputation. He said he'd ask around before he returned to college tomorrow. I told him to get me names of people who might have something against Misti Palmer. He'll call me tonight."

"Good work," said Fen. "I spoke with Sheriff Irons yesterday. He had no new suspects to give me."

Thelma turned from the bacon that sizzled and popped. "He must not be trying very hard."

"You're probably right. He lost a lot of sleep dealing with a flood and two murders at the same time."

"That's no excuse," said Thelma. "When you had a big crime to solve, you'd work from can 'till can't, sleep for two hours, and go again." She paused. "Do you think Sheriff Irons wants more than one suspect?"

Fen considered the question for several seconds, which gave Bailey time to sit up straight and add a question of her own to Thelma's. "How much political pressure do you think the sheriff is under not to look for any other suspects?"

Fen's answer was obtuse. "I've always wondered if elected

officials in small counties were more prone to succumb to political pressure than those in large counties."

Thelma had the last word. "It's a good bet there's cash changing hands. Morality whispers while money and power shout. It don't matter how many people live in the county, money can make crooks out of honest folks."

Silence fell on the room until Thelma asked, "How many eggs do you want with your bacon and biscuits?"

"Two, over medium," said Fen and Bailey at the same time.

Fen then asked, "Are you leaving for college tomorrow at your usual time?"

"A little later," said Bailey. "I want to get in at least eight hours of painting today and tomorrow. I'm hoping to have it all but finished."

"Good thinking," said Fen. "When do you plan on delivering it?"

"The client lives in Austin, so I can drop it off at his office on my way to Bandera. You and Lou will be there by the time I get out."

"What if we're not?"

"Then I'll go on to Bandera and stay with Jeremy."

Thelma sucked in a full breath. Fen waited for the verbal broadside to come, but Bailey headed it off. "Don't worry, Thelma. I'll be at his parents' home, in his sister's room. She finished college two years ago and lives in San Antonio."

Thelma mumbled something under her breath, then said, "I don't like it, but it seems my opinion don't count for much."

Fen ignored the plea for pity and directed his question to Bailey. "If the three of us need to work the case, would you rather stay at Jeremy's parents' home or with us?"

Bailey had an answer at the ready. "With you and Lou." She gave him a conspiratorial wink. "Jeremy's way too cute for me to be around him more than a few days. Bandera isn't that far from the Mexican border. The temptation to get a quickie wedding might be too much for us."

Thelma delivered their plates. "Eat your breakfast before it gets cold and stop trying to get a rise out of me. Keep up your teasing and I'll come to Bandera and make sure you're properly chaperoned."

<hr>

ON MONDAY MORNING, Fen and Lou arrived within seconds of each other at Chuck and Candy's law office. His truck's diesel engine clattered to a stop while her Toyota Camry hybrid did nothing to disturb the peace of the crisp Monday morning.

Fen greeted her with, "I see you survived Thelma's feast."

Lou groaned. "Your belly should be so big you can't see the tips of your boots. How do you keep from looking like a blimp when she cooks for you like she does?"

Fen gave a one-word response. "Moderation."

"Bologna," said Lou. "You ate twice as much as I did, and you don't even have a paunch, let alone a spare tire like I'm carrying around."

Fen countered with, "You could snag husband number four any time you wanted to."

"Wash your mouth out with soap and then cut out your tongue. Three matrimonial mistakes mean I'm off the market."

He opened the back door to the nondescript building and allowed her to go in first. The reception area was empty, which meant Candy was in the conference room, in the break room making coffee, or in Chuck's office. Fen took a step into the hallway. "Is anybody home?"

Candy stuck her head out of the break room. "Come on back."

Fen led the way. By the time he reached the door of the

break room, Candy had poured his coffee into his favorite mug and handed it to him with instructions. "There's an assortment of pastries in Chuck's office. He's soothing his bruised ego for losing every bet he made. Go on back."

Fen followed her instructions as Candy greeted Lou and asked about her days after Thanksgiving. Their voices faded as Fen made his way to Chuck's office. As usual, he sat behind his desk, engaged in a phone conversation. His spacious office had an informal seating area with a sofa, two wingback chairs, and a coffee table. Fen helped himself to a sausage kolache and settled into one of the two chairs.

Lou and Candy came through the door as he popped the last bite into his mouth. Lou turned to Candy. "See what I mean? He eats anything he wants and never gains weight. I'll gain two pounds just looking at that raspberry kolache."

Fen swallowed. "If you're going to gain weight by looking at it, you might as well eat it. Perhaps you'll only gain one pound."

"Good point," said Lou, as she placed the pastry on a paper plate and settled onto the couch.

Chuck finished his call with a quick, "I'll get back to you this afternoon." He made his way to the gathering, snatched two pastries off the platter, and sat in the second chair while Candy settled on the couch.

Chuck said, "Someone else start the meeting while I feed my growling stomach."

Candy took over. "I'll start, but I have little to say. We wondered if the judge might hold a bond hearing over the holiday weekend. He didn't. Brent Stone is still in jail, but his bond hearing should start about now."

Fen said, "That's earlier than I expected."

Candy nodded, as did Chuck. Lou asked, "What's the significance of the earlier-than-usual starting time?"

Fen looked at Chuck, who motioned for him to answer. "It

may mean nothing. It was a four-day weekend, and the judge probably has a busy day planned."

Lou wrinkled her brow. "That answer came too fast and is too simple. What else?"

Chuck swallowed a sip of coffee. "It's possible the prosecution, defense, and judge agreed on a deal this weekend."

"A deal for Stone's release?"

Chuck had already taken another bite, so, once again, Fen answered for him. "It's possible."

"How much money will Stone have to come up with for bond?"

Fen considered shrugging off the question, but Lou wasn't one to quit questioning until she had a complete answer.

Chuck interrupted before Fen could speak. "I'll say the chances are ninety percent that the judge will set a bond at two-thousand dollars or less."

Candy added, "If that's the case, he'll need to come up with ten percent of the total bond to be released."

Lou put together the pieces. "Two hundred bucks is nothing. Elton Palmer must have pulled some strings."

Chuck cautioned her. "Don't get ahead of yourself. We don't know if the defense found another suspect. Also, the evidence against Stone seems shaky to me."

Fen settled his mug on a coaster. "Now is a good time to tell you that Bailey didn't spend all her time painting this weekend. She has a male friend who's from Bandera. He attends college in Huntsville but went home to his parents' house over Thanksgiving. To make a long story short, Bailey's friend knows Brent Stone by reputation. He did some checking and came up with the name of a local motorcycle mechanic who had a motive to harm one of the victims, Clay Trueblood. The mechanic's name is Ray Long. It had to do with money owed, but Bailey's friend didn't know how much."

Lou took down the name.

Candy said, "If Bailey discovered another suspect with a couple of phone calls, there's no telling what Stone's defense attorney found, or will find."

Lou said, "My research shows Brent Stone is no Boy Scout looking to do good deeds, but that doesn't mean he killed either victim."

Chuck's cell phone rang. He stood, moved into the hall, and shut the door behind him. The muffled conversation lasted less than a minute. He returned and said, "The judge released Brent Stone on a personal recognizance bond."

Candy looked at Fen then Lou. "You two better get to Bandera before something happens to Stone. How long before you're ready to travel?"

Fen narrowed his eyes. "You think he's really in danger?"

"From what we've heard about Elton Palmer, I think he may forget justice has rules and processes."

"I'm ready to go. My travel bag and laptop are in the car," said Lou.

"It won't take me long to go home and grab what I need."

Candy nodded her approval. "I'll take care of reservations for you."

Fen had a final thought. "Bailey's going to be mad as a cat with a string of firecrackers tied to its tail because we're leaving so soon."

Chuck reached for another pastry. "Candy will see what we can do about getting her to you as soon as possible."

Chapter Fifteen

Thelma stood with hands firmly planted on her hips. "I knew when you left this morning that you were going to Bandera. It happens every time you talk to lawyer Chuck early in the morning. If you go at a decent hour, you're talking about ranch or oil business."

Fen responded with a humorless smile. It was his way of acknowledging he'd heard her but didn't agree.

Thelma rattled on. "I was so sure you'd hit the road that I packed everything you need for a week. Stay any longer and you'll have to wash clothes or smooth talk someone else into doing it for you."

Fen asked, "Any chance of me getting a sack lunch to take with me?"

"I'll have turkey sandwiches ready by the time you load your truck. Be sure you get all your painting supplies. I know how putting paint on canvas helps you think." She then mumbled, "Lord knows you need help in that department."

"Did you pack Sally's picture?"

"She's where I always pack her. In winter, she goes between your T-shirts and flannel pajama pants."

"Perfect. Lou's already on the road. She guessed that we'd leave today, too."

"Where are you staying?"

"Candy's taking care of it. I'll text you details after she sends me the information."

Thelma wagged her head. "A man who owns a four-thousand-acre ranch is leaving home to stay at a cheap hotel. Isn't that what they call irony?"

"Life is full of ironies, absurdities, and paradoxes. They add humor to our existence."

"I see nothing funny about you going to do other people's jobs."

Fen considered reminding her why he was going, but she'd already turned to build him two sandwiches of leftover Thanksgiving turkey. He also knew she'd worry about him until he returned.

The text from Candy came about thirty minutes after the wheels of his truck started humming on a blacktop road heading southwest. Sparse traffic allowed him to read text messages without endangering himself or other drivers. He and Lou had a small cabin each at a location overlooking the river and the town of Bandera. Candy described it as a special place with character and history, close to the two crime scenes, especially the second one near the park.

Twenty miles later, his phone rang. He checked the caller ID and activated the device. Bailey blurted out, "This stinks. Candy told me she ran into a brick wall with the university president. I don't see why they won't let me skip this week of classes. We won't do anything but review for finals that I'm already exempt from taking."

"Sometimes you have to play the hand you're dealt."

"That's lame. I worked my tail off studying and making top grades so I'd be able to leave early if I needed to. I want to be free to help you."

"You already have by discovering Ray Long, the motorcycle mechanic."

An idea sparked in Fen's mind. "You mentioned Jeremy's older sister. She's closer to Brent Stone's age. I wonder if she knows Brent better than Jeremy. Will you have time to check with her this week?"

"Time is the one thing I have too much of. What do you want me to ask her?"

Fen sensed it was time to challenge her. "I thought you wanted to become a private investigator."

"I do."

"Then let your brain and your gut guide you. You and Lou have already studied the two victims and some other names I gave you. Pretend those are the ends of twine. Start pulling on them and see what happens. Start with Jeremy's sister." He took a breath. "By the way, what's her name?"

"Frieda Blankenship. She's still single."

"Get Frieda's phone number from Jeremy. Have him contact his sister to let her know you'll be calling. At this point in the investigation, you can accomplish a lot by using your phone and your brain. Not every interview has to be face-to-face."

A note of optimism crept into Bailey's words. "It's about time you trusted me to do something. I'll call right away. What else can I do this week?"

"Keep pulling strings. One thing will lead to the next. Send Lou and me reports on everything you do and get here as quickly as you can on Friday."

Bailey must have heard something in the tone of his words that concerned her. "You sound stressed. Is anything wrong?"

"They released Brent Stone on a PR bond this morning. I'm hoping they didn't pin a target on the back of his shirt by letting him run free."

"Holy smoke," said Bailey. "You and Lou better get to him before someone else does."

"That thought crossed my mind."

"I hope you brought your pistol."

Fen considered how best to respond, then decided not to hold back. "There's one on my hip, a backup in my boot, and one more packed in my suitcase."

Bailey let out a two-note whistle. "You must be planning on a shoot-out. That's one more gun than you can hold in your hands. You'd better let me carry one after I arrive."

"I brought it for Lou."

"Lou? She hates guns."

Fen spoke with a firm tone in his voice. "We've been over this a hundred times. Next fall you'll be twenty-one and you can conceal carry a pistol. In fact, I'll buy you whatever you want for your birthday. Until then, practice staying out of situations where you'll need that level of protection."

Bailey kept pleading her case. "I still don't see why you brought a pistol for Lou and not one for me."

"Lou presses people hard for answers. Sometimes too hard. As I said, you're not officially of age. I want you to learn how to get information without making enemies or offending people. Use your looks, age, and brain to your advantage. Your small size makes you look harmless. Don't spoil it by toting a cannon on your hip."

The deep sigh from Bailey told Fen he'd said enough, so he changed the subject. "Be sure to bring everything you need to paint something, or someone. That will be your cover story. I want the three of us to act independently in public. You're already staying with Jeremy's parents. Act like you and he are getting serious and you're there to make a good impression on the family."

A giggle sounded before she said, "At least I won't have to pretend about that part of my assignment." She paused. "That reminds me, we didn't talk about me changing schools this coming semester. I applied at Sam Houston State University. They offer degrees in Art and Criminal Justice."

Fen groaned. "Are you wanting a BA, a BS, or an MRS?"

"Hilarious," said Bailey, without a hint of mirth in her voice. "I plan on being Miss or Ms. Bailey Madison for a long time."

"That's your decision, too, but if things get serious with Jeremy, you'll need to tell Thelma."

Bailey backtracked. "It's not that serious between us. At least not yet."

"I didn't think so."

Bailey ended the conversation with a quick, "I'll call you tonight after I get in touch with Frieda."

"Keep pulling strings and keep us posted."

The call ended, and Fen resettled into the driver's seat, but his thoughts remained on Bailey. Was she ready for a serious romantic relationship that might end in heartbreak—or marriage and children? He didn't think so, but Bailey had a knack for bringing about sudden changes to her life and his.

***

Fen arrived in Bandera with a couple of hours to spare before check-in time at the one-bedroom cabin Candy had rented for him. He hadn't heard from Lou, which didn't surprise him. As a seasoned reporter, she knew most every trick in the book about finding information in both large cities and small towns. He believed she would start with the *Bandera*

Bulletin, the local weekly newspaper, to see what had been said and written about the murders. She'd also add to the list of names of people to follow up with.

Fen dropped by Sheriff Irons's office to get an up-to-the-minute report on the investigation. The expression on Rusty's face showed equal parts happiness to see him and contrition that he'd somehow placed Brent Stone in danger.

"I'm glad to see you," said Rusty. "I hope you intend to do more than paint."

"That's the plan," said Fen. "Tell me about the PR bond."

"Not much to tell. Elton Palmer and Judge Willoby went hunting Saturday morning. The judge killed a twelve-point buck, then I received a call Saturday afternoon telling me the city marshal would deliver Brent Stone to court early Monday morning. I was to have him dressed out in street clothes."

Fen asked, "Did Stone's attorney or the DA have anything to say?"

"I wasn't there, nor were any of my staff. The city marshal's deputies do all the transporting to and from court and act as bailiffs. All we did was check the paperwork and release him when he returned from court."

"What time was that?"

"A little after nine this morning."

"Where did he go?"

"He was supposed to go back to the dude ranch where he works. That's his permanent residence."

Fen asked, "Do you know if he went there?"

Rusty gave a nod and said, "I had my sergeant take him there, but that doesn't mean he's there now. We impounded his truck when we detained him, so he's on foot or on horseback." He looked past Fen and mumbled, "If he's smart, Brent's lying low at the Lucky 7."

"I was thinking the same thing," said Fen, before asking, "Is

Elton Palmer the type of man who'd come after Brent himself, or would he send someone?"

Rusty scratched his chin. "A little of both. If it was twenty years ago, he'd do it himself. Today, I think he'd have his son Cliff soften Brent up before he finished the job."

Fen sensed Cliff Palmer could be one of those ends of twine that he needed to pull to see where it led. He made a mental note to find him. For now, he'd ask Rusty.

"Tell me about Cliff."

Rusty's response began with a sideways glance and a warning. "Watch your step around Cliff. He's what you might expect from the heir apparent to a good portion of the county's wealth. He's into anything that's fast. That includes motorcycles, cars, horses, boats, and women."

"How old is he? Is he married?"

"Almost thirty. One prior marriage to his high school sweetheart. She matured. He didn't."

Fen asked, "Is she still around?"

A shake of Rusty's head gave a partial answer. "Becky miscarried two months after they married. She was five months along. She stuck it out for another year, but losing the child matured her. Not so with Cliff. He's still the wild boy he was in high school."

"Is Becky still in Bandera?"

Rusty leaned back in his chair. "She was way too pretty and ambitious to stay around this county. She's a CPA in Houston, remarried, with her second child on the way. Her parents retired and resettled to help with the grandchildren."

Fen wanted to know more about Cliff. "Any arrests on Cliff's record?"

"There should be, but—"

Fen finished the sentence for him. "But that's not the way things work in this county. I understand. My former father-in-law and Elton Palmer have a lot in common. Both men put their thumbs, and money, on the scale of justice."

Rusty qualified his response to Fen's last statement. "Elton rarely gets involved in criminal cases."

"Rarely?"

"He made exceptions for his son and Misti." Rusty inspected his hands before looking up. "I'm glad you understand the predicament I'm in."

"I understand because I lived it for several years when I was sheriff." He paused. "I'm still living it, but things are slowly getting better."

"Then you know why I asked for help in solving these two murders. I feel like I'm a hot horseshoe, stuck between an anvil and a hammer."

Something was bothering Fen. Something he had to know, but wasn't sure if Rusty had the answer, or if he would tell him. "Was it a coincidence that I was in Bandera when the two murders took place?"

Rusty looked straight into his eyes and gave a simple, "Yes."

"Did you contact a woman named Audrey?"

The matter-of-fact tone continued. "She contacted me after you and KK discovered the second body. She told me you'd come back to help if I needed you." He paused and squinted. "I called a couple of people I know and trust in Austin. They told me Audrey's legit, but for me not to ask questions about her. I take it you know her?"

"We met while I was working on another murder case in Smithville."

"Do you trust her?"

"With my life," said Fen.

"That's good enough for me."

Fen rose from his seat. "Where might I find Cliff Palmer tonight?"

"Anywhere there's a bar with cold beer, hard liquor, and loud music. He hits all the water holes, but you're most likely to see him in the bar and dance hall on 11th Street."

"Next door to the TRAIL BOSS STEAK & GRILL?"

"You can't miss it. Don't be surprised if there's a horse or two tied to the hitching posts out front."

"I may try to find him tonight if I can't find Brent Stone."

Fen extended his hand. "Don't expect to hear much from me for the next several days. I don't always work fast. I've found that asking too many questions at one time makes killers skittish."

On the way to his truck, Fen spotted a sheriff's department SUV pull into a reserved parking spot. The slamming of the driver's door preceded a pleasant smile on a pretty face. "Hello, Sheriff Maguire. Are you back to do some more painting, or is this something official?"

Fen returned the smile. "Hello, KK." He pointed to the camper shell affixed to the bed of his truck. "I'm loaded with art supplies. I ordered snow so I could do a winter landscape."

"You'd better write a long, convincing letter to Santa to get that wish."

He changed the subject. "How's the swift-water rescue business?"

"Not a drop of rain since you left. Did you bring any with you?"

"It's snow I'm after. About a foot would be nice if you could help arrange it."

"That's your Christmas wish, not mine. Have you been naughty or nice this year?"

Fen let out a laugh. "I'll have to plead the 5th on that."

"Where are you staying?" asked KK.

"My travel agent called it a rustic cabin near an abandoned dance hall."

A quick nod told him the deputy knew where to find him. "That's the Silver Spur, or what's left of it. It sits on a bluff overlooking the town. If you enjoy boot-scootin', go to 11th Street."

KK turned to go into the building, but stopped and faced him again. "What kind of mood is the sheriff in?"

"About halfway between happy and worried."

"Hmm," said KK. "I may wait before asking for a few days off."

"You'd better get your name in before the Christmas rush. When do you want off?"

"This Wednesday, Thursday, and Friday to go with my two scheduled days off Saturday and Sunday."

"The worst he can say is 'no'," said Fen as he unlocked the driver's door of his truck. Checking in at the cabin was the next thing on his list of things to do.

Chapter Sixteen

Cowboy rustic described the cabin's exterior to a T. From the native stone walls, down to the rustic Texas star anchored on the wall beside the front door, the cabin looked like it had weathered scorching summers and frosty winters for over a hundred years.

Fen used the combination Candy had sent him to open a lock-box, remove the keys, and unlock a new white door with a sparkling window. The newer interior with all the modern conveniences came as a pleasant surprise. With Christmas around the corner, he wasn't surprised to see a table-top tree decked out with small cowboy-themed ornaments in the shape of a hat, boots, horseshoe and tin star. There was even a Santa face sporting a cowboy hat. With the limited amount of space, the owners had opted to keep the rest of the Christmas décor to a minimum with themed soap dispensers and throw pillows. Enough to remind him of the season, but not get in the way.

Fen unloaded his truck and set up a small easel with a sketch pad in the tiny living room. He made other trips to retrieve an extra box of paints, his clothes and a few groceries.

He was looking out the front window when Lou's Toyota Camry pulled into the gravel driveway of the cabin across from him. She climbed out, scowled, and had a question waiting for him when he arrived. "Are you responsible for choosing these little houses on the cliff?"

"No, but I think Candy made a wise decision. We overlook the town, are next to what's left of a famous dance hall, and have our own tiny homes to stay in. I like it."

Lou remained unconvinced. "There's not a rail to hitch your truck to. Aren't you afraid it will wander off?"

Fen couldn't help but smile. Lou had spent most of her career as a reporter for a major Dallas newspaper. Even though she now lived in a small Texas town, she still identified with big city ways.

Instead of answering her absurd question, he asked, "Did you find out anything useful at the local newspaper?"

"I've seen better circulation in a cadaver, but they somehow put out a decent weekly. The double murder is the biggest thing to hit Bandera in many years. They were all nice and helpful, but I could tell they weren't exactly happy to have one more reporter come to rifle through their back issues."

"Any surprises?" asked Fen.

"Not to me. Small populations mean editors and owners of newspapers take extra care not to ruffle the locals' feathers. They reported the arrest of Brent Stone and heaped praise on Sheriff Irons and his staff for keeping the county safe. Until the sheriff arrests someone else, people will assume Stone is guilty."

Fen asked, "Did your research reveal any alternative names of suspects?"

Lou shook her head. "I believe the only way I'll get useful information in this town is to find people who knew the victims and get them to trust me."

"I'm expecting a call from Bailey tonight. She may have found—"

Lou interrupted before he could say anything else. "She called and said she contacted Frieda Blankenship. I told her I'd be happy to follow up with Frieda if Bailey wanted me to."

"What did she say to that?"

"She wants to do it without help."

Fen chuckled. "Does that surprise you?"

"Not a bit. I'd say the same thing."

Lou rubbed her arms. "It's cold on this hilltop. Let me grab my jacket and you can tell me what Sheriff Irons had to say." She reached into her car, retrieved a puffy jacket and zipped it most of the way up to her neck.

"How'd you guess that I'd go see Rusty when I got in town?" asked Fen.

"It wasn't a guess," said Lou. "Simple logic, based on experience."

"You know me too well," said Fen. "What am I going to say next?"

"You're going to tell me what you want me to do tonight, and then you'll talk about what your plans are. They won't be the same as mine."

Fen didn't contradict her. "Bailey, Thelma, and you are all getting too good at reading my mind. What's with you women?"

"Women's intuition is a marvelous thing. Now, tell me what you expect me to do tonight."

Fen leaned on her car. "Rusty is afraid Brent Stone will have a very serious accident now that he's out of jail. There's a high probability that Elton's son, Cliff, will cause this accident. If it's not successful in putting Brent out of commission, Elton will follow it with another, fatal one. Rusty also said Cliff finds a watering hole in one of the local bars almost every night of the week. KK suggested I go to the dance hall on 11th Street if I wanted to dance. I'd like you to go there and find out what you can about Cliff Palmer. Also ask about Ray Long, the motorcycle mechanic Clay Trueblood supposedly owed money to."

"KK suggested the dance hall?" asked Lou. "You've already talked to her?"

"Only briefly. She came to ask Rusty for a few days off."

Lou was never at a loss for words when chasing a story. "Let's get back to Elton and Cliff Palmer. What makes you think father and son won't go after Brent Stone tonight?"

"The police impounded Brent's truck when they arrested him. A sergeant took him back to the dude ranch where he works. I'll go to the dude ranch and make sure he's still there."

Lou's eyes narrowed. "Do you think he'll talk to you after you roughed him up?"

"I won't know until I try."

Lou scanned the surroundings, but her mind focused on the investigation. "I'm counting on doing an interview with him as a bonus. I sense there's a juicy story to be found with that man."

Fen took over. "My chief concern at this point is Brent Stone's safety. If he's back at the dude ranch, he should be safe. The hired hands sleep in a communal bunkhouse."

Lou counted on her fingers. "Research Cliff Palmer, locate Brent Stone and interview him, and find Cliff Palmer. I may have to ply Cliff with alcohol to get him to talk to me."

"Try charm first. It's cheaper."

"I'm a charm school dropout." She gulped a breath. "Anything else?"

"One more thing, but it can wait until tomorrow. Cliff's ex-wife lives in Houston. Get the background info on her and call her tomorrow. It's a long shot, but she may know something about the victims or Cliff's relationship with them."

Lou asked, "Are you thinking Cliff might be a suspect?"

"It's possible Elton Palmer sent Cliff to lean on Trueblood to stay away from Misti and things got out of hand. Or maybe killing him was the plan all along. What better revenge on Brent Stone than to pin Trueblood's murder on him? Or, like I said before, their revenge on Brent Stone may come in the form of him having an 'accident.' If you find Cliff, see if he, or his father, are set on revenge. If you can't do that, get creative with your questions."

Lou's eyes sparkled with anticipation. "Revenge and bloodshed make for a great story."

Fen held up his hand as a stop sign. "Don't get too excited. There's nothing that points to Elton or Cliff being guilty of anything yet. We don't even know when the two victims died."

"You saw both of them, didn't you?"

"Yeah. But the bodies weren't in good shape, and I'm not a forensic pathologist. We're a long way from solving this."

Lou pressed a button on her key fob and the trunk clicked and yawned open. "This has the makings of a decent short story and a chapter in my future book, but it won't be worth a nickel if you don't solve it."

"Thanks for your vote of confidence," said Fen as he walked away.

"By the way," said Lou. "What are you doing tonight besides going to a dude ranch and talking to Brent Stone?"

"Going to eat a good meal and talk to a waitress I met the last time I was here."

Fen had the choice of going to the Lucky 7 Dude Ranch or filling his empty belly with another steak from the Trail Boss. He chose the latter and arrived about fifteen minutes after five.

The approach of the winter equinox meant the sun bid farewell earlier and earlier with each passing day. In its place was the twinkle of Christmas lights in storefront windows with fake snow in the corners. Evergreen trees, both plastic and real, festooned with cowboy themed ornaments of spurs, tiny pistols, and miniature longhorn cattle had a place of honor in every store and restaurant.

Fen had to park almost a block from the restaurant. The night air and a brisk breeze bit his cheeks and made him grateful for the Stetson that grazed the tops of his ears. He kept his hands shoved into the pockets of his jacket and quick-stepped toward his destination. Western music sounded from the dance hall next door, but it was too early on this back-to-work evening for there to be a live band.

The restaurant hummed with voices layered under a western version of Christmas carols. The mood seemed festive as patrons consumed large portions of food guaranteed to satisfy them. Overfilled plates of turkey and dressing were but a memory as steak and baked potatoes regained their preeminence in this carnivore's paradise.

Fen cast his gaze around the room and spotted a young couple rise from a table for two against a wall. Gladys Mae motioned for him to follow her. "I'm tickled pink that you're back in town. Follow me, hon. It won't take me but a jiffy to clean the table you were lookin' at."

"How's Scooter?" asked Fen.

"Sick of turkey. How 'bout you?"

"I ate one and a half turkey sandwiches on the trip here today. I've had my quota for the year, but I don't set the menu at my house. My cook and housekeeper rules the kitchen."

"I bet she has plenty of turkey left over. Tell her you want turkey enchiladas on Christmas Day."

Fen considered the chances of him breaking tradition and

said, "To pull that off, I'll need to make her think it's her idea. Got any suggestions?"

"The restaurant is using up the leftover turkey in enchiladas next week. I'll give you the recipe and you can put it where she'll find it."

"That might work. What day will it be on the menu here?"

"A week from today. Will you still be here?"

"Most likely." He looked around. "This place is hopping tonight."

"It's twenty percent off filet mignon night. Scooter should be here by now. He gets meals half off, plus the special discount." She looked around. "I wish I had time to talk, but filet night has me steppin' and fetchin'. What can I get you to drink?"

"Coffee and water."

"Coming up."

Gladys Mae brought his drinks then glided across the room to serve other customers. Fen watched her while she made the demanding job look effortless.

It wasn't long before the familiar figure of Scooter Gillespie approached the table. "Gladys Mae told me you needed some company. Mind if I join you, Sheriff?"

Fen held his hand out to the empty chair. "Have a seat, Scooter. How have you been?"

"Tolerable." He paused. "No, better than tolerable. I'm doing good. There isn't much I like more than Christmas and the town's decorations put a grin on my face. Gladys Mae says I'm just a kid trapped in a large body."

Fen had several questions to pose to Scooter, but knew it would be a breach of unwritten protocol if he rushed. Instead, he stuck with something open-ended. "What is Christmas like around here?"

"Busy. There's a lot of retirees from Houston, Austin, and

San Antonio here after Thanksgiving. Cooking and cleaning wore out the grandmas, and grandpas are ready to take off their hearing aids after the grandchildren go back to school. The dude ranches are laid-back and restful, if that's what they want. As soon as schools are out for their winter break, things get busy with kids again. Families come and fill up the hotels, cabins, and dude ranches. Trail rides, chuck wagon cookouts, and old cowboy songs by the campfire are a big hit."

Gladys Mae came back, took orders, and moved on after running her hand over her husband's shoulders.

"She's a good woman," said Fen, after Gladys Mae was out of earshot.

"I'm blessed," said Scooter.

Fen leaned forward. Enough time had passed that he could ask a few questions. "Did it surprise you that Judge Willoby released Brent Stone this morning?"

"Not after the judge killed the twelve-point Saturday morning. From what I hear, it's a real trophy buck. It won't surprise me if he hangs the head in his courtroom."

Fen was on the verge of asking another question when Scooter volunteered more information. "What does surprise me is how fast Brent disappeared."

Fen tried hard not to show his surprise. "I thought the sergeant took him to the dude ranch."

"He did," said Scooter. "Brent went back to work and led a group of guests on an afternoon trail ride. Once they were on horseback, he told the group to pay close attention to the trail they were on because they'd have to find their own way back. He said it was all part of the adventure. When they were at the turnaround spot, he told them to follow their hoof-prints back to the corral. The last anyone saw of him, he was heading west at a lope."

Fen puffed out his cheeks and blew out a full breath. "Where do you think he's going?"

Scooter shrugged. "That's wild country he's headed into. The sheriff and a cowboy from the ranch will track him come daylight."

As Gladys Mae set his salad in front of him, Fen wished he'd brought his horse. He took his phone out of the pocket of his jacket.

Chapter Seventeen

Fen stopped window-to-window with Sam's ranch truck. "Thanks for coming, Any trouble on the way?"

The sound of horse hooves shuffling inside the trailer was the only response to the question. Fen realized how silly his question was. Sam had arrived prior to the agreed upon pre-dawn time at the city park. A streetlight shone down on them and revealed a dusting of confectionery sugar on Sam's coat.

"I see you stopped for a bag of donuts coated with powdered sugar. Did you get coffee, too?"

"Plenty of both. If Thelma would buy us donuts, we wouldn't have to sneak them."

"We're meeting the sheriff at first light. I have the directions on my phone."

Sam replied with, "I looked at a map. There's no need to use your phone, just follow me."

Fen didn't argue, and Sam led them to their destination with no directional errors. The first slivers of purple and orange shone in the east as they crossed over a cattle guard and under an arching metal sign reading Lucky 7 Dude Ranch.

Sheriff Irons followed them in, pulling his own two-stall horse trailer. A man with a bushy mustache stepped down from the porch of the main ranch house and pointed to a spot for them to park and unload. Sam took two horses from his trailer, while KK took two from the sheriff's trailer. She'd traded in her work uniform for the unisex style of western wear: jeans, boots, a felt cowboy hat with a modern western crease, and an unbuttoned coat that almost covered the holster on her side.

Rusty and Fen took care of introductions with the owner of the Lucky 7. After the formalities, the owner asked Sam, "What tribe are you from?"

"Choctaw."

Fen quickly added. "He may have started out in Oklahoma, but he can track a Texas rabbit wearing socks."

"That's good to know. If you find Brent, tell him I said he's fired. Leaving customers to find their own way back was the last straw." He turned to face Sam. "It's easy tracking until you get halfway to the hills. Brent was supposed to make a sweeping turn and come back on a parallel path." He pointed. "I'm thinking he headed due west, toward that tallest hill in the distance. The land gets rough and stays that way. You'll eventually come to a gravel road, but not until you're on the other side of that range of hills. Don't let the word *hill* fool you. You'll find cliffs, box canyons, and places you'll have to get off and lead your horses up and down steep grades."

Sam looked at the hills. "If he's there, I'll find him."

"One more thing," said the owner. "I have chaps if you didn't bring any. Every variety of cactus, thorny bush and tree you can imagine grows around here."

Fen looked at Sam, who said, "I brought our chaps."

"Mine are in my truck," said Rusty.

Two cowboys passed by as KK said, "I'll need to borrow a pair."

"Hold on, you two," said the boss of the ranch. "Roger, fetch a pair of chaps for Deputy KK."

The trailing cowboy had kept his face hidden as he passed. He stopped, turned, and said, "Yes, sir. She can use the ones I have on."

Fen gave Roger a hard stare. "Sheriff Irons and I want to talk to you when we return."

Rusty added, "Don't leave the ranch. On second thought..." He faced the owner. "Do you mind if Roger rides with us for a mile or two?"

"Not at all. He may miss breakfast, but that's a small price to pay for doing whatever he did to get hauled to jail last week."

The four tightened the straps on their saddles, mounted their horses and waited for Roger to join them on horseback. They walked their horses until they were out of earshot of the ranch. Sam led the way after Roger told him to stay on the well-traveled path for two miles.

Rusty rode on the left side of Roger while Fen took the right. KK brought up the rear. Rusty began the mounted interview. "Where did Brent go, and don't tell us you don't know."

"I don't know," said Roger. "I'm an inch away from losing my job and that would mean I'd miss another semester of college. Brent arrived yesterday morning, acting like nothing happened. The only unusual thing was he wanted to take the guests on the afternoon trail ride. He rode off and didn't come back."

Fen tried a different tactic. "You're a bright young man. What's your best guess where he is right now?"

Roger took his hat off and resettled it on his head. "I spent a good part of last night asking myself that same question. Two places come to mind. The first is a box canyon with a cave he told me about."

"Why would he go there?" asked Rusty as the horses walked at a slow, steady pace.

"He'd feel safe there. He said thick cactus guards the front of the small canyon and it has three steep sides. I've never been there and can't tell you where it is."

"Where else?" asked Fen.

"This is a long shot, but do you remember me talking about some women that Brent and me met at a picnic area a while back?"

"The ones from San Antonio?" asked Fen.

"Yeah. Their names are Nancy and June. I never heard their last names. Nancy was one of the few women he'd ever met who could keep up with him drinking and snorting coke."

KK spoke from behind. "We'll need a description of both of them."

"You can't miss Nancy. Her hair is red as a fire truck, and all her exposed skin from the neck down is covered with tattoos. Of course, that's not much help in weather this cold, but it was warm when I met her. She wore shorts and a tank top that day."

"Height and weight?" asked KK.

"Tall and thin. Not much up top, but long legs and a cute face."

"What about June?"

"She's older and rougher looking in the face. Short brown hair and she smoked a lot, which really turned me off."

Fen asked, "Who drove and what make and model of vehicle?"

"Nancy drove. It was a base model '97 Chevy Silverado half-ton that smoked almost as much as June did."

"What color?"

"Mostly white with a gray hood and a dented tailgate."

"Any other things you remember about the truck?"

"The back license plate hung crooked by two pieces of wire."

Rusty took over again. "Did you see Brent talking to anyone else at the ranch yesterday?"

"He probably said something to the people on the trail ride, but that won't help you. We have a script we're supposed to follow. As for the other ranch hands, I doubt it. We didn't figure he was in the mood to answer questions, so we left him alone. It surprised us when he didn't come back with the guests."

Rusty faced Sam and spoke a little louder. "Do you need Roger to ride with us any longer?"

"No."

"Go back to the ranch and stay there," said Rusty. "We're going to pick up the pace and try to be back before dark. If you're not there when we return, I'll be very upset and you don't want that to happen."

"Don't worry, Sheriff. I'm not leaving the ranch until I go back to college."

Roger pulled lightly on the reins and his horse came to a stop, wheeled to the right and he tickled it with his spurs. The horse took off at a fast trot.

KK took Roger's place, riding three abreast on the wide trail. Sam leaned forward and clicked once with his tongue. It was all it took for the horse to respond and move out at a good clip. He didn't look back until he came to a stop where the wide trail turned to the right. "One horse goes straight. All others turn and go back."

The riders changed to ride single file, with Sam leading, Rusty next, KK third, and Fen brought up the rear. They continued the quick, steady pace and kept it for hours. They came to a small stream and allowed the horses to slake their thirst. Fen took a water bottle from his saddlebag and did the same, as did everyone but Sam.

With their horses refreshed, the small posse started an uphill climb through thick prickly pear cactus and thorny mesquite trees. A saddled but riderless horse approached. Sam dismounted, spoke in a soft tone, and took hold of the horse's bridle. He then untied the reins from the saddle horn which allowed him to hold the horse while he examined each side of the gelding. "He has the same brand as the horses back at the ranch. There's no blood on the saddle. He's hungry and will go back on his own to get fed if I release him."

With reins retied loosely, the horse passed the other riders. Sam hooked a foot in a stirrup and pulled himself into the saddle. KK asked, "Do you think Brent is out here on foot?"

"That's one possibility," said Rusty.

Fen didn't think so but kept his theory to himself and voiced another concern. "If we don't find him in the next hour, we'll have to turn back, continue in the dark, or find a place to camp, preferably a cave."

Rusty voiced his preference. "I say we keep riding. We need to know if he's up in these hills or if he had someone pick him up on the county road on the other side. At least it's too cold to worry about rattlesnakes crawling into our bedrolls."

Fen looked at Sam. "What do you say? Can we make it up and over these hills in the dark?"

Sam looked toward the hills. "I can. The sheriff and the woman might. I don't trust you to ride at night."

KK and the sheriff snickered.

Fen accepted the critique. "Sam's right. I gave up chasing escaped convicts at night many years ago and never tried in terrain like this. Let's keep going until we have to walk our horses." He let out a huff and saw his breath. "I'm saddle-sore, hungry, tired, and cold. Another hour in the saddle is all the fun I can stand for one day."

Sam used his reins to direct his horse's head back toward

the hills and off they rode until the sun dipped behind the jagged hills, shooting rays of sunlight into a cloudless sky. Fen's horse stumbled on a steep downhill grade. This caused Sam to look back. "This is far enough. There's a cave up ahead."

KK asked, "How do you know?"

"I spotted it when we crested the last hill. There should be plenty of wood for you to gather."

Fen stood up in the saddle to relieve his aching posterior. "Are you going to kill something for us to eat?"

Sam shook his head and pointed at the ground. "The rider is on foot. My horse and I will follow the man's tracks. There's plenty of moonlight for me to see. You three go to the cave, eat beans, and sleep."

Fen gave Sam a squinting glare. "When did you decide to track him alone in the dark?"

"When we found his horse."

"That means we had time to go back to the ranch and stay the night."

Sam's next comment came with a quirked smile. "You ate too much at Thanksgiving. A couple of missed meals and a night away from central heat will do you good."

Sam's horse shot forward as the mouths of all three hinged open. KK was the first to speak. "I don't know about you two, but Sam nailed me. I have too much backside covering my saddle."

Fen ended the conversation by saying, "The 'Rock-Hard Hotel' awaits us. It may not have central heat, but a cave, a blazing fire, hot beans, and a wool blanket sounds better than another minute in this saddle."

KK asked, "Do you think Sam will be back by first light?"

"We'll find out tomorrow."

Chapter Eighteen

Shards of light entered the cold cave as Fen tugged his blanket to cover his chin. The fire stokers had lost ambition in the predawn hours, resulting in dark, bone-chilling cold. Fen looked from under the brim of his Stetson and considered his options. As much as he hated to face the frosty morning, someone had to resurrect the fire. His first movements to accomplish the task caused every muscle, ligament, and bone to remind him he was on the downhill side of forty. At least he didn't have to dress or put on his boots, as he'd slept fully clothed.

He took a short, dry tree limb from the stack of wood they'd collected the previous evening and stirred the ashes with it. Red coals winked back at him. Next he added small branches, followed by larger ones. By the time KK and Rusty quit pretending they were asleep, flames danced.

Fen looked down at his bedroll, a thin waterproof ground cover, and an army-green wool blanket. The saddle blanket had served as his pillow, with his saddle as a backstop. He once thought the life of a cowboy would be a fun adventure. That was before he turned ten. Today, harsh reality replaced the romance of riding the range.

Rusty gave the first words of the day. "Fen, why didn't you make coffee while you were up?"

Not to be outdone, Fen said, "I called Starbucks and asked if they made deliveries to caves. I'm surprised they're not here by now."

KK had to clear her throat before her first words squeaked out. "I have instant coffee if you have water and something to heat it in."

Fen said, "We can boil water in the empty cans of pork and beans we ate last night."

Rusty replied, "We all should have plenty of water after filling our canteens at the stream we crossed. I'm glad I finally got to use my travel water purifier."

The figure of a man appeared in the cave's opening. KK squealed. Rusty moved a hand toward his pistol in its holster beside him. Fen simply said, "Good morning, Sam. What did you find?"

"Two rabbits, a squirrel, and an armadillo. You need meat to go with your coffee." He walked into the cave with the rabbits and squirrel already skinned, cleaned, and skewered on debarked tree limbs, ready to roast over the open fire. He then produced a pan large enough to boil water for three cups of coffee.

Rusty asked, "Where's the armadillo?"

Sam patted his stomach. "Crispy armadillo and fresh ground Starbucks coffee are almost as good for breakfast as tiny donuts dusted with sugar."

KK said, "This day is getting better by the minute. The only thing that would have made it better is if you'd returned with Brent Stone."

Sam shook his head. "I only locate people. You catch them."

Fen took over. "Sam had a run-in with the law many years ago. I reviewed his conviction, found the previous sheriff had played fast and loose with the law, and took steps to get him a new trial. His case was reversed and remanded back to the sentencing court with instructions to find him not guilty."

Rusty's eyebrows went up. "That rarely happens."

Sam spoke in a matter-of-fact tone. "The man deserved to die, but I didn't kill him."

Fen added a postscript. "The experience left Sam suspicious of everyone who wears a badge."

"I don't like lawyers or judges either."

KK said, "I hope that doesn't include Sheriff Irons and me."

Sam locked her in his gaze. "Sheriff Maguire is the only lawman I trust."

KK shivered, and Fen didn't blame her. Sam possessed skills enough to provide meat for himself and three others after a frosty night in unfamiliar territory. It would be easy for him to make someone disappear.

Fen sensed the need to get the conversation back on track, so he turned to Sam as the three rotated their breakfast over the flames. "Did you have any trouble keeping on Brent's trail?"

Sam shook his head. "No problem. The gravel road the sheriff talked about was on the other side of this range of hills. The man's tracks stopped at the road. He got into a truck with mismatched tires. The truck turned around and headed south after leaving a few drops of oil on the rocks."

Fen looked at Rusty. "He contacted someone and had them pick him up. The questions to answer are, who picked him up and where did they go?"

KK said, "This is what I was afraid would happen."

Fen kept his eye on his roasting rabbit. "KK, if you don't get your squirrel out of the flame, you'll be eating charcoal."

"Oops," she said. "I hoped we'd bring Brent back. There's no telling where he is now."

Rusty seemed more optimistic. "Thanks to Sam, we at least know where not to look."

It may not have been a balanced breakfast, but all three partakers of the fire-roasted rabbit and squirrel agreed it tasted better than the tepid beans they'd eaten the night before.

Water and dirt, mostly rocky soil, extinguished the fire as Rusty flattened tin cans under his boots and placed them in saddle bags. The horses received blankets, then saddles. The sojourners left the 'Rock-Hard Hotel' in better condition than they found it. It now had enough dry wood to start the next campfire.

The trip back to the Lucky 7 didn't seem to take as long. Perhaps it was because of the crisp early winter air or that the path was now familiar. Most likely it was because Sam set a faster pace. Miles passed and the sun warmed Fen enough that he unzipped his coat. Once again, he rode last in line.

A mile past the stream where they found Brent's horse, Sam turned in his saddle and pointed at the ground in a damp part of the trail. "Five horses headed toward the mountains. Only one came back yesterday. Can you tell which one?"

Rusty said, "It's faint, but only one set of tracks face east."

Sam nodded his approval, and the two engaged in a conversation about the nuances of tracking. KK slowed her pace and tried to read the prints on harder ground.

Fen asked, "Do you see the difference?"

"Not now, but I could in that muddy spot we went through."

"Me either," said Fen. "I find it easier to track men on my

computer than on horseback. I call Sam when there's old-school tracking to do. Sometimes it takes both."

KK glanced his way as they rode side by side. "Where do you think Brent is right now?"

"Probably in a warm bed."

"That's not what I meant. What city do you think he went to?"

Fen envisioned a map. "He could have gone to Eagle Pass or Del Rio. Both are border towns."

"Do you think he's in Mexico?"

"Not necessarily, but it gives him one more option to make his apprehension difficult."

KK didn't look convinced, and Fen didn't blame her. It was a wild guess, so he turned the question around on her. "What's your theory? Where do you think he is?"

KK kept her eyes on the trail. "Definitely not in Bandera or Bandera County. He's too well-known to chance staying here. He could have gone to Kerrville or San Antonio. Kerrville has a growing population of about twenty-five thousand, and Interstate 10 runs through it. As for San Antonio, it has a million and a half people. Probably half as many more undocumented people. It's a place where people go to hide."

"You're probably right," said Fen before he changed the subject and asked, "Did Rusty ask you to come with him to look for Brent?"

"I was the first to volunteer when I found out Sheriff Irons was going after him."

"Did you fear for his safety?"

KK shot back, "Didn't you?"

Fen considered the question and gave what he believed was a weak answer. "I never met Elton Palmer, his son, or his murdered daughter. I'm trying to keep an open mind about the father and son's desire for revenge."

"This is Bandera," said KK. "Some people here forget we're no longer in the nineteenth century."

Fen changed the subject. "Tell me about Misti Palmer. Did you know her well?"

"Misti was a spoiled, beautiful rich girl who enjoyed stomping on a girl's feelings and breaking a man's heart."

"Did she ever stomp on your feelings?"

"I never gave her the chance. She tried once, but I didn't play her game."

He kept looking ahead at the trail. "And what game was that?"

"It happened at the dance hall on 11th Street about five months ago. I was dancing with a handsome man who rode into town on a 1985 Harley Electra-glide. He had the leather vest, tattoos, holey jeans, and boots. Misti showed up, looked over the male talent and cast me a look that said she was taking over. I told the guy, who turned out to be a financial planner, that I had to use the restroom. That was a lie. I left and drove to another dance hall in Comfort, a tiny community to the east of Bandera." She grinned. "I wonder to this day if she had to listen to a sales pitch on investing."

Fen said, "I think we have something in common. We're both satisfied living single." He then qualified his statement, "At least for the time being."

"I'll never marry," said KK with a far-off look in her gaze.

Fen didn't let her get trapped in her thoughts. "Never is a long time. You might reconsider someday."

Her gaze remained on a spot on the horizon. "It would take a miracle."

He kept on with another question. "Any other encounters with Misti?"

KK returned to the present. "That encounter was one more than I wanted. I saw what kind of woman she was, and I didn't want to play childish games with her. She could have all the phony bikers she wanted."

They kept riding two-abreast, and Fen asked, "Do you know Cliff Palmer well?"

"Well enough not to want to be around him. Daddy's money spoiled both his children."

"Do you think he'd go after Brent?"

"His daddy says jump, and he asks, 'How high?'"

He waited to see if she'd expand on her comment. It came as they topped a hill and saw the ranch not far ahead.

"Cliff never had to work for anything. He'll inherit everything his father accumulates, then spend the rest of his life trying to spend it all."

Sam unhooked a metal gate and pushed it open while still mounted. The first two riders went ahead, as Fen had one more question for KK. "Do you believe Brent killed Misti and Clay Trueblood?"

"Misti for sure. After all, he broke the conditions of his release."

Fen countered with, "I still wonder if it's safer for him out of jail than in." He quickly added, "That doesn't mean Rusty shouldn't get a warrant for Brent's arrest and do everything possible to find him."

Fen rode ahead and pulled up next to Sam as he took the saddle off his horse. Fen did the same to his horse. Sam took his saddle into the trailer and returned with feed for both horses. Fen spoke as the horses ate. "Thanks for coming."

Sam looked to the far hills. "This is good land. Not many people, very few lights to block the stars and moon. Plenty of deer, too. Thelma would enjoy cooking for guests. You should sell your land and buy a ranch out here. Start over with the woman lawyer from Smithville."

Fen stood dumbstruck as his heart raced. He'd never heard Sam offer unsolicited advice.

He finally found his voice. "You may be right, but I won't consider it for several years."

"I thought you'd say that. Go help Sheriff Rusty. I'm going home."

"Don't forget to stop for donuts but be sure to brush the sugar off before you get home."

Sam flashed a quick smile, but it left as fast as it came. "Take care of Bailey when she comes. Two-legged snakes don't hibernate in winter."

KK was loading hers and Rusty's horses when the sheriff came to where Fen stood. "She's taking my truck and trailer to my place. You and I need to have another chat with Roger. He's bound to have some ideas about where Brent is."

"I was thinking the same thing." Another thought crossed his mind. "When I came back into town, KK was on her way to ask for some days off. Did you approve them?"

"I did, but she changed her mind when she learned I was going after Brent. She told me a few minutes ago she'd work overtime to find him or transport him back to Bandera when he's arrested."

Fen looked toward the bunkhouse. "We should find Roger and see what he failed to tell us."

Rusty smiled. "This will be a lot more fun than sleeping in a cold cave."

Chapter Nineteen

Rusty watched as KK drove his truck and trailer through the entrance of the Lucky 7, with Sam's truck and trailer following. He turned to Fen. "I should have asked if you minded taking me home after we speak with Roger."

Fen dismissed the statement with a wave of his hand.

Rusty looked at the main house, a sprawling building with weathered wood siding everywhere except on the original rock cabin. "I reckon we should tell Jim we need to talk to Roger."

Fen nodded. "Do you smell what I do?"

"Fried chicken," said Rusty. "I wonder if there's any left over. The rabbit for breakfast hopped away a couple of hours ago."

They approached the largest of the many additions to the building as Jim was coming out the door. "Any luck in finding your desperado?"

Rusty fielded the question. "He outfoxed us. Had someone pick him up on the road on the other side of Dove Pass. There's no telling where he is now."

Jim looked to the west. "He's partial to female companionship. I'd be checking motels from here to the border."

"That's not a bad idea."

Fen changed the subject. "Did his horse make it home all right?"

"It's my horse, and he came home ready to eat. Homing pigeons have nothing on horses at a dude ranch. You can take them a day's ride from here and they'll come back." He paused, "Speaking of food, you two look like you could stand a meal."

Rusty said, "We wouldn't want to hurt the cook's feeling by turning you down."

Jim pulled the door open. "Eat all you want. I want to hear more about your trip. My storyteller told the guests a posse was searching for a desperate outlaw. He laid it on thick, and the people lapped it up. They saw you ride off wearing chaps with pistols on your hips and an Indian tracker. It's all they've talked about. I can't wait to read the reviews they'll post on social media. It's given me an idea to incorporate an outlaw chase into our schedule."

Rusty took the idea and ran with it. "If you want to give them a truly unique experience, have them spend the night in the cave we slept in and only give them a can of pork and beans for supper."

Jim considered the suggestion and rejected it. "I don't think the insurance company would go for something that authentic. They'd probably require we put a porta-potty near the cave." Jim grinned and pointed to the serving line. "Fill your plates before they take the food away."

Fen and Rusty took turns telling Jim tales of the trail as they shoveled in food that almost rivaled what Thelma served. Fen slowed and asked, "How would you describe Brent Stone, in less than twenty words?"

"I can do that in less than ten," said Jim. "Good cowboy and a lousy man."

"What makes him a lousy man?"

"Let me put it this way," said Jim. "He has a hard time resisting temptations."

Rusty's fork hovered above his food. "Can you be more specific?"

"The Bible calls them the lusts of the flesh. Drinking, gambling, greed, and especially women."

"Is he a habitual liar?" asked Fen.

Jim took his time answering the question. "I've never known him to lie. When confronted, he owns up to what he's done. Of course, that's only when confronted. He's not opposed to getting by with not volunteering information."

"I experienced that when he was in jail," said Rusty. "When things got too close for comfort, he clammed up and demanded to talk to an attorney."

Warm peach cobbler and coffee ended the meal and the discussion concerning the wayward ranch hand. Rusty leaned back as a ranch hand cleared the table. Jim asked, "Do you want to talk to Roger?"

"I'd rather go home and take a nap," said Rusty, "—but Sheriff Maguire and I had better talk to Roger."

Jim leaned forward. "You tell me if he won't talk or tries to shade the truth. I'll send him packing."

Rusty said, "Fen has over twenty years of experience interviewing people who don't want to talk to him. Where can we find Roger?"

"Go to the bunkhouse. I'll send him to you."

Fen and Rusty opened the door to a large room with rows of top and bottom bunks running down each side of a wide middle aisle. On the end nearest the door, there were two round tables with wooden chairs. The smell of leather and sweat hung heavy in the air. Decks of cards and dominoes rested on a narrow table by the front door, waiting for the next game. The room was void of occupants besides the two lawmen.

They made themselves at home by taking off their hats and hanging them on a rack made of blunted deer antlers. Fen took a step through an open side door and quipped, "If it wasn't for this modern bathroom, I'd think this was an original bunkhouse."

Rusty sniffed and said, "I don't think the cowboys are taking advantage of the showers as much as they should."

The two walked to a table and seated themselves in simple, solid chairs. The front door eased open and Roger came in. He hung his sweat-stained hat on a stubby antler beside Fen's and joined them.

Roger spoke first, which Fen believed was his first mistake. "I hope this doesn't take long. Mr. Frank has been watching me so close I'm afraid to use too much salt on my mashed potatoes."

Rusty asked, "Why do you think that is?"

"Because I spent time with Brent. The boss thinks I'm like Brent, but I'm not."

"Did you know Brent planned to leave yesterday afternoon?"

Roger waited a few seconds too long to respond, and Fen struck like a coiled snake. "You're an inch away from being in more trouble than you can imagine. If you don't want to spend the night in jail, lose your job, and spend your college money on a lawyer, I advise you not to play games. Your buddy Brent caused the four of us to sleep on the ground last night and eat beans out of the can. The sheriff and I are not in the best mood."

Judging from his bobbing Adam's apple, Roger received the

threat and believed it. "I suspected he was leaving when he took bread, bacon and cheese from breakfast and filled a canteen."

Rusty piled on. "And you didn't bother to tell the boss, did you?"

"No, sir."

"I should take you to jail right now."

"Hold on," said Fen. "Let's give Roger a chance to redeem himself." He shifted his gaze to the nervous young man. "Where is Brent?"

"I don't know, and that's the truth."

"You're a smart college guy. Where do you think he is?"

Roger's head dipped. "Like I told you earlier, the first place I'd look is San Antonio. That girl in the old truck seemed to think Brent was something special, and he wasn't pushing her away."

Rusty asked, "Tell us her name again."

"Nan is what Brent called her."

"Nan?" said Fen under his breath. "That's short for Nancy, right?"

Rusty locked his gaze on Roger. "Think hard. Did you ever hear Rusty use her last name?"

"He called her Nan Jerk, or sometimes only Jerk if he was teasing her. I guess it was an inside joke. It didn't seem to offend her."

Fen stuck the name in a mental file cabinet as Rusty drilled down on the details of the woman's physical appearance, identifying scars, marks, and tattoos.

Fen took over and got a more detailed description of Nan's truck, including the mismatched tires.

Throughout the interview, Roger shifted his gaze to the door, as if he was looking for a way to escape. Rusty's phone buzzed. It was the first time in more than a day either one of them had good enough reception for anyone to reach them. By the way he said, "I'm busy," it was an unwelcome interruption of the interview. Rusty listened, rose from his chair, and hastened to the door. He jerked it open, stepped outside, and closed it again.

Fen wanted to keep Roger off balance, so he spoke in a fatherly tone that didn't match his words. "You're getting better at answering our questions. I'd say your chances of being arrested and losing your job have gone down. Of course, the call the sheriff received might tip the scales in the other direction."

Roger's eyes were wide as he gazed at Fen without saying a word.

Fen asked, "What's the biggest lesson you've learned while working at this ranch?"

Roger didn't hesitate. "To pick better friends. I can't believe I'm sitting here talking to two sheriffs about a man who may have killed two people."

Fen leaned forward. "Do you believe Brent killed them?"

The young cowboy took his time before shaking his head. "I never saw Brent lose his temper or heard him speak badly about anyone. That includes some of our guests who pulled some really stupid stunts. One guy tried to stampede the longhorns by firing a pistol into the air. Brent talked Mr. Frank into letting the man and his family stay. I would have sent them home.

"Don't get me wrong, Sheriff Maguire, Brent has his faults, but being mean isn't one of them."

The door opened, and Fen made note of Rusty's changed countenance. Worry lines that weren't there before now creased his forehead. He asked, "Do you have any more questions for Roger?"

"No. He was just telling me he's not convinced Brent has it in him to kill anyone."

"He may be half right," said Rusty as he threw a thumb over his shoulder and growled as he looked at Roger. "Go back to work. We're through with you for today."

Roger sprang from his seat and left without another word. Fen remained seated as Rusty plopped down and rubbed his temples. He spoke while his fingertips made tiny circles. "The report from the medical examiner came back. A gunshot to the base of Clay Trueblood's skull killed him. Also, there was no water in Clay's lungs."

"What about the time and day of death?"

"That's the last item that complicates things. The cold water zapped Clay Trueblood's body of heat. The ME could only guess as to the exact day. It may have been six or seven days before he was found."

"Was it the same with Misty Palmer's report?"

Rusty shook his head. "Different cause of death. You were wrong about the gunshot this time. What you saw was a puncture wound from a stick. What looked like powder burns was debris from the bark. The official cause of death was drowning. The scratches, bruises and contusions, as well as the puncture wound, could have been pre-mortem or post-mortem."

"Who died first?"

"Trueblood by two or three days. The coroner couldn't be any more specific."

Fen put the puzzle pieces together. "We're not dealing with a double murder, but two separate killings. The MOs are completely different." He stared at Rusty. "Are we looking for one killer or two?"

Rusty shrugged his shoulders in defeat. "I thought for sure we had one killer to catch, and I thought it was Brent Stone."

Fen heaved a sigh. "I need to sleep, paint, and come up with a new plan. In the meantime, email me a copy of the coroner's reports, then get some rest."

After dropping the sheriff at his office, the trip back to his cabin overlooking Bandera gave Fen a chance to ponder what actions he should take. He stopped on the bridge where Misti Palmer's life likely came to a violent and premature end. The river was now a peaceful stream.

He reminded himself that he needed to take the advice he gave Rusty and rest. Lou, however, needed another assignment and he had one for her.

Chapter Twenty

Fen pulled into the gravel driveway and parked his truck by the back door of his cabin. Lou must have heard him coming as she wasted no time walking the short distance from her cabin to his. A look of displeasure wrinkled her brow. Instead of going inside, he walked to a wooden yard swing with padded cushions. The swing dangled on chains attached to a metal A-frame.

Lou stood before him with hands tented on her hips. "Well," she said. "Did you catch Brent Stone?"

"No, but I have an idea where he might be. All you have to do is find him."

Lou's collar length hair swung from side to side. "That's not how we play the game. Start at the beginning, give details, and I won't interrupt unless I have to." She paused. "By the way, you smell like a campfire."

"The shower wasn't working in the cave I slept in last night."

"Details," said Lou with chastisement in her single word.

"I'm too tired, dirty, and saddle sore to give details. Here are the highlights. Sam, Rusty, KK, and I tracked Brent until almost dark. Sam kept tracking while the rest of us slept in a cave. I should add, it was a cold and rocky cave. At dawn, Sam returned and told us someone driving a vehicle with mismatched tires picked up Brent, turned around, and headed south."

"Do you know who picked him up?"

"It's only a guess, but I believe it's a woman named Nancy and they're somewhere in San Antonio."

Lou showed her lack of patience as she said, "I need more information than that if you expect me to find them."

"Use your skills to look for a woman Brent calls Nan Jerk."

"That can't be her real name. How do you expect me to find someone with only a nickname?"

"Try Nancy Jurik. I knew a guy in high school with the same last name. It's Polish or German and pronounced *Ur-ik*. People called him Jimmy Jerk."

"I hope you're not too tired to realize this is a long shot."

"It's the best I can do with a chafed undercarriage."

Lou let out a huff. "Somebody woke up on the wrong side of the cave this morning."

Fen tilted his head. "That makes two of us. Who put a bee in your bonnet?"

"You did," snapped Lou. "I've been twiddling my thumbs all day. Why didn't you call or text?"

"No cell service. I could have asked Sam to send up smoke signals, but I didn't think you could read them."

They stared at each other until Lou stuck her tongue out at him and said, "What do you want me to do if Nan Jerk turns out to be Nancy Jurik?"

"Get an address."

"What else?"

"Find out if Brent Stone is with her. Look for an older truck in rough shape with a rear license plate being held on with bailing wire. If the tires don't match and it leaks oil, call Candy and have her run the plates."

Lou narrowed her gaze. "Why don't you want Sheriff Irons to run the plates? Don't you trust him?"

"Rusty's a good man, but there's more to this county than meets the eye. If I don't play my cards close to my vest, there could be another murder."

A smile made a brief appearance. "Three murders would make a real page-turner. Now you're speaking my love language."

Fen stood, but Lou blocked the path to his cabin. "Are you going to tease me with another potential homicide and walk away?"

He gave her a stare he'd mastered as a state trooper. "Concentrate on finding Brent Stone, and I'll throw you another bone to chew on. You'll like it. There's plenty of meat left on it."

"Two can play that game," said Lou. "I went dancing last night. If you were in a better mood, I'd tell you who I danced with and what I learned."

Fen walked by her and mumbled, "It's about time you showed some initiative. I'll call you after I get some sleep."

Fen made it into his cabin and pulled off boots that he'd worn for a day and a half straight. Wiggling his toes brought back feeling but released a pungent odor. He realized his hat was still on when he walked into the bathroom and looked at the reflection. He removed the Stetson and threw it on the small table outside the bathroom. A second look at his face in the bathroom mirror showed a greasy band of hair above his ears and a pink streak about an inch wide running across his forehead. He'd worn boots and a hat much longer than normal, and it showed.

The ringing of his phone caused him to sigh and say, "This better not be a robo-call." It wasn't.

"Hello, Candy. I guess you're calling because you received a copy of the autopsies."

"I'm making sure you did, too."

"Not yet, but Rusty told me what they said. I'm having to recalibrate my thinking about the case, or should I say cases?"

"You sound tired."

"The years caught up with me. I need to trade my bedroll for a thick mattress."

Fen waited until Candy stopped snickering. He regrouped and said, "I'm glad you called. Lou's hunting down a lead for a woman whose name could be Nancy Jurik. She'll need information on where to locate this woman, if that's her real name. I was snippy with her a little while ago. If you could help her get started I'd appreciate it."

"Do you think she and Brent Stone are together?"

"It's the best theory I have."

"I'll get on it. Anything else?"

"Not yet, but I need to talk to Bailey and make sure she's following up with Jeremy and his sister, Frieda."

"I'll call her and relay your message. You get some sleep."

Candy then asked, "What about Ray Long, the motorcycle mechanic? Have you verified Clay Trueblood owed him money?"

"He's next on my list. I was working on the assumption this was a double murder, not two separate crimes." He took a breath. "More proof that I'm losing my touch."

"Nonsense," said Candy. "You're as sharp today as you ever were. All you need is sleep."

"And a long, hot shower," said Fen.

Candy ended the call with, "Take care of yourself and I'll

do what I can for Lou." She paused. "By the way, Audrey's tracking your progress. She's worried."

Fen didn't say it, but he sensed danger, too.

FEN AWOKE with the comforter pulled up to his chin. He slept best in a cold room with plenty of blankets. He checked the time on his phone. The glowing numbers read 4:32. Following the previous afternoon's shower that lasted until the hot water ran out, he'd donned sleep shorts and a baggy cotton T-shirt, turned off the central heat, and crawled under the covers. A quick calculation revealed he'd slept for ten and a half hours.

Not wanting to place his warm feet on the frigid floor yet, he turned on the light and grabbed Sally's framed photo. He imagined her joining him and wished her a good morning. The morning ritual continued for twenty minutes before he braved the cold and padded his way to the thermostat and the coffeepot. He left both to perform their jobs as he scurried back to bed to finish his talk with his late wife. Her silent voice reminded him to be thankful for the women in his life who were filling the void she'd left when her transplanted heart stopped beating. As he thought about Thelma, Bailey, Candy, Lou, and the latest addition, Audrey, he was humbled to realize afresh how much each one meant to him. They couldn't take the place of Sally, but he couldn't imagine life now without any of them.

Fen ended his time with Sally by saying, "This was a much better way to start the day than waking up in a cave." He rubbed his chin and realized he hadn't shaved in two days. He pulled fresh socks on his feet and poured a cup of coffee. He'd rake the stubble off his face after his eyes were open better.

A three-ring binder caught his eye. He took it and his coffee to a leather chair with a reading lamp beside it. The first pages gave a history of the cabins and the ruins of the Silver Spur Dance Hall. It also included information on the mostly completed mini-mansion that was in the process of being rebuilt.

At first light, he put on his coat and walked to the two-story home that looked to be almost ready for occupants. He remembered from his reading that a suspicious fire had destroyed the home many decades ago.

He walked to the back corner of the home and gained access to what looked like a metal pole barn with a tin roof and concrete floors. The ends were open to the elements and window frames void of glass gave incredible views of Bandera and the surrounding land. From the top of the cliff overlooking the Medina River, he could see at least fifty miles. His mind raced. This was where he'd set up his easel to capture a panoramic view of Bandera County. "If only it would snow," he lamented, "this would be the perfect winter landscape."

He spun around when a woman's voice echoed off the concrete and tin structure. "I was wondering how long it would take you to discover this place," said Lou.

"Have you seen this view?" It was a silly question, but Fen posed it anyway.

"I had plenty of time to explore yesterday. Did you read the history of this place or notice the raised bandstand?" She closed her eyes. "I can see World War II pinup girl Betty Grable being introduced to her future husband, big band leader, Harry James. Did you know they met here?"

"I read the history of the Silver Spur this morning."

Lou shivered. "I wonder what other stories this place could tell? Gambling, illegal moonshine, even that the house that burned provided ladies of the evening."

Fen cast his gaze to the river below. "If the walls talk, ask them who killed Clay Trueblood and Misti Palmer. You can see both crime scenes from here."

Lou changed the subject. "Candy found an address for Nancy Jurik. I'm leaving for San Antonio in a few minutes. Do you want me to talk to her?"

Fen spun back around. "Find out if Brent is with her. Report back to me and no one else. I may have to bend the rules a little, and I don't want you involved."

Lou rolled her eyes. "I know what's coming next. You'll do something that won't allow me to write and sell a story to the wire services. The only thing I'll get is royalties from book sales after you retire."

"Deferred gratification pays excellent dividends."

"So says the man with four thousand acres, cattle, crops, paintings, and oil wells."

"I keep telling you that you're one marriage away from having all your financial needs met. What about the guy you danced with the night before last? Is he a rich rancher?"

"As a matter of fact," said Lou. "Cliff Palmer will be rich after his father dies. Until then, his father has him on a generous allowance."

All thoughts of painting a landscape fled as Fen focused his gaze on Lou. "What else did you learn from Cliff?"

"He can dance a mean two-step and he doesn't waste time making a play on a woman."

"That's not exactly what I meant, but it's interesting all the same. I hope you didn't slap him."

Lou lowered her chin and looked up at him as she spoke. "He wanted to play. I needed to work. So, I teased just enough to let him know I was interested but tired. He thinks I'm in town for a couple of weeks doing research for a novel. I want to play him slow and not frighten him off."

"That's probably the best thing to do. When will you see him again?"

Lou shrugged. "He's not the type of man to make long-term plans and his definition of long term is anything over an hour."

Fen realized that Lou had already examined the possibilities of how to extract information from Cliff and developed a strategy.

Lou brought the conversation to a close by saying. "I'm leaving for San Antonio to stake out Nancy Jurik's apartment. I'll call when I know something." She looked out the window one more time. "You should call Bailey."

"I may wake her if I call this early."

"Take the chance. She's miserable about not being here with you."

Fen allowed his gaze to fix on distant purple hills as rays of sunlight shot through a narrow gap. He imagined the miles before him covered in a blanket of snow. Without turning, he reached for his phone. "Moments of inspiration like this don't come along very often. I'll take a few photos before I call Bailey."

Chapter Twenty-One

The desire to sketch and paint hit Fen with enough force that he blocked out anything else Lou said or did. He didn't know how long he stared at the vista. When he focused on his surroundings again, he was alone. It wasn't long before he had an easel set up in the Silver Spur and his pencil had established the horizon line on pristine paper.

The ringing of his cell phone didn't totally break the spell of inspiration, but it was unwelcome all the same. He considered turning his phone off, but he glimpsed the caller's name and answered in a tone that betrayed his focus. "Hello?"

"Hello, yourself," said Bailey. "I thought you'd be more awake after sleeping the clock around."

"I'm wide awake," countered Fen.

"I hope I didn't interrupt your time with Sally."

"That was hours ago. I'm sketching an unbelievable landscape."

"Ah," said Bailey like she'd spoken with a long sigh. "Your muse made a surprise visit. Did you take photos?"

"Yeah," said Fen, with his gaze still locked on the creation that spread out before him.

"I can tell you're locked into something special. I'll call back later."

Fen's gaze shifted to the river and town below him, which allowed him to focus on the conversation. "I hear highway noises. Where are you?"

"On my way to Bandera."

The revelation put the inspiration to draw on hold. "I thought we agreed you'd wait until finals started before you came."

"Jeremy and I talked it over and he came up with a work-around. We're both sick for the next three school days. We diagnosed the ailment as sudden onset college-itis. He's driving home from Huntsville and I'm on my way from Georgetown. We'll stay with his parents and both be free to help you for the next five days."

"Are you both sure you won't be missing anything important?"

"I took my last quiz yesterday and aced it. Jeremy has two end-of-term essays to turn in. He put the final touches on them last night and one of his fraternity brothers will turn them in to his professors on Thursday and Friday. Next week is dead week, followed by finals. All I have left to do is clean out my room."

"What about Jeremy?"

"He has to go back for dead week and take two final exams."

Fen considered the work-around Bailey and her boyfriend had concocted. "Is this an example of optional ethics?"

"I look at it as how to get around silly rules with creative thinking." She turned the tables on him. "I know for a fact you're guilty of not telling the whole truth and nothing but the truth."

Fen thought of his failure to include Rusty in his search for Brent Stone by sending Lou to spy on Nancy Jurik.

It was time to change the subject. "How long before you arrive?"

"A couple of hours. I plan on stopping at the Blue Bonnet Café in Marble Falls."

Fen let out a moan of desire. "They need to put a disclaimer on the menu that they're not responsible for injuries caused by gluttony."

"Do you want me to bring you a piece of pie?"

"You'd better not this time. I'm in work mode until we get these cases solved." He took a quick breath. "I'll be in the Silver Spur Dancehall in front of my easel when you get here."

"Will you give us something important to do?"

Fen considered the question before saying, "Everything in a murder investigation could be important. It's often the little, seemingly insignificant things that blow a case wide open. You know that."

All he heard was a deep sigh of frustration.

"By the way," said Fen. "Did you talk to Frieda?"

"Yeah, but I'm in a construction zone and the road is extra narrow." She let out a yelp.

He heard a loud bang.

The silence lasted only a few seconds, but they might have been the longest seconds of his life.

Bailey shouted, "That was close. Oh no! I have to stop and help."

The call cut off and Fen whispered a prayer of thanksgiving for Bailey's protection. He followed it with a petition for the other people involved in the crash. Visions of crushed metal, shattered glass, and broken bodies flashed in his mind, reminders of the fragility of life from his days as a highway patrolman and sheriff. A sense of helplessness swept over him, as did a cold north wind. He shivered from his hat down to the soles of his boots.

He walked away from his easel. The sketch could wait. Thinking about the case could also wait. He needed to warm himself. More than that, he needed to talk to someone. He pulled out his phone and placed a call to the first person who crossed his mind.

A sleepy voice answered. "What's wrong? Are you all right?"

"Not really. I just had a big scare and need to talk to someone."

"A big scare? Are you hurt?"

"I'm fine, just a little shook up. I was talking to Bailey when I heard what sounded like a car crash. Her last words were she had to stop and help."

"Oh, no!"

Fen quickly said, "I'm pretty sure she's all right, but she's somewhere between here and home, I don't know where, looking at God knows what."

"I'm glad you chose me to call," said Audrey. "Keep talking."

Fen spoke in clipped words forced through a constricted windpipe. "I almost lost her. I can see the crash. The images are so real."

"But we didn't lose her. She's alive and doing all she can to help people. You're the example she uses to know how to react to stressful situations."

Fen took a deep breath and let it out slowly through his mouth. "I'm still shaking, but the counseling session is helping."

"Where are you?"

"In what's left of an old dance hall on top of a high hill overlooking Bandera."

"The Silver Spur?"

"Uh-huh. Have you ever been here?"

"No, but I've heard of it. I'd like to dance with you there."

Fen pulled a red bandanna from the back pocket of his jeans and wiped his cheeks. "You're trying to put different images in my mind."

"Is it working?"

"I can almost hear the music playing and feel you in my arms. It doesn't seem as cold in here now."

"Good. You can think about us whenever you want to." She paused. "Thank you for choosing me to call. You're a good man, Fen Maguire."

Fen asked, "Any other ideas for warming me up?"

"Hot food and coffee."

Fen smiled. "That's what I get for being greedy. Thanks, Audrey. I'll take your advice and go to THE HEN'S NEST for breakfast." He took a full breath then let it out. "Any more words of wisdom?"

"Wait for her to call you back. She'll need to talk. Encourage her to tell you everything."

Fen didn't know how much time passed before he left his easel where it stood, taking only his sketch pad and pencils back to the cabin. The talk with Audrey did more good than he imagined it would. Worry for Bailey was replaced with peace, knowing she was safe and that she'd arrive with a new appreciation for life. The adrenaline rush left him and hunger took its place.

Customers had mostly filled THE HEN'S NEST by the time he arrived. He found an unoccupied table for four with one chair missing. The server named Juanita recognized him and brought coffee. She asked, "Do you mind sharing a table? This is our busiest time of day."

Fen shrugged. "I don't mind at all."

The deep rumble of motorcycles drew closer as two loud ones parked on the far side of the parking lot. It wasn't long before the riders entered wearing black leather from the neck down. Juanita spoke to them and pointed to Fen's table. The tallest, with his black hair slicked back into a man-bun looked at him and nodded his approval. The other's haircut reminded Fen of a blond banker wearing a costume.

Fen took a closer look at the first man and recognized him as being Ray Long, the motorcycle mechanic and suspect in the killing of Clay Trueblood. Was this a lucky coincidence? Perhaps; but then again, the town only had a thousand residents. Chance meetings at restaurants were probably a common occurrence.

After handshakes and introductions, Fen motioned to Juanita and asked if she could bring him a few sheets of plain copy paper. He turned to his tablemates and explained. "I'm a professional artist and I like to doodle. Do you mind if I draw a sketch of each of you? It won't take me long and you can take them with you."

The blond thought it was a cool idea while Ray said, "I like free things, but there's usually a catch. What is it?"

Juanita returned with sheets of paper and said, "Mr. Maguire is an outstanding artist. His paintings are quite valuable."

The testimony seemed to put the men at ease, especially Ray. Fen hurried through the first sketch of the blond sitting on his motorcycle outside.

Juanita took their orders, and Fen knocked out the first sketch. The conversation flowed with talk about the "banker" who turned out to be an insurance adjuster.

The food arrived, which put the second sketch on hold. Fen sketched between bites. By the time their plates were clean, he'd finished the sketch and handed it to Ray.

"Wow. This is fantastic. I wasn't expecting to see the river in the background."

Fen remained silent as Ray admired the sketch with a depiction of Clay Trueblood's crime scene. There was no immediate sign that he recognized the place.

Before Fen could say anything, KK and Deputy Scooter Gillespie entered the restaurant, scanned the occupants, and zeroed in on Fen's table. Both nodded a greeting but only KK spoke. "Sheriff Maguire, I see you've met Ray Long."

"Sheriff?" said Ray with a raised voice. "You said you were an artist."

Scooter spoke next. "He's the best artist you'll ever meet, and he's a former sheriff."

Ray asked, "What's this about, KK?"

"Sheriff Irons wants to see you."

"He talked to me a few days ago. Is he asking, or telling me to talk to him again?"

Scooter hooked his thumbs in his gun belt. "Asking, unless you refuse."

KK shifted her gaze to Fen. "Would you like to join us at the sheriff's office?"

Fen nodded. "That sounds like more than a request."

"It is."

Scooter said, "Come with me, Ray. You'll have to ride in the back, but I won't handcuff you unless you do something silly."

"Why would I do that? I've done nothing wrong."

Chapter Twenty-Two

F en paid the bill and followed the deputies' pickup trucks into Bandera. He caught one of the few red lights, which delayed his arrival enough that Scooter and KK were coming out of an interview room alone when he arrived. Scooter said, "He's not happy, but Ray's waiting for you and Sheriff Irons."

Rusty emerged from his office and extended his hand for Fen to shake. "You look fully recovered from your stay at the 'Rock-Hard Hotel'."

"Hot water and sleep cured most of the aches and pains," said Fen. "You look peppy yourself."

"I'm walking on sunshine. Dora Jean had a big surprise for me when I got home from chasing Brent. After many years of trying, we're having a little cowboy, or a cowgirl. We'd resigned ourselves to being content with each other and spoiling the nieces and nephews."

Conversation took a pleasant turn away from murder and into the changes in Rusty's future. The sheriff of Bandera County rattled on as they went into his office and closed the door behind them.

It took a while before Rusty slowed the pace of his words. Fen let him ramble as his thoughts turned to Bailey and her close call with death earlier that morning. How quickly things can change.

They finished Rusty's one-sided conversation about becoming a dad, and Fen found an opening to change the subject. "I'm glad you had Ray picked up for questioning. It saved me time tracking him down."

Rusty looked at the closed door and stood. "Let's get this over with. Dora Jean told me we're going to San Antonio this afternoon and we won't be back before tomorrow evening. She's in full shopping mode, and I'm not about to slow her down. We won't buy much this trip, but I'll come back knowing more about products for babies than I thought possible."

He kept talking. "I still can't believe I'll be a father. The doctor said Dora Jean getting pregnant is the closest thing to a miracle he's seen in a while. At our age, there was only a five percent chance she could conceive."

"If you don't mind me asking," said Fen. "How old is Dora Jean?"

"Forty-three. We're the same age and married when we were twenty. Many of the people our age are talking about their grandchildren."

It occurred to Fen as he shut the door to the interview room that he hadn't asked Rusty if he'd uncovered fresh evidence. It seemed likely since he'd spoken to Ray recently but hadn't arrested him at the time.

Ray stood when they entered. "What's this about, Sheriff? I have a customer who needs a rebuild on his Gold Wing."

Rusty simply pointed to the recently vacated chair. He and Fen moved to the other side of the table and sat in plain wooden chairs that bore the scars from many years of service.

The sheriff spoke in a tone that combined low volume with empathy. "Sorry to delay you from earning a living, but there's a thing or two we need to clear up. It shouldn't take long, and I appreciate you coming here."

"I didn't think I had a choice."

Fen corrected him as he issued enough of a smile to relate he didn't pose too big of a threat. "There's always a choice. You could have refused, demanded an attorney, or caused a scene. You made the right decision at THE HEN'S NEST."

What went unsaid was the expectation that Ray would continue to cooperate.

Ray's gaze shifted back to Rusty. "Ask whatever you want. I've done nothing illegal and have nothing to hide."

Rusty kept his words soft and nibbled around why Ray was currently sitting in a police interview room. "Do you own a pistol?"

"Sure. Who doesn't?"

"Tell us about it."

"It's a nine-mil Glock. I keep it at the shop under the counter. I've never had to use it, and hope I never do."

Rusty then asked, "Any other pistols?"

The diamond stud in Ray's left ear caught the light as he shook his head. "I have a .243 and two shotguns in my trailer."

Rusty leaned forward. "What about a .22?"

Ray leaned back. "I used to. It was a Ruger six-shot revolver. I bought it from a friend when I was in high school."

Fen asked, "Did you sell it or give it away?"

"Neither. It went missing three months ago."

"Where did you keep it?"

"At my shop. I used it until I could afford something with more firepower. After I got the Glock, I cleaned and oiled the Ruger, wrapped it in a red rag and kept it behind the nine mil."

Rusty leaned forward as he seemed to search Ray's face for signs of deception. "We have a problem, Ray."

"Oh?"

"Clay Trueblood was killed with a .22 then dumped in the Medina. You have a missing .22."

Ray's countenance turned to concrete. "*We* don't have a problem, Sheriff. You do. Someone stole my pistol, and you need to find them."

Rusty countered with, "We have the pistol, and the ballistics show it's the weapon that killed Mr. Trueblood. All we have is your theory that someone stole it. I know for a fact that you never reported it missing or stolen."

Fen interrupted before the two reached an impasse. "I have a suggestion." He waited until Rusty and Ray both turned their full attention to him. "Ray, this could probably be cleared up quickly if you'd allow Sheriff Irons to do a search of your home, business and property."

"What if I don't?"

Rusty had the answer. "I'll detain you right now and take my time getting the warrants."

Fen quickly added, "By giving your permission for a search, you stay out of jail and can work on that Gold Wing. The other way, you'll get your name in the newspaper and people will probably assume the worst."

"What are you looking for if you already have the pistol?" asked Ray.

Fen quickly responded. "Anything related to the murder. Computer records, emails, texts, bank records, phone calls. The list goes on and on."

"I... I don't know," said Ray. "I don't enjoy getting pushed around by cops. It comes with the territory of being a biker." His eyes darted from side to side like he was looking for a way out. He broke the silence by saying, "You're talking about locking me up on a murder charge."

Fen held up a hand as a stop sign. Ray seemed on the verge of demanding legal representation, so Fen said, "You don't have to go to jail. Let us do a search of your property and answer our questions honestly. I think you're telling the truth. That's not an expensive gun and there's no telling when you lost it or someone stole it."

Rusty hesitated but played along. "There's a loose end we have to tie up. I don't have time to spend on it today, but Sheriff Maguire can take your statement tonight."

Ray examined the black lines of grease under his fingernails. "It still sounds like I need a lawyer."

Rusty said, "That's your call, Ray."

Fen added, "With your cooperation or without it, we're going to find out who killed Clay and Misti."

Rusty made a plea. "We know you couldn't have killed Misti. You went to a biker rally in East Texas. What you don't have is an airtight alibi for when Clay died." He nodded in Fen's direction. "Sheriff Maguire is your best hope if you're telling the truth about not killing Clay."

Fen gave him an icy stare. "If you're guilty, I won't lose sleep when you go to prison. If you're innocent, I keep you riding your Harley."

The conversation ended when Rusty asked, "What's it going to be, Ray? Cooperate with Sheriff Maguire tonight at your trailer or talk to a lawyer in jail?"

"You keep making me choose between bad and worse."

"At least you can choose," said Fen. "The killer didn't give Misti or Clay a choice if they wanted to live or die."

Ray let out a moan, looked down, and said, "Search wherever you want. I'll give you the password to my computer and anything else you want." He sighed in resignation. "Come over tonight after seven."

CRUNCHING gravel alerted Fen to Bailey's arrival. He went out the front door and met her where white driveway stones met clumps of grass. Her chin quivered when she exited the truck. All pretense at stoicism vanished like a drop of water hitting a hot skillet. He opened his arms and she filled them. They clung to each other like two magnets.

Instead of going inside, he led her to the yard swing. She took his arm in hers as if it was a child's security blanket and blinked away tears. The swing rocked back and forth as Fen waited for her to speak.

Fen noticed that her burn-scarred hand had a fresh bandage on it. "What did you do?"

"Cut it on car glass trying to remove an infant's car seat."

"Stitches?"

She shook her head. "It was a nightmare, only it was real. Too real."

"Fatalities?" asked Fen.

"Two injured. One seriously. The husband got the worst of it. A four-month-old girl was in the back seat but got out without a scratch." The pace of her words picked up. "I took the baby to my truck while the woman did what she could for her husband. He was unconscious and bleeding from the scalp. A bone in his lower arm was sticking out."

"It's a good thing the baby was in a car seat."

Bailey nodded. "I had to cut the straps that held the seat in place. Have you ever messed with an infant's car seat?"

"Once," said Fen. "I also cut the straps to get the baby out."

"The girls at school kid me for carrying a pocketknife, but it came in handy today."

"Tell me about the wife," said Fen.

"She wanted out until I told her to keep her husband's head from moving. She couldn't use her right arm. I think the impact knocked her shoulder out of its socket. Having something to do calmed her. I took the baby and went back to my truck." Bailey wiped another stray tear from her cheek. "The baby cried until I sang to her. Then we played peek-a-boo like nothing happened while we waited for help."

She sniffed then continued, "It took what seemed like forever, but cops and volunteer firefighters arrived and went to work. The ambulance came and someone decided to airlift the husband to a trauma center in Round Rock."

Bailey shook her head in disbelief. "The truck driver sat on the ground with his head in his hands. The highway patrolman told me it looked like the truck's right front tire had a blowout."

Fen imagined the scene. "That would cause the truck to swerve to the right. I bet the driver over-corrected and lost control."

Bailey looked through tear-clouded eyes. "Three seconds earlier and I'd have been the one taking a ride in a helicopter."

Fen swallowed what felt like a golf ball. He cleared his throat and said, "You kept your head when it mattered the most. I'm so proud of you."

Bailey shook her head. "The biggest hero today was whoever strapped the baby into her car seat good and tight. The highway patrolman said it saved the baby's life." Her mouth pinched. "Now I know why cops give tickets to people who drive with children not properly restrained."

She looked up at Fen. "What will happen to the truck driver?"

"It all depends," said Fen. "State troopers will do a thorough investigation. They'll determine if impairment or negligence was the likely cause of the accident. If so, there are several things they could do."

Fen recognized the stern look on Bailey's face and decided not to go into all the things that could happen. He shortened it by saying, "There are no winners in what happened today. The family, their extended family, the truck driver and his family, first responders, which includes you. Everyone is affected. I wish I could tell you to forget it ever happened, but you won't be able to."

He paused and waited for her to respond.

It didn't take long before she said, "You saw things just as bad and worse. How did you get over them?"

Fen patted the arm that held his so tightly. "You're doing it now by talking and holding onto someone you trust. For me, it was Sally who helped me get past the hardest things. She gave me so much support, I can still feel it."

To lighten the mood, he looked at Bailey. "Pizza also helps. Have you eaten anything since the accident?"

She shook her head.

"Let's go to town and share a large supreme."

She loosened her grip on his arm, wiped a lone tear from her cheek and gave him a weak smile. "Pizza works for me. Where's Lou?"

"Staking out an apartment in San Antonio."

"Cool," said Bailey. "What do you have for me to do?"

"I'm going to interview a suspect tonight. His name is Ray Long."

"I already have a file on him."

"See if you can add anything to it. But first, we're going to lunch, and I'll catch you up on developments in the case."

"All of them?"

Fen gave her a sly glance. "Don't I always tell you everything?"

"Ha! You never tell me everything and it drives me loony."

Fen rubbed his chin. "Then you already know what to expect. I'll tell you almost all, and you can tell me almost all of what you've been doing. Let's start with your relationship with Jeremy."

Bailey's eyes opened wider. "I forgot all about him coming home today, and me staying at his parents' home."

"Let's go," said Fen. "When we get back, I'll show you a view you won't believe."

Chapter Twenty-Three

"Cute name," said Bailey as Fen wheeled his truck into a parking space in front of THE DOUGH JOE restaurant on Main Street in Bandera.

"It's not every day you find a restaurant with pizza and coffee in its name. They also have a bar in an adjoining room, but I guess they ran out of imagination on how to incorporate that in the name."

Bailey looked up and down the street. "Is this one of those towns that specialize in clever names for businesses?"

"GAIL'S NAILS is on the other side of Main Street and Sheriff Irons told me there used to be a coffee shop named PONY ESPRESSO. Also, there's THE HEN'S NEST. I had breakfast there this morning."

This brought a smile to Bailey, the first since she arrived. "I love quirky names like those. Towns and cities need more of them."

The room was without frills other than the usual smattering of Christmas decorations including a tree with the ever-popular cowboy themed adornments. Instead of garland or strung popcorn snaking through faux branches, it boasted a roping lariat. Bailey spotted it and raised a single eyebrow. "They take the old west seriously."

"Think of it as attending a comic-con for cowboys every day," said Fen. "The crucial difference is some of the people you'll see here are real cowboys."

Bailey looked around the room as if she was searching for a face that fit the image her mind had conjured up. A look of disappointment pulled down the corners of her mouth. "They all look normal."

Fen wanted to keep things light, so he said, "Looks are deceiving. Don't turn around, but there's a man in the corner. He's wanted for cattle rustling. If the town marshall sees him in here, there may be a shoot-out."

Bailey made a slow turn, looked at two women displaying Christmas treasures, and spun back around. She punched Fen in the arm hard enough to sting. "Stick to painting. You have no future as a comedian."

A husky woman's voice came from over Fen's shoulder. "Sit anywhere you like. The lunch crowd started clearing out ten minutes ago."

He turned to thank the woman, but she'd already moved to deliver a bill to a large table occupied by what looked like a multi-generational family of eight. A tug on his arm told him Bailey had chosen a table for them. It was the only two-person table in the restaurant, and it sat against the far wall.

The same server who told them to find a seat arrived not long after they'd eased into their chairs. This time, she greeted them with a warm smile. "It's chilly outside. How 'bout something hot to drink?"

"Do you have hot chocolate?" asked Bailey.

"Sure do, and it comes with a dollop of real whipped cream, not the squirty stuff."

"Yum."

"Make it two," said Fen. "What pizza do you recommend?"

"If you like traditional, get the supreme. For something different, try the barbecue chicken or the cowboy pizza. The cowboy has plenty of meat. If you like things hot, get the jalapeño popper pizza."

Fen and Bailey looked at each other, but not for more than a second or two. Bailey said, "One large cowboy."

The waitress's pen hovered in the air as she shouted, "The little lady wants a large cowboy." She looked at Bailey with a straight face and asked, "Do you want him to own a large, medium or small ranch?"

At Bailey's blank look, an explosion of laughter came from Fen and most all the patrons. Bailey hung her head.

"Sorry, hon," said the waitress whose grin exposed perfectly aligned teeth and laugh lines around her eyes. "If you don't say 'pizza' after 'cowboy,' we shout that you're looking for a man. It's part of the cowboy culture to joke around."

Bailey lifted her chin. "Now that you mention it, a large, rich cowboy sounds good. Can I get him to go?"

The woman winked at Bailey. "You're quick as a cat and the prettiest girl I've seen in a long time. The last thing you need to worry about is getting a man."

Fen continued to smirk as Bailey faced him. "Now that you've had your fun at my expense, tell me about the investigation. Start with the suspects and don't skimp on details."

Fen scooted his chair closer to the table, leaned toward Bailey, and lowered the volume of his voice. "Brent Stone has top billing as a suspect. Misti Palmer dumped him a long time ago, but we think they might have come back together for seconds. Most everyone in Bandera County believes he killed her. That goes double for her father, Elton Palmer."

"Why did she dump him?"

"I don't think she needed a reason. Misti has a long history of short romances that trace back to junior high school."

Bailey said, "Fire and ash."

"What do you mean?"

"That's what I call girls and women who go through men like they're a log on a fire. They burn hot for a while, then move on to the next log and treat the first guy like he's a pile of ashes. I can see where a cowboy like Brent Stone might not like being thrown out. Where is Brent now?"

"That's what Lou is trying to find out."

Fen launched into the long version of Brent being arrested and released on a PR bond. He related their tracking adventure with Sam as the tracker, while Rusty, KK, and Fen acted as a modern-day posse.

Bailey snickered when Fen included the parts of beans for supper, sleeping in a cold cave, and the posse returning empty-handed and saddle-sore. Her countenance changed when he told her about Nancy Jurik, who might or might not, be Brent's latest romantic interest.

"Do you think that girl Nancy could be a suspect?" asked Bailey.

"If he's with her, Rusty could charge Nancy with harboring a fugitive. That's a long way from a charge of accessory to murder. As things stand now, she's a person of interest."

Bailey shot him a look that said she only partially believed him. "What is your gut telling you about her involvement?"

"My gut is telling me to drink hot chocolate and eat pizza. My brain is saying several conflicting things."

"And what are those?"

"I believe there's a high probability that someone will harm Brent if he returns to Bandera County. On the other hand, he broke the law by leaving the county without permission. It's very possible that he killed Misti and there's an outside chance he killed Clay Trueblood, too."

"Why would he kill Clay?"

Fen puffed out his cheeks. "I have nothing to base that on other than he's running from the law and the two murders happened close together."

Hot chocolate arrived and put the conversation on hold while both sipped, then sipped again and again. Bailey raised her head and wiped the whipped cream from her nose. "Don't tell Thelma, but this is the best hot chocolate I've ever had."

Fen moaned in agreement. "What happens in Bandera, stays in Bandera." He paused. "There's an exception to that. You need to call Thelma before she hears about the accident today."

"I'll call her from your cabin."

Bailey drained her cup and got back on track. "Do you know who'd want to kill Brent?"

"It's only an educated guess, but based on what Sheriff Irons has said, Misti's father and her brother are the likely candidates. Elton Palmer is a wealthy rancher and county commissioner. His son does what Elton tells him to do, as do most people in this county."

Bailey's eyes shifted back and forth as if she was looking for an answer. Fen asked, "What are you thinking?"

She raised her gaze to meet his. "Lou needs to do more than locate Nancy Jurik and Brent Stone. She needs to warn them."

Fen gave his head a firm shake. "If she does, she'll be complicit in helping to hide a fugitive from justice."

"Oh," said Bailey. "I hadn't thought of that."

Fen finished his hot chocolate as Bailey hit him with

another question. "Who are the other suspects? What about the guy you're going to see tonight?"

The oversize mug clinked when the porcelain rested on the table. "Ray Long," said Fen. "I had breakfast with him this morning. That was before deputies took him to be interviewed by Sheriff Irons and me. We almost blew our chance to get him to talk when he found out his pistol was used to kill Clay Trueblood."

Bailey sat up straight. "That's sounds like enough to convict him."

"Not necessarily. He claims someone stole his pistol several months ago."

"Did you believe him?"

"Not completely. Clay Trueblood owed him money for a motorcycle repair bill."

"How big of a bill?"

"I'll find out the full amount tonight. He's promised to give us computer access to his financials."

"That's a motive to go along with the means. The old stolen gun story sounds sketchy. Why didn't Rusty arrest him?"

"News of a child on the way disrupted Rusty's focus on work today. He'd mentally checked out, so I sort of took over then delayed the interview until tonight."

"A child? I thought Rusty was old, like you."

Fen pretended to be offended. "He and his wife are only forty-three. That's young. My old age won't start until after my seventy-fifth birthday, and that's subject to an extension or two."

Bailey grinned then asked, "Any other suspects?"

"I've already mentioned Nancy Jurik. It's possible Brent talked her into killing Misti for him."

Bailey wrinkled her nose. "That sounds unlikely. Who else?"

"Cliff Palmer," said Fen. "It's unlikely that he killed his sister, but he might have had something against Clay."

Bailey shook her head. "Unless you have more on Cliff, that's too far of a stretch."

His gaze shifted to the door, where a trio of Asian men decked out from head to toe in garish western wear entered the restaurant. Bailey said what Fen was thinking. "Lord, save us from Kung-Fu cowboys."

Fen looked at her. "You sound like Thelma."

"Sorry. I've picked up some bad habits at college. Catty, judgmental descriptions slide off my tongue before I can stuff them back in."

The server put the pizza on the table and told them to enjoy.

"We will," said Fen and Bailey at the same time.

After finishing his first slice, he looked into Bailey's blue eyes. "I want you and Jeremy to get more information on Cliff from Frieda. You might as well include Cliff's ex-wife, Becky, too. She's the least likely to be involved, but you never know."

Fen lifted his gaze. "That reminds me. Lou went to a bar and danced with Cliff. Call her and find out what she learned about him."

Bailey put half a piece of pizza back on her plate. "Wait. Lou told you she danced with Cliff Palmer? You should have a full report of what she found out."

Fen let out a low growl. "We had a slight disagreement, and I didn't follow up."

"A disagreement about what?"

Fen looked down and to the left, then he eked out, "I don't remember. Lou said something, I snapped at her, she didn't like it, then I said something else, and—"

Bailey finished the rambling sentence. "And now I have to call Lou and do what you should have done."

Fen nodded. "It wasn't my finest hour."

"I'm glad to see you're still human."

The restaurant was mostly empty when Fen and Bailey pushed their chairs back. It always amazed him how the petite blond could pack away pizza like a three-hundred-pound offensive lineman and never gain a pound.

The brief trip home took them south down Main Street until they turned right on Cypress Street and traveled past the city park, made a couple more turns and approached the bridge over the Medina. Fen stopped at the center point of the concrete structure. "This is where we believe Misti went into the water."

Bailey nodded in a way that told him she already knew. "It's such a pretty place. The cypress trees look like they've been here a thousand years. I wonder how many lovers have stopped on this bridge."

Fen's thoughts turned to Sally and then to Audrey. He didn't have time to analyze why both women came to mind before Bailey's phone erupted in a calm-killing electronic jumble of notes.

Bailey puffed out her cheeks. "Here goes nothing." She pushed something on the phone's face and spoke in a cheery voice. "Hi, Thelma. What's up?"

"Don't you *what's up* me, young lady. I want to know why it took me over five hours to hear you almost got yourself killed today."

"The Lord protected me," said Bailey in her impression of a cherub's voice.

"He must have, but you're not a cat with nine lives. I have several reports on what happened, and none of them match. I'm ready to listen and you'd better be ready to talk."

"All right, but I need to make it quick. I'm standing on a

bridge, looking down at the Medina River. There's a sign that says we're not supposed to stop on the bridge."

"Who's *we?*"

"Me and Fen."

"That figures. He's on his third set of nine lives. The way I figure things, you've already gone through five or six. The longer you stay around him, the more you're pressing your luck."

Fen spoke up. "I can hear you, Thelma."

"Good! Get Bailey somewhere safe and keep her there."

Bailey took over. "Let us get off the bridge and up the steep hill to Fen and Lou's cabins. I'll call you back to tell you about the accident, and I won't skip any details. It scared the daylights out of me, but hot chocolate, pizza, and a long conversation with Fen eased my mind. He brought me back to normal."

"Your idea of normal and mine aren't exactly the same, but it does me good to hear you say you've already talked about it. I'll be waiting for your call."

As she stuffed her phone in a pocket, Fen looked at her. "You always know exactly what to say to calm Thelma down."

Bailey wiggled her eyebrows. "That's because she doesn't know everything I do."

Fen put his palms over his ears. "Please don't say another word. I'd rather stay blissfully under-informed."

A car approached from the downhill side of the road. Fen and Bailey scurried to the truck. On the way up the hill, Bailey said, "Are you painting today?"

He nodded a positive response. "There's a home up here under construction. Go to the northwest corner and you can get into the old dance hall from there. That's where I set up this morning. Bring your easel and a sketch pad. It'll inspire something in you."

"I need some*one* to draw."

"I have plenty of photos to choose from. There's one of Sam leaning off the side of his horse looking at the trail when we were tracking Brent Stone. I think he'd appreciate a sketch for Christmas."

Bailey's eyes lit up with excitement. "That sounds totally rad! Send me the photos."

Chapter Twenty-Four

F en sent Bailey five photos of Sam tracking Brent. As expected, she chose the one he'd described to her. Because of Sam's unusual body angle, it would be the hardest to draw and paint. Yet, the scene would depict something truly unique, a twenty-first century man practicing skills passed down through generations. He wondered what title Bailey would give the work.

"That was a quick phone call you made with Thelma," said Fen as he set up his easel.

"I told her about the photos you took of Sam and sent them to her. She liked the ones that showed his face. Her excitement caused her to stop lecturing me about defensive driving. Instead, she told me to get to work on the drawing. I told her she could give him the pencil drawing as a Christmas present. She wanted to commission a painting."

"What did you say to that?"

"That she can place the order, but there's no way I could charge her."

Fen organized his pencils. "Generosity has a way of coming

back to bless you, but will you have time to paint it before Christmas?"

"Thelma asked me the same thing. I told her I already delivered the portrait of the woman and her cat to the guy in Austin. He liked it so much that he gave me a big tip. As for the one of Sam squatting and looking at the ground, it won't be that hard. I'll tighten up the distance, show the horse's reins in his hands, but not the horse. I'll also blur the background like I did on my latest portrait."

Fen nodded his approval. "It will still be a challenge to get it finished, but by focusing on Sam, you can cut the time required and complete it without compromising quality. Many artists don't take time management into account when they paint or sculpt. There wouldn't be as many starving artists if more of them used simple business practices."

Bailey stared at the photo and enlarged it on her phone. "I have a feeling the painting of Sam leaning off the horse to see tracks will be a signature piece for me. It doesn't show his face, but the braided hair, buckskin coat, jeans with chaps, and moccasins tell the story of a modern Native American performing an ancient skill."

Bailey slipped her phone into the pocket of her jacket and the two got to work. Fen estimated they'd sketched less than an hour when Bailey's phone rang again. She didn't turn on the speaker, but she didn't need to for him to know who she was talking to.

"How long before you get to town?" asked Bailey.

Fen kept sketching the distant hills.

"Yes, I know where it is... the Dairy Queen on Highway 16 in twenty minutes."

Fen looked at her after she hung up. "You'd better pack up."

Bailey came over and looked at his sketch. "I'm trying to imagine what the land will look like covered in snow."

Fen stood back. "Do you know why I'm drawing it as it looks now?"

"Not really, but I bet you're going to tell me."

"It's like drawing an animal or a person's body. You need to know what lies under the skin. When it snows, I'll know what amounts to the bone and muscle structure of the land. That's why I'm pushing you to take a class in human anatomy next year."

Bailey looked at him. "I learn something new every time we draw or paint together."

"You'll learn more from people who specialize in portraits."

Bailey gave him a quick hug. "You'll do for now." She efficiently gathered her tools of the trade and left, leaving only a pleasant memory of their time together.

The shortest day of the year quickly approached which meant Fen had to pack his pencils and schlep everything related to art back to his cabin sooner than he wanted. He preferred to draw and sketch in natural light, but the changing seasons made outdoor painting difficult. Back in his studio, it was much easier and more comfortable to paint. He'd made a considerable investment in lighting that self-adjusted to maintain consistent illumination regardless of the time of day or changes in the weather. This was especially good for the later steps of painting when shadows and details meant the difference between very good and excellent. For pencil sketches, he had to get outside to find inspiration. He knew it sounded silly, but the land had to speak to him.

He'd no more than set up his easel in the cabin when his phone rang. Lou greeted him with a deep yawn. "Sorry about that. It's been a while since I sat in my car, waiting for someone to leave an apartment."

"Did you find Nancy's truck?"

"I'm looking at it. Dirt and bumper stickers are holding it together. It has a flat tire."

"How close are you to a grocery store?"

"There's a convenience store half a block away. Does that count?"

"Absolutely. Nancy impresses me as an impulsive woman who waits until the last moment to do things. I bet there's not much in her pantry or refrigerator. Look for her to either call out for delivery or walk to the convenience store."

"If you're right about her going to the snatch-and-grab, I'm going to follow her and strike up a conversation."

"That's exactly what I don't want you to do. Stick to the plan."

"I like my way better. If you want to know if Brent Stone is still with her, all I have to do is ask her and see how she reacts. I'm very good at spotting lies." She mumbled, "I should be after marrying three of the best liars that ever lived."

Fen allowed silence to speak for him that her idea wasn't acceptable.

"Fine," said Lou with a huff. "What if I wait until she goes to the store, and I go to her apartment and knock on her door? I could pretend I'm taking a survey."

"No," said Fen as he stepped on the first word of her next sentence. "He'll either not answer the door or not believe you're a survey taker. Either way, he's likely to run."

Lou put steel in her voice. "There you go again, not trusting me."

"Trust has nothing to do with it," said Fen. "In this case, I don't trust myself to make the right decision with Brent."

He explained the dilemma he faced. One phone call to Rusty and officers would arrest Brent if he was hiding in

Nancy's apartment. That was one option, the one that followed proper police protocol.

"Calling Rusty could also result in Brent's death."

He heard Lou's deep inhale of air, but the beep in the background seemed to stop her words in mid-air. Then, she said, "Bailey's calling. I'll talk to you later. Don't worry, I'll sit here and cuss you for being a hard-headed man. I promise I won't do anything for now."

The call ended, and Fen shook his head. He wondered again how his formerly male-dominated life had become so crowded with females, each one with a different idea of how he should run his life and the murder investigations that came his way.

"Lou will throw a wild-eyed fit if she discovers I'm setting her up, along with Bailey and Jeremy, to discover if Brent is in Nancy's apartment."

He'd used simple reverse psychology. Lou understood his dilemma. She'd tell Bailey. Neither of them objected to bending the rules, and San Antonio was only fifty miles away. Bailey and Jeremy would think nothing of making the trip. They and Lou would come up with a plan to get Bailey inside the apartment. Her age, petite stature, and ability to act like a scatter-brained adolescent wouldn't raise suspicion.

Fen nodded approval to his plan. He'd know later that night if Brent Stone was there, Lou would come back and get a good night's sleep, and Bailey would help the case move forward.

This still left Fen with the problem of deciding what to do with the information they gathered, but he'd worry about that later. He had an interview to conduct with Ray Long and needed to focus. Bailey and Lou were competent, and Jeremy provided plenty of muscle. "Safety in numbers," said Fen aloud.

He gave a passing thought to supper, but the cowboy pizza had filled him to the point of discomfort. Instead, he used the spare time to visualize what his painting would look like. He mentally divided a canvas into various distances. First, the horizon line, the sky, distant hills, middle distance from the hills to the town, the town itself, the park and river below, and something very close to give perspective. There were so many decisions to make: What time of day? Bright sunshine or something more muted? What type of clouds, if any?

Thoughts of painting had to wait. He opened his computer, moved and clicked the cursor until he landed on a website. It revealed Ray Long's phone number, which he called.

"Long's," said the man in a hurried voice.

"Ray?"

"Yeah."

"This is Fen Maguire. Did anyone from the sheriff's office come by and take anything from your office today?"

"No. I've been expecting them, but they never came."

"Do you have your computer with you?"

"Yeah. I run everything on a laptop."

"Do me a favor," said Fen. "Unplug it and take it home with you. I'm leaving in a few minutes."

"You barely caught me. I was about to walk out the door."

"Can you run your business without your computer for a few days?"

He hesitated. "I ran it for years without a computer. Sometimes I think it's more trouble than it's worth. I'd rather turn a wrench than stare at a screen."

"It might be a couple of days before we can get it back to you. Be careful driving home," said Fen.

"Are you trying to tell me something?"

"Yeah. On second thought, stay in your shop until I get there. I'll follow you."

Fen went to his truck. A sense of dread had crept in as he spoke with Ray. It reminded him of slate-gray snow clouds moving in from the northwest. He hurried to his truck, brought it to life, and spun gravel. After negotiating the hairpin turn on the way down the steep hill, he pulled out his phone and placed the call.

Bailey answered. "Hey. I didn't expect to hear from you tonight."

The sound of highway noise came through, which confirmed his suspicion that she and Jeremy were most likely on their way to San Antonio. Instead of gloating over predicting the future, he asked, "How proficient is Jeremy with computers?"

"That's a strange question," said Bailey. "What's up?"

"I'm on my way to pick up Ray Long's laptop. I need to know if you and Jeremy have the expertise to get into it and look for evidence."

Bailey spoke with confidence. "I'm pretty good, but Jeremy is way more proficient than me. He started building computers in elementary school and writing software in middle school. If something's on a computer, he can find it."

"Perfect," said Fen. "I'll have an assignment for you two tomorrow."

"Text me the time and place you want to meet."

"I'll be in the ruins of the dance hall," said Fen. "Come after breakfast."

"We'll be there."

Ray's motorcycle shop proved to be a modest tin building down a pothole-infested asphalt road off Highway 16, about halfway to the small community of Medina. A graveyard of motorcycle frames and parts sat on the far side of the building with a tiny office on one end and what amounted to a double garage with two roll-up doors. It was the type of one-man shop that survived by word of mouth and the skill of the owner. Perfect for a free-spirited man who liked to work alone.

Fen pulled into the driveway, and Ray came out of the office carrying his laptop in his left hand and a pistol in the other. Fen rolled down his window. "I'll follow you."

Ray passed the computer through the open window and stuffed the pistol into an inside pocket of his leather jacket. He zipped the jacket to keep out the cold and threw a leg over his flat-head Harley. The motorcycle responded with deep thumps of exhaust, which turned into an ear-splitting roar when he turned off the side road onto Highway 16.

They'd traveled about two miles when they passed another side road with a sheriff's department pickup truck half hidden in a line of trees. Fen glanced down at his speedometer—Ray was going fifty miles an hour in a sixty-mile-an-hour zone. The officer was too far off the main road to run radar anyway. Darkness prevented him from seeing who was in the truck.

Another few miles had Fen following Ray down a short lane off the main highway and stopping in front of a specialty school bus. It looked like Ray had converted a school bus previously used for special needs students into his RV. From the outside, it lacked curb appeal, but on the inside, it was a compact marvel of style, comfort, and functionality.

Ray explained after Fen finished giving compliments, "My former girlfriend and I rebuilt this from the tires up. That includes the engine and transmission. It has everything a newer motorhome has except a fancy exterior and slides that always leak. We pulled a trailer with our bikes on it all over the country."

Fen noticed the lack of a woman's touch now. "What happened to your girlfriend?"

"It's a simple story. She wasn't ready to settle down. I was. We went to Sturgis. She pointed her bike west when the rally ended. I drove back with only my bike on the trailer. I keep thinking she'll come back. Until then, I'll fix bikes, save money, and keep this bus ready to go on the road again."

"Are you still in touch with her?"

"She calls when she hits a rough patch. It's often enough to give me hope."

Fen asked, "Did Clay Trueblood owe you money?"

Ray retrieved a scrap of paper and wrote on it. "This is my password. Look for a file labeled accounts receivable. You'll find Clay and a lot of other people who owe me money. Collecting from nomads isn't the easiest thing to do." He took a breath. "I've been down and out and stiffed a bike shop or two when I was younger. I count it as payback for the things I'm guilty of."

Fen stood. "I'll get your computer back to you as soon as I can."

Ray tilted his head like a confused puppy. "Is that all? I thought the cops were going to tear my business and this bus apart looking for evidence."

"They still might."

Ray declared, "There's two sets of law in this county. Have you figured that out yet?"

Fen responded with a partial answer. "Actually, there's three. Sheriff Irons is a straight shooter. Most of the deputies on his team are, too."

"Not all," said Ray. "When you put on leather and ride a chopped Harley, you learn pretty quick which cops are straight and who's crooked, especially when the chosen few get complaints from *proper* citizens."

"That's expected," said Fen. "It doesn't change the fact that people with money and influence play by the rules most of the time."

Ray responded with, "I don't know about that. I think

they're just smart enough to stay out of sight and let someone else do the dirty work."

Fen kept talking. "It's a third group that I'm concerned about. There's a current of evil running through this county. It's below the surface, but it's as dangerous as the Medina after a ten-inch rain."

"That's not very comforting," said Ray.

"Good. It will keep you on your toes. Keep driving under the speed limit and it's not a bad idea to carry that Glock. Make sure you don't take it to any prohibited places, like bars or banks."

Fen followed his own advice and kept his truck five miles an hour under the posted speed limit. He slowed when he came to the road where the sheriff's department pickup was parked earlier. It had moved on.

Chapter Twenty-Five

Rays of sunlight shot out like golden daggers over the distant eastern hills as Fen approached the Silver Spur with an easel, a sketch pad, and pencils. He also brought a thermos of coffee. Breakfast could wait. He had only minutes to experience the day's transition from first light to dawn and capture the sight with photos and more detailed sketches.

He closed his eyes and imagined the scene before him covered in nature's visual equivalent of white fondant. The image he saw with his mind's eye exceeded his expectations.

After taking photos, time lost meaning as he picked specific areas and focused on details to draw. He was on his third sketch when Lou's voice sounded from over his shoulder. "Rembrandt wearing a Stetson is at his work again." She followed the sentence with a sneeze.

Fen kept drawing. "You missed Rembrandt by five centuries and a few thousand miles. I heard you arrive last night. You three stayed longer in San Antonio than I thought you would. Did you have trouble making a plan for Bailey to find out if Brent was in Nancy's apartment?"

He shot Lou a glance. She glared, crossed her arms, and said, "You rat. You set us up."

"You're only partially right. I set you up to succeed."

Lou's gaze shifted back and forth until her eyes widened. "You sneaky snake. Not only did you set us up to discover Brent, but you did it so you could claim no responsibility in knowing what the plan was."

Fen kept sketching. "You and Bailey are very much alike. You each have enough rebellion in you to bend rules. Sometimes, the best way to get you to do something is to tell you not to do it."

"Wait a minute, Buster. You never told Bailey she couldn't knock on Nancy's door."

"Exactly," said Fen, "I did that on purpose."

She countered with, "And I thought you were a pig-headed fool for not letting me handle things. What was your reason for allowing Bailey to go in and not me?"

Fen grinned. "You weren't the right tool for the job."

"What's that supposed to mean?"

"You could have easily found out if Brent was in the apartment by badgering Nancy with tough questions. That was sure to cause Brent to run with or without Nancy. Or you could watch the apartment until you were sure he was there by the amount of delivered food."

"That second way could have taken days."

"See what I mean?" asked Fen. "You didn't want to take that much time, and I don't blame you. That's why I told Bailey to call you. I knew you two would come up with a plan for her to get Nancy to open her door without raising suspicion. The only thing I didn't know is how she'd do it."

Lou huffed air through her nose and said, "Bailey pretended to be a pizza delivery girl. She stated the address on the order was wrong, and that they could have the pizza because of the late delivery. Instead of waiting for Nancy to object, Bailey walked into the apartment and put the pizza on the dining room table. From there, she could see into the kitchen. Brent's hat was on top of the refrigerator."

"Don't you see?" asked Fen. "Bailey was the right tool for the job. A bubbly college girl didn't raise suspicion. Now we know where Brent is and where he's likely to stay. You had a good night's sleep while Bailey did something very useful and showed off a little for her boyfriend."

Lou had a parting shot. "You could have told me your plan."

"Don't underestimate Bailey," said Fen. "The time she spent on the streets of Houston taught her how to read people, even you. She's better than most seasoned detectives in spotting deception."

Fen changed the subject. "What time is it?"

"Eight-thirty."

Fen took out his phone and punched the screen. Bailey answered on the third ring with a lighthearted, "Good morning."

"Yes, it is," said Fen. "Lou tells me you had a successful trip to San Antonio last night."

"We did. It was so easy. Do you want to hear about it?"

"Have you had breakfast?"

"Jeremy's mom makes a mean omelet."

"What are your plans for the morning?"

"Not much. Do you want to meet somewhere?"

"Is Jeremy close by?"

"He's sitting next to me. His mom brought out a stack of family photos for us to look at. I didn't know normal families took so many pictures of their children."

It occurred to Fen that the premature death of Bailey's father and her mother's slip into depression, alcohol, and drugs meant few family photos. He put the thought aside and said, "Ask Jeremy for the name and address of a place we can meet around ten o'clock. It needs to be a place where I can get something tasty, but not a full meal."

"I'll call you back."

Lou filled her coffee cup from Fen's thermos and sipped. "One redeeming quality about you is you make excellent coffee. Husband number two's coffee tasted like he used dirty socks for a filter."

Fen's phone rang, saving him from another of Lou's ex-husband stories.

Bailey kept the call short and simple. "Ten o'clock at Cowgirl Coffee on Main Street."

"Lou and I will meet you there."

Following the call, Lou looked around the dance hall. A shiver started at her shoulders and worked its way down to her knees. "Do you think this place is haunted?"

"Probably," said Fen without thinking. "Do we need to call Ghostbusters?"

"I bet their PKE would flash and beep."

Fen turned to her. "I remember watching that movie with Bailey. They used some sort of gizmo to detect ghosts. What did you call it?"

"A psychokinetic energy meter. PKE for short."

"If they could develop something similar that would detect killers, I'd be out of a job."

Fen shifted his attention more fully to Lou as another chill brought her shoulders up and shook her body. An earthquake of a sneeze followed, and she asked, "Do I need to go with you to see Bailey and Jeremy?"

"The reason I'm meeting them is to hand over Ray's computer to see if they can find something interesting on it. Bailey says Jeremy is a computer genius."

A closer look at Lou revealed a flushed face. "You'd better get to your cabin before I have to carry you."

"All three of my ex-husbands carried me over the threshold. No offense, but I'd rather crawl back to my cabin than relive the memory of being carried into a rented room."

A racking cough from Lou punctuated her statement. She caught her breath and whispered, "Aren't you going to tell me the details of your meeting with Ray?"

"I'll put everything in an email. You can read it in bed."

"That's the best idea you've had in a long time." Lou sneezed again.

"I'll bring you some chicken noodle soup."

Lou shook her head. "You work on the murders. I'll take care of myself."

Fen threatened her with something he knew would change her mind. "When the three of us work a case, Thelma makes Bailey call her twice a day. It will take Thelma only a day to realize you're sick."

"Not if you lie about it."

Fen wagged his head. "I don't always tell Bailey everything, but I won't lie to her, and she won't lie to Thelma."

"Can you cut to the end? I'm freezing."

Fen gave his head a single nod. "Here's the bottom line. Thelma believes the only cure for a cold is chicken noodle soup. If Bailey or I don't convince her we're nursing you back to health, she'll pack her soup pot, drive here, and stay in your cabin until you're well."

A look of panic widened Lou's eyelids. "Bring me a gallon when you come back from delivering the laptop. Tell Bailey to load up on vitamin C. I'm going back to bed."

FEN LOOKED in the mirror while holding his razor under hot, running water. After a quick examination, he ruled the morning ritual a success and grabbed a towel to remove residual dots of shaving cream. The ringing of his phone in the next room caused him to loop the towel over his shoulders and take the few steps necessary to retrieve it.

"Good morning, Audrey," he said with a lift in his voice. Even though the boundaries to their relationship were firm, the occasional extra phone calls were becoming more common.

"I hope I didn't interrupt you. Nothing's wrong other than a touch of pre-Christmas loneliness."

He replied with, "My loneliness gets worse the closer I get to the 25th. I look for this year to be especially difficult."

"You must miss Sally something terrible."

"She never grew up when it came to Christmas. It was like she went on a sleigh ride of joy after Thanksgiving and took me along to listen to the bells."

"Oh," said Audrey with disappointment dripping from her simple response. "I shouldn't have called."

"No!" said Fen. "I'm glad you did. You're my future, and I hope I'm yours. It's these four and a half more years of transition that I'm finding difficult. This year, I'm feeling guilty for wanting to spend time with you instead of with my memories of Sally. Isn't that silly?"

"Not at all, and there can be significant benefits in waiting. I have my reasons for agreeing to such an agonizingly slow courtship, and you have yours. I rushed into a physical relationship once and became an unwed mother. I learned the value of listening to that *still small voice* and being willing to wait." She paused. "That doesn't mean I like it."

"Nor do I." He took a breath. "Perhaps we should change the subject?"

"Good idea," said Audrey. "How's the investigation progressing?"

Fen groaned. "I'm conflicted about that, too. I know where the prime suspect to one murder is, but I believe he's safer there than in jail."

"Do you think he'll abscond?"

"There's no reason for him to."

"Then leave him there. The one thing you don't want is the scandal of a prisoner being killed in his cell. Having him, or her, disappear is the lesser of the two evils."

Her words confirmed what his heart was telling him to do.

Audrey continued, "How close are you to knowing who committed the murders?"

"There are suspects for both crimes, but something's missing. I feel like I'm looking for two specific rocks through muddy water."

Audrey spoke with confidence. "Keep at it and give it time. The waters will eventually clear."

"I hope so. Lou's sick and I'm turning over a laptop to Bailey and Jeremy. The owner of the computer is Ray Long."

"Ray Long? Wasn't it his pistol that killed Clay Trueblood?"

"That's right. Clay owed him money for a motorcycle repair. Bailey and Jeremy will try to find other evidence on the laptop today."

"Rusty has more than enough to arrest Ray Long for killing Clay Trueblood. What's he waiting for?"

"For me to give him the green light."

"What are you waiting for?"

Fen didn't know how to explain his hesitation, but he made a stab at it. "Ray may be a motorcycle gearhead with a dislike for cops, but not without reason. He's a thoughtful man, a strategic thinker. If he were to kill someone with his own pistol, he wouldn't have left it where the cops could find it."

"Are you saying someone is trying to frame him?"

"Unless I discover something else, that's the direction I'm leaning."

Audrey's sharp mind took in the information like a computer absorbs data and spit out a response. "If you're right, there may be only one killer."

"Or two," said Fen. "I can't rule out anything or any of the suspects yet."

Audrey finished the conversation by saying, "Good hunting, my love." She amended the salutation. "Or should I say my future love?"

Fen responded without thinking. "I'll respond to either."

Chapter Twenty-Six

With no parking spaces open on Main Street, Fen used the lot behind the building that housed the Cowgirl Coffee Company. It turned out to be fortuitous as the coffee shop occupied the second floor of the two-story building and a stairway facing the back parking lot was the only means of access.

As usual, he arrived a few minutes early and settled into a comfortable chair while waiting for Bailey and Jeremy to arrive. The business had an upscale, funky vibe that included a collection of gnomes. The menu displayed a surprising variety of sweet and savory breakfast and lunch dishes. As usual, he ordered plain coffee. Shots of espresso made him too jittery. Not a good thing for an artist's hands.

Bailey led the way through the door and walked a straight line to his table, with Jeremy ambling behind her. "Good morning, again. Did Lou tell you about last night?"

He so enjoyed seeing her happy. "I hear congratulations are in order for a mission accomplished."

Jeremy spoke up. "All I did was drive and worry when

Bailey went inside. Lou wanted to go with her, but Bailey stood her ground. We agreed that if she wasn't out of the apartment in four minutes, we were coming in to get her."

Bailey wiggled her eyebrows. "I was out in three. All it cost was a medium pepperoni pizza." She took a breath. "When are you going to arrest Brent?"

Fen held up a hand to silence her and leaned forward. "No names. You know better than that when we're in public."

He looked down at the bandage. "How's the hand?"

"I pulled another tiny shard of glass out of it today. I think I got it all. Somehow Thelma found out about the cut and called before you did this morning. I had to send a photo to convince her it wasn't serious or infected. Jeremy's mom talked to her and backed me up."

Fen nodded his approval to Jeremy. "Your mom must be a straight-talking woman."

"Sometimes too straight. She didn't mind telling me what she thought of the girls I dated in high school." He looked at Bailey and winked. "Of course, there wasn't much to choose from in a town this size."

Fen asked, "What does your mom think of Bailey?"

Bailey looked at the tall, handsome man by her side. "Good question. What does your mom think of me?"

Jeremy chuckled. "I think she likes you more than me after you told her how you handled yourself at the accident."

Bailey swatted away the compliment. "It scared me down to my socks. I shook like a leaf in a dust-devil on the drive to Bandera. Ask Fen. He'll tell you how scared I was."

"There's a time to be scared and yesterday was it for Bailey."

She interrupted. "Let's move on. Is that the laptop you want us to investigate?"

Fen raised a backpack to the top of the table. "Here it is.

You'll find a piece of paper with the password on it when you flip open the screen. The power cord is in there, too. Look for hidden files or anything else that looks suspicious."

Jeremy's smile pulled up the corners of his eyes. "This is so cool. Last night I went on a real stake out and watched Bailey complete a covert mission. Today, we're searching a computer for incriminating evidence. I feel like I'm living in a spy movie."

Fen leaned forward and whispered. "Do you know what the first rule of being a spy is?"

"Uh... no."

"Secrecy," said Fen in an even quieter voice.

Bailey expanded on Fen's word. "No one but Fen is to know about this. Not even Lou. Fen will tell her what she needs to know, when she needs to know it, and don't ask why."

Fen added, "This isn't playacting. Two people are dead and we're trying to make sure the body count stops there."

Bailey took Jeremy's hand. "I trust you never to say a word about this to anyone. I have a strict *one-and-done* policy when it involves working on cases with Fen. Do you understand?"

"I do. One betrayal of your trust and you're done with me."

"Forever," said Bailey with cold steel in her voice.

Fen leaned back and lightened the mood. "You haven't ordered anything to eat or drink. What would you like?"

Jeremy spoke before Bailey could. "Nothing for me. I want to get started on this project."

"Me too," said Bailey. "The public library is in the next block. We plan on staying there until they kick us out."

Bailey picked up the backpack and slipped her arms through the straps. It was too big for her slight frame, so she tightened the black straps until it pressed against her shoulders and lower back. "I'll call you when we leave the library or if we find something important."

Fen nodded his approval and watched them until the door

closed behind them. Until now, his stomach hadn't registered a complaint about not being fed breakfast. That changed with a resounding growl. He'd noticed another customer eating a fried egg, ham, and avocado breakfast sandwich on a toasted brioche bun. "The perfect amount of food," said Fen under his breath. "I'll be able to devote all afternoon to reviewing the suspect's files."

He'd finished most of his sandwich when the door opened and KK strode across the floor to his table. Instead of a uniform, she wore jeans, boots, a long sleeve shirt, and a puffer vest zipped up halfway. She wore her hair down and her makeup was thicker than usual. The bulge on her hip contrasted with the friendly smile.

Fen took a last bite as she said, "Mind if I join you?"

He increased the pace of his chewing and pointed to the chair across the table. After swallowing, he said, "That breakfast sandwich was downright tasty. Are you here for an early lunch?"

She took off her cowgirl hat and placed it crown down on the table. "I saw your truck and thought I'd be neighborly. How's the investigation progressing?"

"Hard to tell," said Fen. "I believe most of the chess pieces are on the board, but I can't seem to put the king or queen in jeopardy. Any ideas?"

She shrugged. "Guesses are cheap. The county's full of them."

"What's the consensus among the locals about who killed Misti Palmer?"

"That's easy," said KK. "When we find Brent Stone, we'll have one murder solved."

"You're probably right," said Fen. "Finding him may take a while, but it's only a matter of time before he surfaces." Fen leaned forward. "Are you worried he won't live to go to trial?"

KK blinked three times. "I wasn't expecting that question. We may portray a county that's stuck in the 1800s, but Sheriff Irons wouldn't allow a lynching in the nearest oak tree."

"You're right about Rusty, but he can't sleep in the jail like sheriffs used to." Fen lightened the mood. "Now that he's going to be a proud papa, his mind will be on other things. That might give someone a chance to take revenge for Misti's murder."

KK shook her head. "I know the officers. They may look the other way when certain people do things that aren't on the up and up, but they draw the line at killing a prisoner or allowing anyone else to do it. Believe me, Brent Stone is safer in our jail than on the streets of San Antonio, Eagle Pass, Piedras Negras, or anywhere else in the US or Mexico."

Fen pressed her, but gently. "I don't believe it's true, but I'm hearing whispers that Elton Palmer would get his son, Cliff, to do something bad to Brent if he got the chance."

"No way," said KK with more force than necessary. "Elton wouldn't tell him to do anything like that, and Cliff wouldn't do it, even if his father asked him to."

"How well do you know Elton and Cliff?" asked Fen.

"Not that well. I see Cliff at the dance halls from time to time."

"What's his favorite?"

"The one on 11th Street." KK tilted her head. "You should go. All work and no play makes a man grumpy, old, and gray."

Fen released a laugh. "You're too late."

KK gave him what he interpreted to be a coy look and said, "I bet you still have plenty of rodeos left in you."

Fen cleared his throat. "I'm just an old guy with too many memories watching from the bleachers."

In a sudden turn of events, KK changed the subject. "When are you going to talk to Ray Long again?"

"What makes you think I haven't already?"

"You and Rusty weren't in with him long enough yesterday."

"You're right. Rusty had more important things to do yesterday and today. He asked me to talk to Ray. I may go see him this afternoon or tonight. Do you want to go if I can arrange it?"

The question brought forth a look of surprise. "Me? I'm just a deputy who splits time between patrol and training. You'd be better off with a supervisor."

"I don't believe you," said Fen with a kidding lift to his voice. "The extra makeup you're wearing tells me you have other plans for the day. Who's the lucky man?"

Her left eye twitched, but she made a quick recovery. "I don't know if you've noticed, but there are very few men to choose from in this town."

Fen needed to transition into a conversation that might produce something useful. "If I can't get you to talk to Ray with me, at least give me your thoughts about him. I found his pistol at the crime scene and we also know that Clay owed him money. What does that tell us?"

KK didn't hesitate. "It tells me you may not be in town much longer."

"Is that because you believe Ray killed Clay Trueblood?"

"Isn't there enough evidence to support that conclusion?"

"Ah," said Fen. "I know what you're thinking. Given the town's reputation, speedy justice can weigh just as heavily as sure justice."

KK didn't directly respond. Instead, she said, "When you talk to Ray, he'll tell you a long, sad story about him going to a biker rally in South Dakota with a woman he'd lived with for years. All we know for sure is they left town together, and he came back alone. I tried to track her down. It's like she ceased to exist after the rally."

"That's interesting," said Fen. "One more piece of circumstantial evidence against Ray." He looked down into his empty coffee cup. "My coffee grounds say my days in Bandera may end soon."

KK rose to leave. Her departure allowed Fen to sit and ponder the conversation. Not wanting to talk on his phone in such a public place, he paid the bill and went to his truck. Once there, he punched a number on speed dial. If anyone could locate a missing person, it was Candy back in Newman County.

Following a brief conversation, he turned off the truck's diesel engine and walked to the library. He found Bailey and Jeremy sitting shoulder to shoulder, both looking at Ray's computer screen.

Bailey looked up. "What's wrong?"

"Nothing. I have another assignment for you. I want you two to go to the dance hall on 11th Street tonight. There're several people I want you to watch, but not talk to."

Jeremy responded with a wide grin. "This is turning out to be the best Christmas ever. I thought all we'd do is sit around the house with Mom and Dad looking at pictures of me growing up."

Fen remembered something else. "When did you say your sister was coming to town?"

"Tonight. She likes to dance, so it will be no trouble talking her into meeting us there."

He looked at Bailey. "You know what to do."

She nodded. "Gather information on suspects you've already identified and have reports emailed to you before dawn."

Bailey turned to Jeremy. "Do you see that look on Fen's face?"

"What look?"

"It's the way a hunter looks when he's tracking his prey and sees a fresh footprint."

Fen left the library but didn't allow a smile to break through until he was back in his truck. "Bailey's progressing well. She has a long way to go, but she has what it takes to make an excellent detective."

Chapter Twenty-Seven

F en knew he had to guard against being overconfident, especially after Bailey's comment about him being near the end of the hunt. Perhaps she'd spent more time studying the suspects and had narrowed down the list more than he had. The thought niggled his mind until he determined his next step would be to return to his cabin and pore over the names of anyone who might have a motive to kill either Clay Trueblood or Misti Palmer.

He allowed the glow plugs in the diesel engine to warm before turning the key. The truck's engine clattered to life, and he eased along backstreets until he turned onto the street that led to the bridge over the Medina. He crossed it and climbed the steep, curvy road leading to his cabin and the Silver Spur. A deputy sheriff's pickup truck told him he had company. But who? Rusty wasn't due back in town until that evening.

A broad smile and the somewhat rotund shape of Deputy Scooter Gillespie revealed the visitor's identity.

Fen parked in the driveway that ended at the back door of his cabin and received a hearty "Howdy, Sheriff Maguire."

"Hello, Scooter. You need to stop calling me Sheriff Maguire. People will think I work for a living instead of sitting around drawing pictures."

Scooter continued the good-natured banter. "I may have been born at night, but it wasn't last night. I bet you were up before dawn working on at least two or three things at the same time."

"I hate to disappoint you, but all I've done today is draw a few sketches and eat a late breakfast at the Cowgirl Coffee Company."

Scooter shook his head. "You also talked to Jeremy Blankenship and his cute blond girlfriend. That was before you spoke with KK."

Fen tilted his head. "If I didn't know better, I'd say you were spying on me."

Scooter's belly jiggled as he laughed. "Ain't much else to do around here."

"You remind me of one of my best deputies, Waldo Williams. The other deputies called him *Where's Waldo*. He wasn't much on giving traffic tickets or ordinance violations. Instead, he was a professional information gatherer. He knew the men and women who were most likely to commit something serious and would let me know what was about to go down, or who to look for after it did. Most of the time, Waldo knew more than any ten other deputies."

Scooter shrugged his shoulders. "I think Waldo and I would see eye to eye on being a good cop."

"Let me ask you something, Scooter. Were you working the north end of the county yesterday evening?"

"Yeah."

"Did you see me going to or returning from Ray Long's place?"

"Can't say that I did. Someone's been helping themselves to

cattle from the ranches between Medina and Utopia. I think I know who it is, but they're slippery as a greased oyster."

Fen gave further details. "Someone in a sheriff's department pickup was parked on a tree-lined lane about a mile from the turnoff to Ray Long's bus. Are you sure that wasn't you?"

"I'm positive, and I can't think of who it might have been. Do you want me to find out?"

"Don't go out of your way," said Fen. "I was in law enforcement long enough to know officers sometimes find a quiet place to rest their eyes for a few minutes. The truck wasn't there when I came back to town."

Scooter moved on. "The reason I came by was to tell you tonight's special at the Trail Boss is chicken-fried steak. Gladys Mae says for you to come hungry. She'll see that you have plenty to take home for another meal."

"Thanks, Scooter."

"By the way, you don't need to worry about bringing chicken noodle soup to that newspaper woman in the other cabin."

"You spoke with Lou?"

"Yep. She came out wearing a robe, house shoes, and a coat with a hood. It surprised me she knew who I was. I could tell right off that she was sick. That didn't keep her from asking me a bunch of questions."

"That's what she does best," said Fen.

Scooter continued his story. "Lou thinks a lot of your ability to solve crimes, but she wasn't as complimentary about you remembering things not related to crime. She said you'd forget to bring chicken noodle soup, and you'd have to return to the store for it."

Fen rolled his eyes. "Guilty as charged."

"Not to worry," said Scooter. "Gladys Mae fills empty gallon buckets of ice cream with soups and freezes them. Her specialty is chicken noodle. I fetched Lou a gallon while you went to the library. Lou wanted me to tell you she was armed and dangerous if you knocked on her door this afternoon."

Fen heaved out a breath that combined regret and thanks. "You saved my hide. I owe you, Scooter."

"No problem, but if I get to be the one to put handcuffs on the killer, it would make my day."

Fen noticed that Scooter had used the singular noun of killer. "Do you believe there's only one person responsible for both deaths?"

"I ain't smart enough to figure that out, but the thought crossed my mind."

"It crossed my mind, too, but I can't find anything that links the two murders."

Scooter climbed into his truck and left. Fen went back to square one with his files of suspects. He started with two people he'd ruled out. The first was Cliff Palmer's ex-wife, a woman named Becky, who was now living in Houston with her new family. Lou's and Bailey's research was solid. Becky left Bandera in her rearview mirror many years ago. She'd severed all communication with Cliff, Misti, and the patriarch, Elton.

Fen moved the laptop's cursor to the next file and said, "Let's try Roger, Brent Stone's cowboy buddy at the Lucky 7."

He reread all his notes from his encounters with the young man. Once again, he concluded Roger was a decent young man, working hard to get back into college. As for a motive, there was none. His relationship with Brent was cursory, brought on by boredom. As for any link to the two victims, none existed.

Scratch another name from the list of suspects.

Fen moved on to examine the files of those he still considered suspects. Topping the list was Brent Stone, Misti Palmer's jilted boyfriend, who fled the county without permission.

A painstaking reading of the file revealed a smattering of redeeming qualities, but it was easy to believe that the hard drinking, drug abusing, womanizing cowboy could have killed the spoiled woman who'd thrown him aside like she'd done to others.

When considering motive, means, and opportunity, motive was the strongest. Means and opportunity were murkier because the medical examiner couldn't give a clear estimate of the time of death for either victim due to water temperature and the condition of the bodies.

Fen knew that Brent Stone would have an uphill battle in court, especially if Judge Willoby was on the bench. That assumed that he'd make it to trial, which was an open question if Elton Palmer had anything to say about it.

He wondered if Brent might be too good of a suspect. Was it possible that someone had chosen him to be the prime suspect? It wouldn't be the first time Fen had seen this take place. But who would be clever enough to orchestrate this?

The next file bore the name of Cliff Palmer. Fen realized that it was a bit of a stretch to think a brother would kill his kid sister, but perhaps Cliff wanted all the inheritance once his father passed. The youngish man liked expensive things and seemed to lack the initiative or brains to earn them on his own. He'd likely go through his half of an inheritance with little trouble. Another ex-wife or two would all but guarantee he'd die with little to show for his life. Once again, means and opportunity were unclear.

The next file was on Elton Palmer, the county commissioner and father of Misti. "No way could he have killed his own daughter," said Fen. "If Brent Stone disappeared or met an untimely death, Elton would be my number one suspect."

But Fen wasn't in the business of solving uncommitted crimes. Yes, it was true he was bending the rules by not revealing Brent's location. He'd justified the omission as his way of protecting Elton and Cliff by removing the temptation to kill Brent.

The image of Nancy Jurick came to Fen, so he opened her file. Was it possible she was in league with Brent Stone? She was harboring a fugitive, so her moral compass didn't point true north. Yet, their relationship didn't start until after Misti dropped Brent like he was a hot horseshoe. An accomplice? Possibly, if she was high enough. Perhaps she could be a useful witness, either for or against Brent. She fit the type of person district attorneys love to threaten with prison if they don't turn state's evidence.

Fen looked at the lone remaining file with the name Ray Long on it. Unlike the others, he had a solid alibi when Misti died. But his was the only name associated with the death of Clay Trueblood. An unpaid bill for a motorcycle repair years ago might be motive enough for a spur of the moment killing. Also, KK had hinted that the mechanic wasn't as peaceful, forgiving, and benevolent a man as he presented himself to be.

Fen wondered if Ray had been too willing to allow a search of his home and business. Was there a garage or storage shed somewhere that held hidden secrets? That seemed possible, even likely if the computer held nothing of value.

Other possibilities occurred to Fen. Was Ray being set up to take the fall for a crime he didn't commit, or was the overactive imagination of a former sheriff turned artist running away with him? Two murder set ups, with two different victims that had nothing in common? That made no sense, but it wouldn't stop him from mulling it over again and again. Thoughts like that would hound him until he found the truth.

Fen closed his computer, retrieved a large canvas from the back of his truck, and placed it on an easel in the tiny living room. For the next hour or two, he stared at the blank canvas, envisioning the high hills in the distance, the gaps in the hills, the city with its dinky water tower, the courthouse on high ground, and the Medina River snaking its way through the county. In his mind's eye, he could clearly see what it looked like without snow, but he'd set his heart on a blanket of white. The weather would have to cooperate and the chances of that happening were slimmer than him solving the two murders without the killer or killers making mistakes.

"Road trip," said Fen to the blank canvas. "It's time I gave this sleepy little town a good, hard shake." He put on his boots and hat, grabbed his coat, and went to his truck. Before he opened the door, he went back into his cabin and fixed his holster on his right hip.

He whispered to himself as he locked the cabin's door. "Next stop, San Antonio."

Chapter Twenty-Eight

Fen was about ten miles into his trip when he placed the call to Audrey. Her response made him think she was out of breath. "Hello... handsome. This is... a welcome... surprise."

"I must have caught you at a bad time. Should I call back?"

"No!" She gasped for another breath. "My personal trainer is trying to kill me. I just finished...a five-mile run... on the treadmill. I'll go outside... and walk around... the parking lot... to cool down."

The sound of a passing vehicle with loud pipes told him she'd left the gym. Background noise and heavy breathing subsided enough for Audrey to ask, "Is this call business or pleasure?"

"Both."

"Interesting. Let's take care of the business first."

"Good idea," said Fen. "You know I do my best thinking when I'm focused on art. Right?"

"Correct. Your paintings sometimes speak to you and guide you. It's the spookiest thing I've ever heard of, but if it works, who am I to question it? Did your painting tell you who committed the murders?"

"Not yet. I stared at a blank canvas for much of the afternoon. A feeling of danger settled over me the longer I sat looking at nothing."

Audrey huffed out a full breath. "A shiver just went down my spine. If you, Bailey, or Lou are in danger, you need to go home."

"It's not any of us. I've had a feeling for a long time that someone is trying to set up Brent Stone for killing Misti Palmer. That feeling grew stronger and stronger today. The interesting thing is that I believe Nancy Jurick is in danger, too."

Audrey waited a few seconds before asking, "Do you have a plan, and is it legal?"

Fen said, "Yes to having a plan. As for it being completely legal, I'd say it passes Bailey's test."

"That's a pretty low bar. You'd better let me be the judge of legality."

"I'm letting you know up front that I'm going to do it even if you advise me not to."

"I understand but use a hypothetical situation and fake names instead of telling me the details outright. It's an old trick attorneys use to sidestep ethics."

Fen launched into a thinly disguised tale. "A long time ago, in a land far, far away—"

Audrey let out snickers that went on for several seconds. She brought her giggles under control and said, "Sorry, I was imagining how that would sound being read aloud by a panel of ethics judges."

Fen tried again. "There once was a woman with a sketchy past and dubious morals. It would be easy to believe that she would steal or do anything to make her life easier. The daughter of a rich man died in a forest fire and everyone blamed the woman. The rich man swore an oath to avenge his daughter's death. Our accused woman went and hid in a cave a long distance away."

Audrey interrupted him. "Introduce the hero. He's the one I'm most concerned about."

"The hero, as you call him, came to town and had other ideas about the woman's guilt. He searched for the woman and found her with the man who owned a cave and took her in."

"I like the hero," said Audrey. "I can see me sharing a cave with him someday."

Fen abandoned the story. "I'm an artist, not a storyteller. Making up lies doesn't come easy to me. Talk of sharing a cave is very distracting."

Audrey shot back, "Forgive me, my hero of the story. I won't interrupt again."

"Where was I?" asked Fen.

"I'd tell you, but I said I wouldn't interrupt."

Fen let out a low growl and continued, "The man who came to town, the one you call the hero, found the cave, but didn't tell the king's knights he knew where the woman was. Days passed and the man was told in a dream that the woman and her friend were in danger."

"Interesting," whispered Audrey. "The hero is full of surprises."

"The hero went to the cave and told the woman and her lover they were in danger. He even rented another cave for them to stay in."

"For how long?" asked Audrey.

"A few days, at the most. The man was close to finding the person who started the fire that killed the rich man's daughter."

Several seconds of silence passed before Audrey asked, "Who rented the second cave?"

"The hero."

"Did he put the cave in his name when he rented it?"

"He did. It was a one-room cave in a much bigger cave with lots of little caves."

"There's a problem with your story. Two people, a man and a woman are checking in under the name of the hero. You'd get by with it if only one person stayed in the room."

"I thought of that," said Fen. "If asked, which never happens, he gives the name of the fairest damsel in the land as the person who shares his cave."

"Let me get this straight," said Audrey in an accusatory tone. "You may have to use my name if you're asked to explain who was with you when you rented a hotel room for a wanted man and his girlfriend?"

"Uh... yeah, but the chances of that happening are less than one in a million. All I'll do is put my name on the room for two when I check in and hand over two room keys to the guy and the girl."

Audrey asked, "Is it a nice cave I won't be staying in with the hero?"

"Only the best for the fairest damsel in the land."

"That makes thinking about it worse than ever."

Fen wondered if he'd pushed her too far. "If you're not comfortable with the plan, I'll think of something else. The last thing I want is for me to do something you're not comfortable with."

"Stop!" said Audrey in a no-nonsense tone. "You're trying to protect someone you believe is in danger. The very least I can do is keep my mouth shut. Attorney-client privilege protects everything you told me. You needn't worry about me. The only thing I'm upset about is not being able to live in your fairy-tale world for four and a half more years. You'd better use that vivid imagination to plan one heck of a honeymoon. If you don't, I will."

"Why don't we each plan one and go on back-to-back honeymoons?"

"Now you're talking like a real fairy-tale hero."

They both remained quiet until Audrey got back to the business at hand. "By the way, how are you going to get the guy and girl out of their cave and go to the cave that sounds like a fancy hotel?"

"Do you want to hear another fairy tale?"

"Absolutely not."

"Yeah. It's best you don't know."

FEN SCANNED the parking lot of Nancy's apartment complex. It held a rather motley collection of cars, trucks, and vans. Most were ten to twenty-five years old with scratches, dents, and dings. Nancy's truck fit the profile, and she'd parked it in a space under her living room window. An hour after security lights came on, Nancy left.

He'd parked his truck near, but not too close, to her second-floor apartment. He waited until Nancy left before going to the convenience store down the potholed street that ran in front of the complex.

He looked for something decent to eat at the convenience store, bypassing the hot dogs and self-serve nachos.

Fen settled for a protein bar and a small container of milk. He'd thank himself later for practicing discretion. There was a time in college when he devoured gas station foods without hesitation. Those days, like his taste in clothes, music, and food, had changed.

He returned to the apartment complex and ate the protein bar in small bites. He was sipping the last of his milk when Nancy's truck made its not-so-grand appearance, with one headlight shining bright as the other made a dim attempt at staying legal. The truck's exhaust system belched its last noisy puff. It reminded him of a derelict exhaling the last full puff of a cigarette and the subsequent racking cough that followed.

Only Nancy exited the truck. She carried white plastic sacks that looked like they contained Styrofoam boxes of food. Fen thought of the chicken-fried steak he was missing. "Whatever it is she's carrying has to be better than that cardboard bar I choked down."

He waited five minutes, then waited five minutes more before easing out the door. With jacket unzipped, he walked on a cracked sidewalk, trudged up a flight of stairs and strode down a balcony overlooking the parking lot. Loud music from more than one apartment sounded as he passed several windows and doors.

Fen stopped beside the door marked 223 and listened. A television blared from the other side. He gave three firm knocks. The sound of people scurrying inside mingled with a television jingle of a commercial for a car company. He waited and knocked again.

A voice sounded from the other side of the door. "Who is it?"

"The owner of Little Italy Pizza. I need to talk to you about a problem we had with a delivery a few days ago."

The door cracked open and the woman he knew to be Nancy Jurick said, "I'm not paying for the pizza. That girl gave it to me."

Fen held up his palms. "I've come to give you coupons for two more free pizzas. Our delivery specialist told me about how nice you were to her. The coupons are our way of saying thank you. Can I come in? I want to get your version of the story. I'm starting an advertising campaign using quotes from nice people like you. I'll make up a name for you if you don't want to be identified."

Fen took a step forward, and the door opened all the way. He blocked Nancy's view of the doorknob as he closed the door behind him and locked it.

Nancy stood about five feet from him. "This really isn't a good time. Why don't you make something up for me to say about your pizzas while you're giving me a fake name?"

Fen put his left index finger perpendicular to his lips and closed the distance to Nancy. He also pulled back the corner of his jacket and hooked it behind the pistol on his hip.

She stood with mouth agape as he whispered, "Stay quiet and nobody gets hurt. I'm here to help."

He didn't wait for a response before raising his voice. "Brent, this is Fen Maguire. Come out of the bedroom. I know you're in there. Nancy brought home too much food for one person."

The door stayed shut, but Brent shouted, "I don't believe you're alone. Cops don't come alone." He spoke louder. "Send Nancy to the window. I bet there's a SWAT team waiting for your signal."

Fen kept his eye on the bedroom door. "Nancy, go to the window or open the front door. It doesn't matter. No one else is outside."

She moved to the window, and he heard the rustle of blinds behind him. She hollered. "No one's on the balcony."

"I'm not going to jail. They'll either kill me or send me to prison for the rest of my life."

"That's why I've come alone. There's another way. It will keep you out of jail. If you stay here, they're bound to find you. I did." Fen kept talking. "Do you remember the girl who brought you a free pizza? Her name is Bailey, and she works with me. If you're going to hide, don't leave your hat on the refrigerator."

Nancy spoke next. "Come out, Brent. What he's saying makes sense. He knew about the pizza and could have come back with cops that night."

Fen didn't want to waste any more time negotiating. "I'll give you sixty seconds to think it over. You have two choices. You can come out and listen to my plan or I'll call for backup. They'll arrest you and transfer you back to Bandera County."

It didn't take long for Brent to open the door. Fen drew his pistol but pointed it at the cheap beige carpet covering the living room floor. Empty hands went to shoulder height.

Fen put the pistol back in its holster. "Smart decision. Let's see if you can make another good one."

Brent and Nancy sank into the couch while Fen dragged a wooden chair from the dining room and sat it in front of them. It took longer to explain his plan than it did for Nancy to pack her suitcase and change into something more appropriate for a five-star hotel.

Fen gave them a few parting instructions. "You'll ride with me and enter first. Go straight to the bar while I pick up the key cards from the desk. Brent, you're to stay in the room. Nancy can leave if she wants or needs to."

"What about food?" asked Nancy.

"Room service. Charge it to the room."

"Can I get a bottle of whiskey on the way?" asked Brent.

"Don't push it," said Fen. He turned to Nancy. "Happy hour is on you two. Three nights at about a thousand dollars a day for food and lodging is the extent of my desire to keep Brent alive."

Brent said, "I'm still having a hard time believing anyone would do so much to help a saddle bum like me."

Fen set his jaw. "If you leave your hotel room, you'll experience a different side of me. I found you once. I can do it again."

Chapter Twenty-Nine

Fen didn't often second guess his decisions, but he made an exception for Brent and Nancy. Not only did he question treating them to a multi-day stay in one of San Antonio's finest hotels, but doubts caused him a good chunk of a night's sleep once he returned to his cabin in Bandera. The dominant side of his brain that functioned in facts, hard evidence, and logic made hash out of the hunch that propelled him to believe the cowboy and the party girl were in imminent danger.

Dawn's light finally poked through the curtains. He threw back the covers, disgusted with himself for entertaining such a feather-brained plan. He turned on the light and there was Sally's photo, staring at him with eyes that could still see his innermost thoughts.

He took the photo in hand, swung his feet back into bed, and pulled the duvet up to his chin. The need for wisdom, understanding, and support was stronger than his desire for coffee on this December morning. A simple question formed within him and worked its way out. "Sally, did I make a huge mistake? They could be in Mexico by now. If they are, it's my fault."

He stared at Sally's lips, wishing they would move and either confirm that he'd acted foolishly or wisely. No response or even an inkling of communication came from the woman who had a way of expressing truth and love in the same sentence.

He moved on to stare at her eyes. "*Windows to the soul,*" he whispered. "Speak to my soul with your eyes."

The longer he looked, the more compassion and love he saw. The sensation reminded him of the time he and Sally climbed into an outdoor hot tub during a Rocky Mountain resort snowstorm. He'd worn his Stetson, and she stuffed her long, blond hair under a knit cap. Steam rose from the water, giving them their own personal cloud. The memory was so real that his first inclination was to paint it. He shook his head. "Some memories are too perfect. I'd ruin that one if I tried to take it out of my mind."

Fen took his time basking in the warmth, but like the fog above the hot tub, it faded, leaving only a pleasant memory and a sense that he'd done the right thing by trying to protect Brent and Nancy.

The ringing of his telephone slammed the door shut on his early morning ritual with Sally. A glance at the phone told him the identity of the caller and the time. He'd been in his memories' hot tub for half an hour.

"Good morning, Bailey."

Excitement propelled her words. "We need to meet. I have a ton of things to tell you. Where did you go last night?"

Fen considered how Bailey knew he'd gone somewhere without telling her. Then, the answer came to him. "Lou must have told you."

"She said you didn't get back to your cabin until after

eleven o'clock. She's feeling much better and credits Gladys Mae's chicken noodle soup for the speedy recovery."

"Thelma and Gladys Mae think alike."

"When and where do you want to meet?"

"My cabin in two hours," said Fen, before he amended his plan. "I'll call Lou and make sure she's well enough to come."

"She is," said Bailey with confidence. "Lou even made a late appearance at the dance hall last night."

"That's a surprise. Yesterday morning she looked pale and pasty."

Bailey shot back, "Being accused of flirting with another woman's man put the color back in her cheeks. I'll let her tell you the story."

Fen was on the verge of asking for details when Bailey said, "Did you hear that? Jeremy's mom has an old brass bell with a wooden handle like schoolteachers used to signal children to come in from recess. Breakfast is on the table. We'll be at your cabin in two hours."

FEN HAD the foresight to stop at a grocery store before leaving San Antonio the previous night. A breakfast of two microwavable biscuits with sausage patties sufficed for his first meal of the day. He wished the cabin's food and condiments cabinet contained packets of jelly, but he settled for coffee to get the dry biscuits down.

He checked the weather forecast on his phone and frowned. The temperatures were supposed to drop in the next few days, but there was no mention of any type of frozen precipitation. After showering and shaving, he still had time to stare at the blank canvas for about twenty minutes. He determined that wasn't enough time to do anything to his canvas, so he put on his coat and hat and went to the yard swing.

Lou must have been watching for him because she came out fully dressed, with coffee mug in hand.

"Mornin'," he said.

Lou proved she felt better by her quick response. "Why do people who live in small towns say *mornin'* instead of *good morning?*"

Fen played along. "*Duh-no.*"

"That's very cute," said Lou, as she eased onto the seat beside him.

"Bailey called. She and her main squeeze will be here in about twenty minutes."

"Don't let Thelma hear you calling him that."

Lou propelled the swing back a few inches and allowed it to rock forward. "Bailey called me, too. We're supposed to meet in your cabin, but it's too small. Let's have it out here."

Fen shrugged. "Fine with me, but will you be warm enough? It would be a shame if you have a relapse."

"Look at what I'm wearing. I'm dressed for an expedition to the Antarctic. Besides, I had a bowl of soup for breakfast. I hate to say it, but Thelma's right about chicken noodle's medicinal value."

Fen looked toward the Silver Spur ruins. "Bailey told me you had some sort of trouble last night. She didn't go into details."

"It involved one of our suspects and that female deputy you've been hanging around."

Fen turned to face her. "The only female deputy I know in this county is KK, and I haven't been hanging around her."

"What do you call going on an overnight trip and sleeping in the same cave?"

Fen gave her a quick response. "I call it a manhunt." He added, "Sheriff Irons and Sam were there, too."

Lou cut her gaze his way. "I've counted the number of times you and that woman have been together. Have you?"

"Uh, no, and so what?" said Fen. "She's a competent deputy who's trained in swift-water rescues and recoveries. We're working on two murders that involve the river."

Lou had more to say. "Name any other deputy you've spent half as much time with."

Fen considered her words and came back with, "If you're saying I'm interested in Deputy Krump, you must be suffering from what they used to call brain fever."

Lou shook her head. "Now you're reminding me of husband number one. He was a handsome man, but thick-headed as a block of concrete. I flirted with him for six months before he realized my hand on his thigh didn't mean I'd dropped my pencil and was trying to find it."

Fen swallowed. "Do you really think she's interested in me? I'm old enough to be her..."

"Much older brother," said Lou. "Or she's imagining you as her rich husband who'll leave her a fortune."

Fen rubbed his freshly shaved face and considered Lou's words. She stood and looked to the east. "I wouldn't be too worried about it. You're her backup plan. KK has her eyes on Cliff Palmer. He's more her age and not near as cautious, smart, or picky as you. It won't be long before she has him wrapped in her web."

"What makes you say that?"

"The way she threatened me for dancing with Cliff last night. She'll run any competition out of the county. Elton Palmer wants a grandson to pass on the family name. KK's ready and willing to fill the role of wife and mother."

The sound of an approaching vehicle put an end to the

conversation. "That should be Bailey and Jeremy," said Lou. "I haven't made up my mind about him yet. So far, he doesn't remind me of my former husbands. That's a wonderful thing." A white cloud was released into the frigid air as she gave a mournful sigh. "He still has the potential to be a scoundrel though. After all, he has that XY chromosome defect that ruins most men."

Fen's thoughts turned from Lou's jaded opinion of men to the laptop and any secrets Jeremy found buried in depths of the machine's memory.

As Bailey walked to the front yard of Fen's cabin, she looked at him and asked, "Where did you go last night? Gladys Mae and Scooter expected you to come for chicken-fried steak."

"I went to San Antonio." He changed the subject. "Will you two be warm enough if we sit outside and talk?"

Lou added, "I've seen phone booths larger than the living rooms in these cabins."

Bailey blurted out, "It feels pretty good out here. Jeremy's mother is either cold-natured or has a woman thing going on. It must have been eighty-five in Frieda's bedroom last night."

Jeremy was more diplomatic. "I told Bailey and Sis to close off the vent, but they were too busy having a slumber party."

Fen brought the meeting to order. "Now that we know everyone will be warm enough, let's have a seat at this patio table." The four of them settled themselves in a chair as Fen said, "I'll begin by telling you why I went to San Antonio last night."

Bailey said, "I bet it has something to do with Brent Stone. Did you arrest him?"

"Not yet."

Lou pulled out her phone, placed it on the table, and activated the recorder. She looked at Fen. "Don't you dare tell me I can't use this."

"You can, but the same rules apply as with all our investigations. No stories go to the press until I say so and I'm going to edit what goes out. Much of what you're about to hear concerning Brent and Nancy will need to remain secret for around ten years."

Lou groaned. "Here we go again. You're taking food out of my mouth."

"I'm leaving plenty of meat on the bone for you," said Fen.

"It's the meat you're cutting off that interests me now."

Bailey whispered to Jeremy, "They play this game every case we work."

Lou shot Bailey a look of disapproval and shifted her gaze back to Fen. "Spill it, Sheriff Maguire. What can't I print for ten years?"

"I moved Brent and Nancy from her apartment to someplace safer last night."

The revelation only whet Lou's appetite for more information. "Where did you move them to, and why?"

"I'll wait until after the case is over to tell you where. As for why, I believe a yet-to-be identified person or persons will try to harm Brent and possibly Nancy."

"Who else knows about this?"

"No one."

Bailey asked, "Sheriff Irons doesn't know?"

Fen shook his head. "No one but us four."

Lou leaned forward, but Fen cut her off before she could pepper him with more questions. "That's all I want to say about Brent and Nancy. Jeremy, it's your turn to tell us what you found on Ray Long's computer."

Chapter Thirty

Bailey rose from her chair, walked to her truck, and came back to the table with Ray Long's computer. She brought it to life, then placed it between herself and Jeremy.

"Ray kept his books on this computer. There's evidence he transferred files from an old computer to this one, but that was over ten years ago."

Fen added, "That was many years before he and his girlfriend went to Sturgis and she deserted him."

Jeremy took over again. "It appears they ran the repair business together. Her name is on most of the paperwork until it suddenly stopped."

Bailey looked at Fen. "The date corresponds to when Ray told you his live-in ran away to Oregon."

Fen asked, "Is there any record of correspondence after Ray returned from the rally in Sturgis?"

"None," said Bailey. "That doesn't mean they didn't text or call, only that they didn't correspond by email."

Fen took in the information and asked, "Did you find the bill for repairs to Clay Trueblood's motorcycle?"

"We found several invoices, demands for payment, late payment charges, and emails threatening litigation."

Fen spoke mainly to himself. "Ray might not be a killer, but he's very accomplished at dancing around the truth." He looked at Jeremy. "Anything else of interest?"

"Not that Bailey and I could find on the computer, but my sister had plenty to say about Cliff Palmer."

Bailey took over. "According to Frieda, he's a detestable, sarcastic creep."

Fen waited for specifics that didn't come. "Can you explain why Frieda would say that?"

Jeremy chimed in. "Frieda can't talk about him without turning the air blue with curse words, and she rarely uses that kind of language. It all goes back to him taking liberties with her while dancing at the bar on 11th Street. Not last night, but several years ago. She refused his advances, and he conducted a campaign to ruin her reputation. Being told *no* isn't something he responds well to."

Fen turned to Bailey. "You were up late with Frieda last night. Did she say anything else about Cliff you'd like to share?"

"She was very thankful that KK danced with him all night."

"Not all night," said Lou. "I waited until KK went to the restroom then I moved in for a dance."

"I'm glad you did," said Bailey. "I was on the verge of doing the same thing."

"You missed a very unpleasant experience, both during the dance and after KK returned. In less than three minutes, I had my caboose grabbed and my life threatened. Cliff thought it was a hoot that KK was so protective of him."

Jeremy added, "Probably because he gets his face slapped so often."

Seconds stretched into a long pause as Fen tried to form a picture of what looked like broken tiles. He gave up and said, "I need to paint. If you want something to do, stake out Nancy Jurick's apartment. I'm fresh out of ideas."

Fen left them sitting in the yard. All he had was hunches, guesses, and what looked like an incomplete list of suspects. Once inside, his phone rang. He looked at the name on the screen and punched a green circle. "Hello, Candy. Did you find Ray Long's former partner?"

"It wasn't easy, but I located her. She's in a grave in Portland, Oregon."

Fen's confidence took another blow. "That's not what I was hoping you'd say. It means I've believed another talented liar. I used to spot them better than I do now."

"Have you hit a roadblock?" asked Candy.

"There's a bridge out sign on a narrow, twisted path. The problem is between my ears. I can't seem to move forward."

"Then turn around and go back to where you started. Take another path. You may be closer to your destination than you think."

"Thanks. I'll follow your advice."

Instead of staring at a blank canvas, Fen used a hard graphite pencil to separate the sky from the distant hills. He consulted photographs he'd taken from the ruins of the Silver Spur Dance Hall to map out the exact location of each undulating hill and the passes. It was an exercise in practicing patience that forced him to engage all his mental energy.

He knew that wasn't exactly true. He learned a long time ago that the more he devoted his conscious mind to the details of art, the harder his subconscious worked to solve problems that had nothing in common with what he was putting on a canvas rectangle.

It took over an hour, but he slipped into *flow,* that state of concentration where time has no meaning. His glances at the photographs slowed and then stopped. The images were so imprinted in his mind, he no longer needed a photograph to show him the next peak or canyon. The pencil became part of his hand and moved effortlessly.

The spell broke at fifteen minutes after six that evening when his bladder overruled his brain and demanded a break. Wanting to return to the mental state of flow as quickly as possible, he rejected the idea of slapping lunch meat and cheese between two slices of bread. Even the lure of coffee wasn't enough to distract him. The fact that it was cold leftover coffee from breakfast may have contributed to his decision to gulp a glass of water instead.

When he returned to the canvas, he was surprised by the progress he'd made. He studied it more closely and whispered, "Not bad. Not bad at all."

Now his focus would be on the second half of the panoramic view of the hills. Flow came again, more quickly than it had that morning. He was nearing the right border of the canvas when his phone came to life. The horn of a cruise ship couldn't have startled him any worse. Flow and whatever muse accompanied her fled the room. He grabbed his phone and stabbed the screen with his index finger.

"What's happened?" he asked, somehow knowing the call didn't bring glad tidings.

"Fire!" shouted Lou. "Flames are shooting from Nancy's windows and smoke is pouring out the roof."

Fen didn't hesitate. "Get plenty of photos. They'll help your book sell. By the way, has anyone called 911?"

"Someone did. I hear sirens getting closer."

Fen looked at the microwave's clock. "Is it really after two in the morning?"

"Bailey and Jeremy took the first shift. I arrived at eleven."

Fen said, "Let me guess. You got hungry, went to the convenience store and missed the person who started the fire."

Lou shot back, "You're wrong. I picked up food on the way. But I absolutely refuse to wear adult diapers on stakeouts, no matter how big the story is."

Fen sighed. "Come back to your cabin when you can and get some sleep."

Lou responded with a question that sounded more like a plea for relief. "When are you going to stop playing around and solve these murders?"

"Soon."

"How about tomorrow?"

"I'll have to talk to Rusty first. He'll need to gather all the suspects."

Lou lowered her voice. "You know who the killers are."

"I will for sure after you, Bailey, and Jeremy go to the county courthouse in Kerrville."

"Why all three of us?"

"Bailey needs to learn how to find official documents quickly. You're the perfect person to teach her. As for Jeremy, it won't hurt him to learn, too. I have a feeling this won't be the last time those two work together on a case."

Lou spoke with a hint of compassion in her voice. "Are you all right with that happening?"

"I'm still getting used to the idea."

Lou changed the subject. "The firefighters are pulling the first hose up to the apartment. Tell Bailey to pick me up at ten o'clock sharp in the parking lot behind the Cowgirl Coffee Company."

Fen did a couple of quick calculations. "That will give me time to do what I need to do. I'm sending you an email telling you the documents I need and the approximate dates. One of them might not exist."

"How do you expect me to find something if it doesn't exist?"

Instead of answering that question, he said, "Stop talking and take a video and stills of the fire."

Chapter Thirty-One

The alarm on Fen's phone brought him out of a fitful sleep at six o'clock. A busy day awaited him, so he threw back the covers and turned on the bedside light. He took hold of Sally's framed photo and said, "Good morning. It's going to be a day where a lot of things can go wrong. I could use some help and you're in the place where people call to get it. If possible, put in a good word for me. I'd hate to make a mistake and ruin someone's life."

He took a breath. "If it's all right with you, we'll talk on the drive to San Antonio. But first, I need to get ready for the day and make some phone calls."

Bailey's name, phone number, and smiling face appeared on his phone's screen. She began with a question. "Did I interrupt your time with Sally?"

"I told her we'd have our time together in my truck on the way to San Antonio."

"Lou sent me an email saying Jeremy and I are going to Kerrville with her at ten o'clock. She also told me about the fire.

You were right. Somebody tried to kill Brent and Nancy. Are you going to talk to them?"

"Not just talk. I'm bringing them to a meeting here in Bandera."

"When and where?"

"I need to talk to Sheriff Irons first, then I'll let you know. For now, you know who to concentrate on. You should have time to go over the files with Jeremy if you haven't already done that. Try to find the motives. Once you know that, everything will make sense."

"You already know, don't you?"

"You'll feel better if you discover the motives behind the murders on your own."

"Always teaching," said Bailey. "That's just one thing that makes you so special."

"You won't think I'm so special if I go to bed with egg all over my face."

"You won't. All the gears will mesh together, and you'll give Sheriff Irons credit for solving the murders."

"I hadn't thought of that. Great idea. Put yourself in my boots and think of ways to make sure he receives the credit."

Bailey sighed. "Like I said, you're always teaching."

The phone went silent, and Fen's thoughts shifted to Brent and Nancy. He considered the two and said to the empty room, "If they left the hotel, my reputation will go from the penthouse to the outhouse. What was I thinking?"

FEN KNOCKED on the hotel room's door. Seconds passed without a response. He knocked again and waited. Once more, only dead silence came from the room. With hand raised, he was preparing to pound the door when it swung open.

"No need to break the door down," said Brent. "Nancy's still asleep, and I was taking a bubble bath."

Fen examined the out-of-place cowboy. He wore a fluffy white hotel robe with matching slippers. His face was clean shaven, he'd slicked back his shiny black hair, and he smelled like a field of lavender.

Walking past him, Fen said, "You're adjusting well to city life."

"Thought I'd see what it's like to live like a fat-cat. It ain't bad, except I can't get no fresh air."

Nancy came in wearing the same outfit as Brent. Her hair was a bird's nest of tangles. She spoke through an opened mouth yawn. "What's going on? Why are you here so early?"

Brent sat on the suite's couch. "Nan, I called for more coffee. Let me know when you're ready for breakfast." He looked at Fen. "I'm diggin' room service."

"It will be on your own dime after today. We're going to Bandera after you two get dressed."

"I don't want to go yet," said Nancy. "Our three days aren't up. You promised us three days."

Fen pursed his lips together as he thought about how to respond. He asked, "Did you have renter's insurance on your apartment?"

"You saw that dump. I trusted the smoke detectors in that place as far as I could throw them. I sure wasn't going to bust my buns to buy nice things to go in it."

"Did you have anything valuable there?"

She snorted through her nose. "Do I look like a girl who stuffs her mattress with hundred-dollar bills?"

"Be thankful you didn't. Someone fire-bombed your apartment last night."

Brent moved to the edge of his chair. "Everything's gone?"

"I stopped on my way here and spoke with a fire department lieutenant. They were looking for Nancy's body."

She put her hand over her mouth to cover the gasp that escaped. She looked at Brent. "It wasn't much, but it was a roof over my head. Now, I'm back to where I started: homeless with only a beat-up truck to my name."

"Sorry to break this to you, but it's gone, too. You parked too close to the building. The fire took out a total of eight apartments."

Brent put an optimistic spin on the news. "It's time for a fresh start for both of us."

Fen said, "This room plus food cost me about a thousand dollars a night. I'll give you what I would have spent if you'll clear out before eleven this morning."

"Two thousand bucks?" asked Brent.

"What's the catch?" asked Nancy.

"Sheriff Irons is having a little get-together this evening. You and Brent may have a few uncomfortable minutes, but they'll pass."

Brent asked, "Do you and the sheriff know who killed Misti?"

Fen nodded.

"And you're going to prove who killed her?" asked Brent.

He nodded again.

"What if we refuse to go?" asked Nancy.

"You'll go, either in my comfortable truck or in the back of a police car."

Nancy stood. "Order me a full breakfast. If I'm starting over with nothing, at least I'll do it on a full stomach."

Brent looked at her and shrugged. "When the only direction we can go is up, then we'll start climbing right now."

Fen stood and rubbed his stomach. "Breakfast sounds like a good idea. I'll be at the hotel restaurant waiting for you."

His mind raced as he rode the elevator down to the main floor. By the time he sat in the restaurant's booth, Fen had a plan to present to Rusty. He placed the call and received assurances from the sheriff that he'd make sure everyone on Fen's list would be present.

The next phone call went to Bailey. Highway noise told him the trio hadn't waited until ten o'clock to leave for Kerrville. "Can everyone hear me?"

"They can now."

He explained the plan and said, "I need you to be back by four o'clock this afternoon with the documents."

Lou said, "We'll be back by three. I need to set up cameras and interview Brent and Nancy before the meeting."

"I can't guarantee they'll want to talk to you."

"Introduce me, then leave us alone. I'll handle getting them to talk."

"They're all yours until the meeting starts."

"Good. How do you want them to look?"

Fen could feel his eyebrows come together. "What difference does that make?"

"You wouldn't understand," said Lou. "Stop at a thrift store and purchase both of them different clothes, something that they'd wear to church."

"They don't impress me as the church-going type."

Lou let out a huff of exasperation. "If church doesn't work for you, pretend they're going to a funeral. Everything they owned is gone. Get them something clean, conservative, and warm."

"I see what you mean," said Fen. "I hadn't thought about clothes."

Bailey added, "Ask Nancy where she normally shops and tell her how much she can spend. She'll take over from there."

"That's what I'm afraid of."

Fen ended the conversation by saying. "Make sure you're back on time with those documents."

246

Chapter Thirty-Two

Lou leaned toward Fen and whispered, "Elton Palmer's face has more wrinkles than a cheap blouse left in the dryer overnight."

Fen responded with a meaningless grunt. He cast his gaze around the circle of chairs and their occupants in the middle of what used to be the Silver Spur's dance floor. If due north was twelve o'clock on the face of a clock, Elton would have his back to a frigid wind.

The county commissioner spoke in an accusatory growl. "Whose idea was it to meet here?"

Fen answered, "It was mine. Sorry about the cold. I wasn't expecting a cold front to blow through."

Rusty added, "Blame me, instead. I wanted a place that would ensure privacy. We'll be discussing some very important things."

"What things?" demanded Elton.

"Family secrets, who killed your daughter, and why."

"I already know who killed Misti. All I want to know is have you found Brent Stone yet?"

"He'll join us in a little while. But first, I'm going to confiscate pistols from everyone who isn't a certified peace officer. If you're packin', stand up and put your hands out like you're trying to fly. KK, Sheriff Maguire, and I will collect your hardware."

"I don't like this," said Elton.

"Me either," said Elton's son, Cliff.

"I don't mind," said Jeremy as he stood. "It's in a shoulder holster under my jacket."

Fen cut his eyes at the young man, who stood still until he was relieved of his pistol.

Fen redirected his gaze to Bailey, who gave him her most angelic look of innocence. "You told me I couldn't carry. Jeremy is almost twenty-two and is an excellent shot."

Fen's gaze shifted to KK, who stood in front of Ray Long with hand extended. "Give it up, Ray. I can tell it's in the pocket of your jacket."

Ray popped up from his chair while reaching for his pocket. KK took a step back, drew her pistol, and pointed it at the mechanic's chest.

"Stop!" shouted Rusty, who moved to where they stood. "Keep covering him, KK." He shifted his focus to Ray. "You're a lucky man. I would have shot you."

Rusty retrieved the pistol and told KK to collect the pistols from Elton and Cliff Palmer. She did so with no further complaints or objections.

Fen and Rusty went to what had been the raised bandstand. They unloaded the pistols, placed them and the ammunition on a bandanna the sheriff pulled from his pocket, then returned to the circle of chairs.

Elton found his voice again. "Was that necessary?"

Rusty ignored the question and drew in a breath. "The next thing I'd like to do is make sure we all know each other. I believe everyone from Bandera has either met, or has heard of, Sheriff Fen Maguire. He volunteered to help me solve the murders of Misti Palmer and a man from Kerrville, Clay Trueblood. You may not know much about Fen, but he knows more about you than you can imagine. I'll let him introduce the others."

Fen cast his gaze around the room. "It's true that I have a thick file of information on each of you, and it's because of the work completed by the two ladies seated on each side of me. They'll introduce themselves." He nodded at Lou.

"I'm Lou Cooper, a journalist. Fen uses me for deep-dive research, personal interviews, the occasional misleading media story when it helps advance his investigation, and anything else he can think of. In this case, my assigned duties involved conducting a stakeout on a suspect and dancing with a person of interest." She gave an unsmiling look at Cliff. "You really shouldn't grope women when you're dancing."

Lou allowed the words to settle before she turned to Bailey. "Your turn."

"I'm Bailey Madison... artist, college student, and private detective in training. Fen is my guardian and mentor."

Fen added, "Don't let Bailey's petite stature and little-girl face fool you. She's tough, smart, can hotwire a car in seconds, and outrun cops any time she wants. She's a chameleon, who can make herself look and act like a girl of twelve or a twenty-five-year-old businesswoman."

Jeremy slipped his hand up. "Everybody knows me and my family. I guess you could say Bailey's my girlfriend."

Bailey glared at him. "There wasn't much conviction in that last statement."

Jeremy beamed a smile. "Bailey likes me enough to change universities. She's definitely my girlfriend."

Fen pressed on. "After that cheerful note, we need to

change gears and get down to business." He stood. "Before we leave this place, you'll know who killed Clay Trueblood and Misti Palmer."

He walked between chairs to go outside the circle and began a slow trek around it. "I'll begin with a confession. So many things about these murders posed challenges, and I'm guilty of making assumptions that caused confusion and delays. Let's start with the river. When we found two bodies in the Medina on the same day, I assumed we were dealing with a double homicide. Similar looking wounds to the back of the victim's necks reinforced my theory. I was wrong. The coroner's report showed the causes of death were different and the crimes occurred at least two days apart."

"That's an understandable mistake," said Rusty. "The wounds looked the same."

"My point is," said Fen, "I almost ruled out the possibility of two killers. After all, what are the chances of two people with so little in common being killed and dumped into the same river and discovered on the same day?"

Fen looked at Elton and then his son. "Why didn't you report Misti as missing?"

Cliff's response was a snort before saying, "Misti went wherever she wanted to and stayed as long as she was having fun."

"Move on," said Elton. "I don't want to think about Misti in cold, muddy water."

Fen moved to stand behind Ray Long. "Let's talk about one of the best motorcycle mechanics in the county. Ray appeared on our radar early on. He's still owed money for the work he did on Clay Trueblood's motorcycle. When I interviewed him, he acted like people owing him money didn't bother him. That was just one lie he told me."

Ray spun around in his chair. Fen's voice cracked like a

whip. "Don't deny it. You gave me your computer and Jeremy found the files you thought you'd deleted. You lied about not going after Clay for the money and you lied about not sending bills and threatening letters to other customers who don't pay on time and in full."

"That's not illegal," said Ray.

"True, but it shows you to be a liar. You even lied about still being in a relationship with the woman you lived with. She left you in Sturgis and went to Portland. She never responded to any of your emails."

"So what? I know in my heart she'll come back."

Fen lowered his voice and shook his head. "She's not coming back. She can't."

Ray sat with mouth hinged open for several seconds. "Did you find her?"

"Yeah."

Fen chose silence to do the work of revelation for him. Then, the weight of the woman's death fell heavily on Ray. His head dipped, his shoulders shaking. Fen looked at Jeremy. "Would you and Bailey take Ray to the parking lot to give him a little time by himself? Watch him from a distance but don't be gone for over five minutes."

The only sound besides three pair of retreating footsteps, was that of the lonesome, stiff wind until Elton broke the silence. "Did Ray kill Clay Truebood?"

"No, but someone worked hard to make us think he did." Fen put a touch of sarcasm in his next sentence. "Do you know who that person is?"

"How is Dad supposed to know?" asked Cliff in a terse voice.

Fen faced Cliff. "You and your father claim to know who killed your sister. Doesn't it stand to reason you two have an opinion about who killed Mr. Trueblood?"

Elton didn't let his son answer for him. "It has to be Brent Stone. You were right the first time about this being a double murder by the same person."

Fen lifted his chin. "We'll find out if you're right by the time we leave today."

Muted voices approached. Wiping his eyes and nose with a red bandanna, Ray trudged back to his chair and slumped into it. His chin rested on his chest as he pulled the collar of his coat up, making himself look like a turtle.

Fen kept his gaze on the corner of the building. All was peaceful until Scooter rounded the corner, followed by Brent Stone and Nancy Jurick, both in handcuffs.

Elton shot from his chair and threw back the corner of his coat. He reached for his pistol, but the only thing he had to point with was his empty hand. Cliff was much slower on the draw, but just as ineffective. KK drew her pistol and hollered for Scooter to move.

Rusty commanded, "Put it away, KK. Scooter has everything under control."

She kept pointing. "He doesn't have their hands behind their back."

Rusty put steel in his voice. "I said put your weapon away. Do it or lose it."

Stunned, KK stuffed her pistol into her holster and crossed her arms. Rusty took a quick step towards her. Fen eased behind her.

Rusty closed the distance even more, which further distracted her. Fen reached around her and jerked the nine-millimeter from its resting place. By the time Rusty was within arm's reach, Fen had unloaded her firearm.

Scooter didn't give her a chance to speak. "Kathy Krump, I'm arresting you for the murders of Clay Trueblood and Misti Palmer. Hands behind your back. Sheriff Maguire is going to handcuff you while I read you your rights. I think it's fitting that he'll use your handcuffs."

The recitation of the well-known paragraph began and stopped after the first sentence when Rusty cut in. He looked KK in the eye. "Do I need to repeat the part that gives you the right to stay silent? I strongly advise you to do so."

KK raised her chin and said, "Take me to jail."

"I will, but not until Scooter finishes and we all hear what Sheriff Maguire has to say."

Chapter Thirty-Three

Scooter posted himself behind KK and said, "You need to sit down. I'll take you to jail as soon as both sheriffs finish. It shouldn't be too long."

Rusty moved to where Brent and Nancy stood and removed their handcuffs "Thanks for playing along. You'll need to come to my office and give formal statements. Brent, your truck is already there. The DA dropped all charges against you. I tried to talk Jim into letting you come back to work, but he doesn't want you at the Lucky 7. Your saddle and everything you own are in your truck."

"Good," said Brent. "Nancy and I need a fresh start. I have a decent nest egg in the bank."

Fen moved to the center of the circle. "Earlier, I made a confession. I said that I made assumptions that caused confusion and delays. What I didn't tell you was Kathy Krump's carefully orchestrated plans to kill two people and pin the blame on others was very effective. Hence the confusion on my part."

He took a deep breath. "I have another confession. I trusted

KK and didn't verify the information she spoon fed to me and others."

Rusty held up his hand. "I'm one of those *others*."

Cliff took his turn, hurt and confusion in his eyes. "I still can't believe she killed Misti."

"That's because she led you to think that way. She was very strategic and calculating."

Elton said, "You need to explain."

Fen faced Elton. "KK was not only a deputy, she was also a swift-water rescue expert. She risked her life to save others and taught others how to follow her leadership. There are few jobs that generate more trust in people's minds than that one. I've fired and arrested dirty cops before, but never a female cop who saved lives in floodwaters. Most people have an innate trust of first responders."

Nods of understanding came from most in the circle, so Fen continued. "This case didn't really begin until I put away all assumptions and started over."

Jeremy raised his hand. "What was the first thing you realized wasn't true?"

"Great question, and it demonstrates my point about not verifying information. Clay Trueblood's shirt was torn open when they pulled his body from the river. I noticed a star tattoo on his chest. So did KK. Her reaction wasn't enough for others to notice, but I saw her face. When the justice of the peace asked if anyone recognized the victim, no one spoke up. I confronted KK about knowing the victim after recovering the second body. The wild guess I made paid off, and she admitted to having an identical tattoo over her heart. She said she was once engaged to Clay Trueblood and that she'd tell Rusty she knew the victim."

"Which she did," said Rusty. "Like Fen, I trusted her too much. I also didn't have the time or inclination not to trust her.

She told us the engagement ended long before she became a deputy in Kerrville and received search and rescue training."

Fen took over again. "We had two bodies after recovering Misti. Both had what looked like gunshot wounds to the base of their skulls. KK stated we had a double murder, meaning one person was responsible for two murders. And everyone agreed with the obvious statement."

"Isn't that what really happened?" asked Elton.

"Yes, but KK arranged a triple-win situation for herself. She had Brent Stone set up for being responsible for Misti's death. But what she really hoped would happen was that you and your son would take the law into your own hands and kill Brent. Everyone in town knows you hated him because you orchestrated their breakup. If by chance, you didn't kill him, then Brent still remained the prime suspect."

"They were a terrible match," countered Elton as he stared at Brent. "He's nothing but a pothead and a saddle bum."

"That may be, but I'm explaining how KK used the breakup as a motive to wave under everyone's nose."

He turned to look at Brent and Nancy sitting on the other side of the circle. "You two played right into KK's hands when Brent left the county without permission."

Fen cast a quick glance toward Rusty. "Did you invite KK to come along on the manhunt to find Brent?"

"She volunteered and wouldn't take no for an answer."

Fen turned back around and locked his gaze on Brent. "KK didn't know that I would join Rusty or that my ranch foreman would be tracking you. I can only imagine what she would have done if Sam hadn't been with us and she'd caught you on the open range."

Lou chimed in. "She firebombed Nancy's apartment, trying to kill Brent. My guess is she would have..."

Her words trailed off when Fen gave her a hard stare.

Elton squinted. "You said that KK arranged things for a triple win. What did you mean?"

"She didn't have to kill Brent if he was convicted and went to prison. The advantage of killing him was speed. Dead men can't fight to prove their innocence. She hoped you would do the dirty work for her, but a prison sentence would do nicely, and that was all but certain, especially after Brent made himself look guilty by running."

"And KK's third plan?" asked Elton.

Fen looked at Cliff. "What's the last name of the first victim?"

"Uh... I don't remember."

"Exactly," said Fen. "He was just some guy from out of town. Don't forget that KK initially pushed the story that this was a double murder. Once the coroner's report came back, she put a leash on people's minds and led them to believe two different people committed the murders.

"KK found out that Clay Trueblood owed a large amount of money to Ray Long. As a backup plan, she made sure I knew about the debt. She also made sure I found the pistol that killed Clay Trueblood, which belongs to Ray. He said someone stole it from his shop some months ago."

"That's because they did steal it," said Ray. "After hearing all this, it had to be KK. She started coming to my shop about five months ago even though she doesn't ride any more. I had no idea she was setting me up."

KK spoke for the first time. "Your theories lack facts, substance, evidence, and motive."

Fen couldn't help but smile. "Thank you for joining the conversation. Let's see what we can do about providing those things you mentioned." He turned to where Bailey, Lou, and Jeremy sat.

"I appoint Lou to begin. Tell us where you went today and what you retrieved."

Lou held up a document. "This is a certified copy of the marriage license between Kathy Lou Krump and Clay Scott Trueblood. It took us twenty minutes to get this. We spent five hours searching for a divorce decree. I'm of the opinion that it doesn't exist."

"Thank you, Lou. Bailey, you're next. Tell us what you learned from Jeremy's sister, Frieda Blankenship."

Bailey stood and spoke in a confident tone. "Frieda remembers Misti Palmer very well. She described Misti as a wild girl who liked older men and fast motorcycles."

"That's hearsay," said KK.

Bailey held up a sheet of paper. "Frieda gave me a list of eight people who have first-hand knowledge of the intimate relationship between Misti and Mr. Trueblood."

Rusty spoke up. "I've contacted four of the people on the list and have signed affidavits from three so far. I'll keep going until I have all eight. I'm sure hotel records and credit card receipts will include plenty of dates, times, and other useful facts."

Fen lowered his voice and said, "Breaking up a marriage sounds like a motive for murder to me."

"Me, too," said Rusty.

"But that wasn't your only motive, was it, KK?" asked Fen.

Her face set like stone, KK said, "You're the one talking. Tell me what else I was thinking."

"I'll let Elton and Cliff help me." He cast his gaze at the father and son. "Elton, do you want a grandson to carry on the family name?"

"What kind of question is that? Of course I do."

Fen nodded. "Cliff, does your father pressure you to settle down, get married, and sire babies until you get a son?"

"At least once a day, every day."

"Have you noticed KK being protective of you in public? Jealous?"

"Yeah. I kind of liked it."

"Pretend the murders never happened. Were you considering marrying KK?"

Cliff's Adam's apple rose and fell. "I hate to admit it now, but I was close to asking her and almost did one night when I'd had too many shots of tequila."

"Have you considered why she killed your sister?"

"No, but you just told us why. Misti broke up KK's marriage."

Fen spoke a single word and let it hang in the air. "Money."

Elton let out a wail. "Please stop."

"No, Dad. I want to know."

Fen moved a step closer to Cliff. "Love and money were the two motives behind the murders. By killing your sister and marrying you, KK would put herself in line for your sister's inheritance. Of course, she had to first get rid of the husband she'd not yet divorced."

"You'll never be able to prove that," said KK.

"He doesn't have to," said Cliff. "I know the truth when I hear it."

She let out a harsh laugh. "You wouldn't know the truth if it bit you on your lazy backside. I had you wrapped around my pinkie."

Fen heaved a sigh. "I have more bad news for you, KK. The apartment you firebombed, Nancy Jurik's apartment, had hidden security cameras. You should have put a ski mask over your license plate and not just your head. You'll receive additional charges of arson and attempted murder once the state fire marshal completes the investigation."

KK's shoulders sagged, seemingly resigned to her fate. "When did you first suspect me?"

"It took me much longer than it should have," said Fen in a voice void of emotion. "Once I opened my mind up to considering all possibilities, it went to work. I can't believe I ignored the matching tattoos. And the ease with which the pistol was found—that should have set off the alarm bells. But you overplayed your hand by putting the note in the mailbox at my ranch. It was too perfect. You used distilled water to seal the envelope, and you discovered where I lived with no problem. You acted too much like a cop."

"Is that all?"

"When we talked about staying single, you were too adamant about never marrying. It was out of character when I considered that you were so interested in and protective of Cliff. At one point, you spoke an outright lie about not knowing Cliff very well."

Fen was on a roll with plenty more to say. "It made no sense for a burglar to pass over a nine-millimeter for a .22 at Ray's shop. I showed him a detailed drawing of where I found his pistol. He didn't react at all. That led me to believe he didn't kill your husband. Eliminating suspects is just as important as putting them on the list."

He summarized. "You almost got away with murder... literally."

Rusty stood. "Almost doesn't count. Scooter and I will take you to jail, and Lou will film the perp-walk."

***

After everyone had disbursed, Fen walked back to his cabin with Bailey holding his hand. "Are you all right?" she asked.

"This one was tough on me. Such a waste of young lives, plus a talented officer."

"Are you driving home tonight?"

"No. I'll stay a few more days. Believe it or not, there's another cold front coming in tomorrow night and they're predicting snow. What about you?"

"Jeremy and I are both leaving in the morning. I don't want to wear out my welcome and he has those pesky finals to take."

They kept walking until Fen said, "Do you want to go inside, or sit on the swing to tell me what's on your mind?"

She squeezed his hand. "The yard swing."

They both plopped down, and Bailey set the pace of the swing's movement along with her words. Both were slow.

"I decided what to do this coming summer."

"Uh-huh."

"First, I ruled out studying in Rome. I can do that later when it wouldn't bankrupt me. Getting a good nest egg first is important."

Fen nodded. "That's a good, rational decision."

"I also contacted the cruise line. I negotiated a deal with them, and I won't be gone all summer."

"This sound interesting."

"The deal involves you."

Fen's left eyebrow raised. "That's even more interesting."

"They really want you to teach on the cruise for artists. I sort of fibbed and told them you wouldn't go without me. They said they wouldn't pay me, but I could attend the classes at no charge. I told them we needed separate cabins. You'll get a nice balcony cabin, and they agreed to comp me a guaranteed single inside cabin. I didn't know what that meant exactly, but I know what the word *comp* means—complimentary. I like the sound of free."

"Have you looked up what a guaranteed single cabin means?"

"Uh-huh. They choose the cabin. I'm most likely to get a single bed in a tiny room with no windows in a lousy location on the ship."

Fen nodded. "That's usually what free gets you. When do we go?"

Bailey stopped swinging. "Did you say *we* can go?"

"Yes, but I reserve the right to tweak the plans."

"What do you mean?"

"I'll pay extra and get a two-bedroom suite. I'll take the largest bedroom, and Jeremy can take the other."

"How did you know we planned for him to go, too?"

"I wasn't always a grumpy old man."

She smiled and placed her head on his shoulder. "You'll never be old and grumpy."

As with many of my stories based in Texas, I have incorporated real locations, and even some businesses, among the fiction. If you visit Bandera, you will find the setting in the book is as close to real as I could get it and make the story work. Fen and his crew frequented several real businesses you will find around Bandera. However, all the character names are from my vivid imagination.

I hope you'll plan a stay at the Silver Spur Dance Hall, which sits high above Bandera on Mt. Rugh. You'll be able to see the view from the dance hall floor that inspired Fen's painting. It's a 'don't miss' view of Bandera and the surrounding countryside.

The Dough Joe, where Fen treated Bailey to a 'Cowboy Pizza,' is a local coffee shop and pizzeria. The story of the waitress teasing Bailey about ordering 'a large cowboy' is an example of my overactive imagination, so don't be afraid the server will embarrass you. You'll enjoy excellent food and service. I want to thank the owner, Owen, for giving me permission to use the name of his delightful business.

Other places we enjoyed visiting were the Frontier Times Museum, The Hens Nest cafe, and the Trail Boss Steak and Grill!

Be sure to put Bandera on your bucket list of places to visit. Thanks for being a fan!

Bruce

If you enjoyed this book, please consider leaving a review at your favorite retailer, Bookbub or Goodreads. *Your* review could be the one that helps another reader discover their next great mystery!

To get in on the fun in my reader community, scan below or go to brucehammack.com/the-fen-maguire-mysteries-reader-gift/ to join my mailing list and receive a free Fen Maguire short mystery eBook.

Happy Reading!

Bruce

About the Author

Drawing from his extensive background in criminal justice, Bruce Hammack writes contemporary, clean read detective and crime mysteries. An avid Hercule Poirot and Sherlock Holmes fan, he believes the world can never have too many whodunits!

He is the author of the Smiley and McBlythe Mysteries, the Fen Maguire Mysteries, the Star of Justice series and the Detective Steve Smiley Mysteries. Having lived in eighteen cities around the world, he now shares his home in the Texas hill country with his wife of thirty-plus years.

Follow Bruce on Bookbub or Goodreads for the latest new release info and recommendations. Learn more at brucehammack.com.